On the Sly
(The Grange Complex Book 2)

by

Joanna Mazurkiewicz

One

Ellie

I held the invitation between my sweaty palms, standing outside the door to apartment thirty-one, feeling like I had swallowed a ton of bricks. One night of anonymous, hot sex sounded great in theory, but in practise I wasn't quite sure if I was cut out for it. Last week when I had come back from my shopping trip, there had been a white envelope on my doorstep, a stylish, shiny invitation to a private party. There was no return address or even the name of the host on the back.

"Are you planning on going in?"

A clipped annoyed voice pulled me out of my thoughts. A blond woman stood behind me in an expensive black cocktail dress. For a split second I was ready to run away, but instead I nodded shyly and knocked. It was time to let go of my insecurities and just get on with it.

Behind the apartment door I could hear other people enjoying themselves and soft slow music. It seemed like the party had been going on for a while. A few seconds later, the door opened and a tall, good-looking man in a well-tailored suit appeared, eyeing me with interest. I couldn't avoid his eyes: they were a piercing cobalt blue that stared right into me. He looked like the sort of guy that no one would mess around with. Tall, confident and intense looking, he was certainly imposing. I told myself that I was ready for this, but my head kept on rehashing events from a few weeks ago, reminding me that my confidence had shrunk after my foolish affair with a married man.

"Veronica, nice to see you again," the handsome man said with a bright smile, looking behind me. "How are you?"

"Fabulous, darling. As usual, you look well," the pretty woman replied as she passed me on the way in.

His eyes sparkled with mischief when he finally glanced at me.

"I see that you received my invitation. Welcome to my home. I'm Harry, the host," Harry said with a bright smile. I waited, worried that he would make out who I was, but when his face didn't show any kind of recognition, I relaxed. No one in Edinburgh knew who I was and the surname that I had chosen to use was common enough.

"Yes, I did," I said, trying to sound like I was excited rather than nervous. Only two weeks had passed since my purchase of the apartment had gone through and I hadn't had a chance to make any new friends in Edinburgh yet. I was hoping that my old bunch of girlfriends would reach out and we would go out like we used to. They didn't; they all pretended to be too busy. Deep down I knew that it was because of the mess of the scandal. They didn't want to be seen with me.

"The rules at my parties are simple and straightforward. Everyone here is single and available for sex. I don't expect you to drop your knickers down for anyone straight away. We are all civilised adults, but I always mention that my bedrooms are available to use if needed. Most people show up here to get to know each other first, before any kind of interaction can take place."

Harry was having this bizarre conversation with me on the threshold and we hadn't even been properly introduced yet. Meanwhile, my heart hadn't stopped racing since I made the decision to come here. I really needed to get a grip on myself. This was my opportunity to be anonymous for at least one evening. I needed to blow off some steam from all the stress in my life and everything that had recently gone wrong. I had given Andrew my heart and he stomped on it and then wrecked my whole life. I was tired of feeling sorry for myself.

"I'm Ellie Frasier," I introduced myself. Harry kissed my palm and opened the door wider to let me through. I caught the scent of his cologne and I liked it. It was very masculine. I reminded myself that I needed to hook up with a complete stranger, someone I wouldn't ever have to see again after tonight.

"I hope you enjoy yourself tonight, Ellie," Harry added. He seemed charming and very confident. The kind of guy that I needed to avoid like the plague. I bet his blue eyes hid a corrupted soul and a darkness that could swallow you. After my affair, I had learned how to recognise those types of men.

Harry's apartment was much bigger than mine with a large open plan living room and a bog standard kitchen. There were people standing around, chatting and drinking as if it were a normal get-together. The invitation had said that food and entertainment would be provided and I assumed that the pole in the middle of the room was supposed to arouse the atmosphere of power and make you surrender to it. My heart leapt in my throat and I was seized by an intense moment of total deja vu. A year ago I had taken some pole-dancing lessons to impress the man that I'd thought I loved. My teacher had always praised me and I managed to start creating my own complicated routines. All of this had to stop when I was forced to leave Glasgow.

I used to attend parties like this one all the time when I was Daddy's favourite daughter. Now I was no one, just a broke twenty-five-year-old woman trying to make it as a reporter and erase the memories of a scandal that everyone still fed on.

I circled around the room for some time, watching the men and women. A few handsome guys smiled and showed an interest, but I was too scared to actually approach anyone. Everyone here was so glamorous and probably wealthy. Doubts started creeping in, making me feel vulnerable and quite lost.

"Champagne?" asked a shorter, dark-haired guy that suddenly appeared at my side, holding out a glass of bubbly for me to accept. He had a very thick Edinburgh accent and nicely cut suit. I hesitated for a split second before I accepted it. He wasn't bad-looking, not really my usual type but cute enough. He had bulky, defined eyebrows and a nice smile, so I assumed that he would be appropriate. Not too handsome or ugly either. I imagined him undressing me and then letting me forget who I was, at least for a night. Tingles of excitement travelled down my spine. It was obvious why he was here.

"Thank you. I'm Ellie," I finally said, smiling.

His eyes gleamed with curiosity and many unanswered questions. "Gavin."

"It's nice to meet you, Gavin."

"Ellie—I like that name. You're new here, and presumably available and open to possibilities?"

I nearly choked on my champagne when he asked that question. Yes, I was available and I wouldn't mind getting myself acquainted with this stranger at all, but this whole thing was happening fast, maybe way too fast. My own deep-seated insecurities were slowly accelerating my sudden panic. Maybe I wasn't ready, maybe it was too soon? In the end I decided to improvise.

"You could say that, Gavin," I replied, moving my finger over the edge of the glass. "Have you been to many parties such as this?"

He arched one bulky eyebrow, moving closer to me. I had to admit, I wasn't too keen on his aftershave. It was strong and too overpowering.

"A few, and I never leave empty-handed. I'm feeling particularly on edge tonight and you're very beautiful, Ellie."

Wow, he didn't waste much time. I drank some more champagne, feeling braver than usual. I felt sexy wearing my long red dress that emphasised my slender figure. I could do this. Sex was something that I wanted and Gavin appeared to be aiming for exactly the same thing.

"On edge, hmmm… what do you mean by that?" I teased, biting my lip. Soft, sexy music was blasting from the speakers that were set at the corners. A few couples had already formed. The invitation had said that there was going to be some sort of entertainment later on, a stripper or a dancer, so the pole in the middle suddenly made sense.

"I'm going to cut to the chase, darling. I haven't fucked for over a week and I want you, so how about I take you to one of the bedrooms back there and we get to know each other better?" Gavin asked, shooting me a heated look.

I dragged air into my lungs. I wasn't expecting this to be that easy. Here was this guy offering to bang the problems out of my head with his cock.

I decided it was just going to be one night where I didn't have to worry about expectations and unfulfilled promises. I finished the champagne in one go and tossed my brown hair behind me.

"Okay. Lead on, stranger," I said. Gavin smirked, took me by the elbow, and we started walking towards the corridor. Five minutes later, I found myself in a big stylish bedroom and my excitement grew. Gavin shut the door, looking like he was ready to get straight down to business.

"Come here, Ellie," he ordered, his thick accented voice sending a shiver down my spine. I dropped my purse on the bed and obeyed him, keeping that sinful smile on my face.

His movements were quick and he had his lips on mine before I knew it. The kiss was greedy and it took me by surprise. Gavin cradled me against his wide chest, moving his palms down to my buttocks and then squeezing. Heat brewed between us and I knew that I was wet enough to actually go through with this whole thing. He caressed my lips with his tongue, and I moaned into his mouth. My pulse was racing with excitement.

He pulled away, still holding my head close to his mouth and staring at my face for a little while. "You look really familiar. Are you sure that we haven't met before?" he asked suddenly.

"No, I don't think so," I said, feeling like someone had just doused me with ice-cold water. The spell had been broken and I knew that sooner or later he would know who I was. My pictures were mainly online on all the gossip sites, and the occasional tabloid used my father's name to gain more exposure and probably sales. After all, my affair had shocked many important and influential people that were close to my father.

Ugly, wracking memories slipped in and I panicked. My renowned surname had been splashed all over the news. Andrew and his accusations were titillation in my social circle. My father's disappointment and his raging anger followed.

"I do recognise your face from somewhere—"

"You're wrong. I'm just a stranger, a nobody. We've never met," I cut him off, trying to get away, but he gripped my wrists tighter and pulled me back to his chest, smiling wider.

"I think you're lying to me, flower," he said.

"Right, I think I've made a mistake. I shouldn't have come here," I snapped, getting aggravated. He laughed, not loosening his grip at all, pretending like we were playing a game. I knew that I had to get out of this room, get away from him. A one-night stand seemed like a really bad idea all of a sudden.

"Oh no, you're not going anywhere, sweetheart," he growled and then started forcing himself on me, trying to merge his mouth with mine. "We are going to fuck like you've promised and you'd better be good."

Mack

I went to take a piss just to get away from all the stares and judgmental looks in the other room. I was trying to find the loo, getting lost in this huge apartment, when I heard a scream. The noise came from the room opposite. I stopped for a second and waited just to be sure that I wasn't being paranoid.

"Get the hell away from me. I said that I don't want you to touch me!"

"Shut up and get down on your knees. Your sweet mouth is going to suck my cock," said a strong masculine voice behind the door.

"No, let me go, arghhh…"

I barged inside the room, not wasting any more time. The woman sounded like she was in distress. My eyes swept the room quickly. A guy that I had seen earlier on was holding a petite woman by her wrists, close to his chest. He lost his pathetic smile when he saw me.

"What the fuck do you want, mate? This is a private party," he snarled, not letting go of the girl.

"You're hurting the lady," I stated, staring straight at the dark-haired woman who was trying to move away from that asshole and looking pretty frightened.

"She's fine, mate. Get the fuck—"

I was next to him before he had a chance to draw another breath and finish his sentence. I fucking hated assholes who didn't respect women. Maybe this was rash and impulsive, but I threw a punch and he went down, crashing against a small chest of drawers. My knuckles stung, but hell, I was ready to beat the shit out of him. He just needed to continue to provoke me.

"Did he hurt you?" I asked the woman, who stood shocked and frozen, staring at me with her mouth wide open. I'd gotten mixed up in someone else's business again. This wasn't good. The woman shook her head, while the guy on the floor cursed a few times, trying to get up.

A few seconds later another man appeared at the door, the one that greeted me at the entrance.

"What the hell is going on in here?" he shouted, spotting the asshole on the floor.

"This imbecile was trying to force the lady here into something that she didn't want to do, so I took care of the problem," I told him.

"She wanted my cock, Harry, and that asshole fucking hit me!" shouted the guy I had tried to teach a lesson only a second ago, obviously without results. He was bleeding, but I didn't care. The shithead needed to be put in his place.

Harry looked furious.

"Gavin, you have crossed the line this time. I'm done with your bullshit," Harry said and started dragging the idiot away from the room by his collar.

I exhaled when the asshole was out of my sight. I shouldn't have gotten involved in this kind of mess when I had more important things to worry about. Someone had dropped an invitation on my doorstep and I'd contemplated for some time if it was the right thing to do to attend. I was frustrated, fucked off by the situation that I had found myself in. Endless hours of surveillance and preparation were for nothing and I figured I needed to take a break, ease the tension.

"Th-thank you," stuttered the woman, glancing at me. I finally remembered that she was still in the room. When I looked at her my dick twitched. What the hell? I hadn't gotten sticky about anyone else since my Charlotte.

The woman wiped her tears away, but she looked pretty shaky. She was beautiful; I couldn't miss that. Her wide hazel eyes were staring straight at me, like she was seeing into me, into my soul, aware of my unhealed scars and sorrowful emotions. Her skin was smooth and slightly tanned. I had a sudden urge to run my finger over her arm, touch it and caress it. Hell, my dick was reacting to her, but this was not the time or place for this kind of crap. She was upset.

"You won't be staying here. Let's go. I'll take you home," I said, not wanting to see her around any other assholes that only wanted to use her. I had showed up here thinking that I could just fuck someone, release some of my frustration and pain, maybe find a woman that could temporarily heal me with her touch, but I thought wrong.

She glanced at me, hesitating. I had no idea what got into me, but I grabbed her hand and quickly left the room. The contact with her skin sent ravaging heat down to my fucking boxers.

"I live in apartment thirteen," she blurted out when we passed through the corridor. People were staring, glancing at us as we walked past them. I held her hand tightly, wanting to devour her body slowly, with care and desire. We took the stairs, not speaking to each other, and I was baffled when I realised where she lived. I had to make sure it was safe inside.

"Would you like to come in for a coffee?" she asked. Her hands were still shaking and I should have said no, but I wasn't an asshole, so I nodded.

"Sure, lead on."

Two

Mack

I was feeling a little odd. My own place was two doors away and I hadn't even realised that I had a neighbour. I took my jacket off and put it on the chair.

"Thank you again," she said, standing close to me. I inhaled sharply, aware of the fact that I wanted to take her to my bed and fuck her slowly until dawn. "What would you like to drink?"

"White coffee please, and stop thanking me. It's fine. You don't have to worry about any other assholes. I hate guys like that. They don't know how to treat women, particularly a beautiful woman like you," I stated. She smiled widely and my dick twitched. This was wrong. I needed to remember that she was a victim and probably traumatised, not someone that I should be fantasising about. She went away to the kitchen to take care of the coffee. I dragged my hand through my hair, remembering my place, the undercover operation that I was supposed to be involved in.

I looked around her stylish apartment, feeling slightly tense. I shouldn't be mixing with any other residents from the complex. This was against the rules, but this evening I wasn't playing by the rules. Tonight I was just myself. Tobias Stanley, the man that was so scared that he had to function as Mack McCune.

When I heard the smash of broken glass, I was on my feet again, hurrying to see what happened.

The beautiful stranger was kneeling on the floor picking up what looked like a broken glass, muttering quiet, angry words to herself.

"Don't touch that; you might hurt yourself," I said, squatting in front of her. We both reached for the same piece and our fingers touched. An instantaneous stronger dose of heat shot down my body, igniting an already burning desire. She had soft, delicate skin and I didn't want to let go of her hand.

"I'm so clumsy tonight," she mumbled, looking at me with embarrassment. Fuck, even after the incident with that prick, I saw want and need in her eyes. This was dangerous. I lifted myself up, knowing that my cock was hard as granite—this wasn't good.

"Don't worry about it."

Her breathing was irregular and those eyes were hypnotising me, letting me know that she wanted me to ravage her slowly and with precise care. We were close to each other and I had to let her know that whatever was in her eyes wasn't a good idea, but then she moved forward and kissed me.

For a split second I was ready to push her away and tell her that she didn't want this, but a sudden craving for more stopped me. I had no fucking clue what was happening, and her lips tasted sweet as champagne and felt so unbelievably soft.

I entwined my fingers into her hair and brought her body closer. She probably felt my hardness pressed over her sex. Well, I couldn't exactly hide it. I couldn't explain this attraction, but I kept devouring her mouth, teasing her tongue until she moaned into my mouth. This woman left me breathless and I didn't want to let go of her.

Finally, I pulled back, breathing hard. She was flustered and that turned me on even more.

"We shouldn't be doing this. You aren't ready," I rasped.

"I can't be alone tonight; please don't make me be alone," she said with determination in her voice, looking broken. I dragged my hand through my hair, wondering what the hell was wrong with me, denying her pleasure.

She had showed up at this party because she wanted to spend a night with someone. She wanted no-strings-attached sex, like me.

Anyway, who was I to judge her? I fucking came here to release the same frustration, a longing for something else, a nagging and craving that I couldn't satisfy. I was fed up with my daily routine. That short asshole at the party acted quicker than everyone else in the room. He saw her and went straight for it, obviously not knowing how to act like a decent human being.

I couldn't deny the instant attraction, the thrill of excitement that spread in my bones. I didn't know her, but there was something about this woman that made me want her. Maybe it was her determination and that hunger for intimacy I saw in her eyes. I had no idea, but at the end of the day we both wanted the same thing.

She was my type—short, slender and probably experienced enough in the bedroom. She was so small, fitting in my chest perfectly. I smiled and couldn't wait any longer. I crushed my lips against hers, tasting her mouth and letting go of whatever resistance I held. This time my kiss started gentle, but that only lasted for a second or two, and I instantly demanded more.

"I hate wasting time, Angel, so let's just get on with this. My cock is aching for you," I said, my voice stern. It'd been a while since I let the other side of me take control. I let her see my dark desires just once, and once was enough. I didn't want to be the regular normal guy for the woman that stood in front of me. I wanted her to see the real me. It'd been two years and it was time I remembered what I truly enjoyed, and how much I needed to dominate another being.

She smelled fucking unbelievable and I wanted to take her right there, to devour her completely. Her eyes were telling me that she was ready for whatever I wanted to throw her way.

"I love the way you took control and led me out of there with a simple command."

"Want me to take control again? I asked.

"Please," she replied.

I smiled wolfishly, whilst keeping my eyes on hers. I lifted her up, so her legs were wrapped around my waist, her sex perfectly aligned over my stiff cock. She was small and weighed almost nothing. Our entrance to her bedroom was abrupt but passionate, and the rush of heat and blood through my body felt so damn good. I had no fucking idea what had gotten into me, but I wanted to thrust my cock into this stranger's wet folds. She blew my senses apart and my groin was burning like hell.

Ellie

I was panting with excitement. This man, whoever he was, woke a craving in me for wild and adventurous sex. The attraction was there, terrifying and yet thrilling. I had to take a risk, so I kissed him. I couldn't stand another lonely night. I didn't want to be that self-conscious girl with a shattered confidence anymore. The cruel memories were feeding on my soul. I had to be close to another human being to break the cycle, to move on with whatever life I chose for myself.

"Take all your clothes off," he commanded, standing by the bed and staring at me with his hard eagle-like eyes. His order sent a shudder right down to my core, lighting up the dead cells. I was out of my dress before I knew it, standing in my white lace bra and knickers, expecting him to follow me, but he hadn't moved. His eyes took me in and began moving slowly down my body. I waited patiently, not quite sure what to expect.

"I said all the clothes off!" he ordered with a hint of impatience, but his domineering voice was a real turn-on. No one had ever talked to me like that in the bedroom, not even Andrew. My pussy was wet for him; it throbbed with need and I craved his touch. I had never been prudish or shy, but in all my deepest fantasies I never imagined submitting to a dominant lover. There was something about Mack that made me want to please him.

I stepped off the bed and let my bra fall to the floor. My knickers followed. This huge man in front of me had a wide strong jaw and light blond hair. He was tall, wide shouldered and strongly built. Our kiss was sensual but rough, and I loved every second of it.

He took off his jacket and started unbuttoning his shirt. My heart stuttered between my ribs when my eyes took in the sculpted muscles on his chest. He had a scar on the right side of his abdomen, wide and long. I was curious and almost asked where it came from, but I forced myself to keep quiet. He wasn't at all like any other men that I'd ever slept with—I had never in my life been this excited about what was about to happen.

"Trousers off," I said approaching him and wanting to run my fingers over his arm, but he grabbed my wrist and pulled me close to his chest.

He leaned over and growled into my ear, "Tonight this pussy belongs to me—it will feel pleasure because I want it to, it will be wet for me because I want it to be wet, and you will come when I say because I want you to. But, my Angel, not until I say you can."

He moved away from me and spread my legs wide apart and sat between my knees, looking at my nakedness intently.

"You have such a pretty sex," he said, sliding his fingers up my slit. "You can beg and plead all you like—I quite enjoy it when you do—but like your pussy, your orgasm belongs to me."

I began to tremble as he slid his fingers through my wetness. He started to massage my clit with his thumb hard and fast, taking me by surprise, then thrust two fingers into my hole. Massaging my inner walls with his fingers, he suddenly bit down on my nipple, surprising me. I moaned loudly and bucked my hips up to meet his hand, feeling a new rush of wetness gather between my thighs.

"Oh God, please… I need this, I need to come," I started to beg as I met the thrust of his hand. He removed his hand and I felt bereft at the loss of him. "No. Please, no," I whined.

"Angel, your orgasm is mine to give as I please. Now, no more moving or I won't let you come. Do you understand?"

I nodded my head and he bit my inner thigh with a sharp growl. It shocked me. It hurt, but not in an unpleasant way; more like he was letting me know he was in charge, he was the boss. "Yes, yes, I understand. I'll be good now."

"Get on all fours now and be quiet," he ordered, pulling away all of a sudden. My head spun and I wasn't ready for it, but I obeyed him, feeling that he had more cards up his sleeve. For a moment the room was absolutely silent. I could only hear the sound of our heavy breathing and feel our vibrating excitement. I had no idea what was happening to me, but his touch made me responsive, twisting me into a mush of submission. In the bedroom, I had always been in control; men were pleased when I turned into a dirty-talking slut, but not this time. This stranger switched my usual role around.

My thighs were shaking with anticipation and my pussy was drenched. I was on my knees with my ass in the air, waiting for him to plunge his hard dick inside me. I heard him rip something off, probably a packet for the condom. Good that he was so well prepared.

When he thrust himself inside me, I crumbled, taking all of him in, crying out. He gripped my hips and started fucking me. Fast and hard. Bringing me to the edge of orgasm, letting me feel it build to that delicious edge of the cliff, then slowing right down to stave off my release, then moving fast again. It was agony, a delicious torture.

"This will be quick but intense, Angel," he rasped and bit my ear.

I had never experienced anything like it. This stranger, whoever he was, pulled the pieces of my shattered soul back together. He was rough but sensual, fucking me until I was out of breath, heart jackhammering in my chest. He pounded into me fast and I panted and moaned, begging for more. He didn't let me rest until we were both on the edge.

Then he wrapped my hair around his hand and pulled my head back towards him. "Come now, my Angel. Squeeze my cock nice and tight and come."

I had no control; I had no options. My body responded to him and I writhed on his beautiful cock, letting my orgasm take over as I moaned and screamed. I felt his release build as he pulsed inside of me. Within moments he was ready again and I was losing touch with reality. My hips moved back and forth, up and down his cock. It was like a punishingly sweet race, only I wasn't keeping up with him.

I didn't care what his name was, who he was or where he came from. That night all I cared about was the fact that he didn't let me sleep, not once.

He was assertive, commanding and passionate. He abused my body in every delightful way, eased the uncontrollable rhythmic throbbing, and shattered any doubt and hesitation. I collapsed on his chest hours later, exhausted but satisfied. Every ounce of pleasure had been wrung from my body. My whole body was numb, heart speeding. It wasn't long before I drifted to sleep, knowing that I was no longer alone.

Mack

I was dreaming about Charlotte touching me. She was tracing the muscles of my arms, smiling at me, humming our favourite tune. It was bliss. I groaned, remembering our intimate moments together. Then I shook myself awake, moving on the bed. It took me a few seconds to realise that I was holding a warm petite body in my arms and I wasn't dreaming anymore. I rubbed my eyes with my free hand, inhaling the soft smell of amber and vanilla. My morning wood was rubbing itself over her ass. I took a deep breath, remembering last night quite clearly. I shouldn't have fallen asleep. I should have left after she was out, snoring next to me. Eventually I managed to wriggle myself off the dark-haired woman that I fucked last night. She muttered something in her sleep, but didn't wake up. Lucky me.

I had an urge to kiss her soft, slightly tanned skin like I used to caress Charlotte's, but instead I dismissed that thought. That would be a mistake. One night, that's all there was to it. This woman was beautiful. And obedient. It had been a while since I had someone so gentle in my bed, someone who made me stiff and ready for more. I didn't know her name and that was all right. What might have mattered was that she lived two doors away from me. But it looked like Lurkin wasn't moving in after all, so one night with her didn't matter. I'd be relocating, abandoning this part of Scotland and starting over somewhere else. That bastard was getting away again.

I found my clothes around the bed, put my boxers and trousers on, and headed out. For a split second I wondered if I could slip back to her bed and just wait until she woke up, but I didn't want to make her feel uncomfortable. My cock was hard again and that wasn't good. I dragged my hand through my hair, seeing flashes of her on top of me. It was supposed to be just one night. I didn't need to leave my number. I couldn't anyway.

Her heavy panting, her soft mouth, everything about this woman felt right. It was a shame that yesterday was my last and final night in the Grange.

I had been working as an undercover detective for over ten years and I was one of the best. Always driven and committed to get the job done. I'd been assigned to live in the complex for over a week, waiting and preparing for another operation, but something had happened yesterday. Rob Pollock, the powerful drug supplier, had changed his mind. Someone must have spooked him. It was time to move on and report at the headquarters in Glasgow.

I unlocked the door to my apartment and walked inside. It was 7:00 a.m. on Sunday morning. In a couple of hours I could forget about the past week, move on. It was a real shame. After years of preparation, I nearly had him. Adrian Lurkin, that was the name that he was using these days. He was the biggest supplier of heroin and cocaine in Scotland and I knew that I should have put him behind bars years ago.

Last night I managed to empty the frustration and anger the past eighteen months had seeded in me. Now I was back to my usual self: a miserable, fucked-up thirty-something guy with anger management issues. My thoughts escaped to the woman two doors down and I clenched my fists, wondering what the fuck was wrong with me. I had had one-night stands before, years ago before everything went to shit, but this time everything felt different. The sex was better, mind-blowing, more intense, and I wanted to sink my cock inside her tight heat again.

My phone started ringing, and my stomach twisted with nervous energy. It hadn't rung for a week, so why now and why so early in the morning? I cursed under my breath and picked it up.

"Hello."

"Stanley, there has been a shift in the operation. The sale went through as planned just this morning. A large sum of money has been transferred to the landowner. You're staying and we are back in the game," said the gruff voice on the other end of the line that belonged to Superintendent Colman, my superior. I looked down at the phone, thinking that he couldn't be serious. Yesterday I had different instructions; I was being transferred.

"You're kidding," I snarled, although I knew that my boss never joked around when it came to the job.

"We don't know what's happened, but we know for a fact that the suspect is going to be there this afternoon, so get ready. In a couple of minutes you'll get an envelope with more details. Stephanie has broken her foot, so I'm pulling her off the case, but Claire has volunteered to replace her."

I shut down, blood stopped circulating through my body.

"Claire?" I questioned, losing my breath. I hoped this was a joke. "I would rather be here on my own. Without a wife, I can bond with him quicker."

"We have discussed this before, Stanley. You will be more believable as a married couple. I'm not cutting her off just because of some kind of misunderstanding that should have been settled years ago," Colman stated, not taking any shit from me as usual.

"Fine, but she better stick to the plan."

"Be respectful. I've got enough on my back as it is. She's a good detective."

I gripped the phone so tightly that my knuckles went white. Fucking Claire, why did she have to get involved? Of course, she would be excited at the idea of seeing me again. We had worked together in the past, and she knew me better than anyone else. My wife Charlotte had trusted her and she had paid for that trust with her own life.

A moment later there was a thick white envelope pushed under my door. I picked it up and tore it apart. Inside were the newest pictures of Rob Pollock. He hadn't changed much, but he'd probably gotten richer. I had to gain his trust and get close to him so he would offer me a job. That meant that I had to stay in the Grange for longer than I originally anticipated. So there was another problem. The woman a couple doors down the hall could complicate things. I should have listened to the voice of reason. Shit.

I needed to get to the shower and clear my head, think about how things were going to pan out for the next couple of weeks. I kept reminding myself that it had been five years since my wife had passed away. I had begun living a normal life again; at least I'd been attempting it. I took on any and all assignments because I enjoyed the buzz, deep down hoping that I would die as I always wanted to: by serving my country. Some days I wondered why God let me live. I didn't deserve it. While the danger and adrenaline kept me going, I tried not to think about that day. Charlotte was gone and there was nothing that I could do about it.

While the warm water surged over my body, my mind kept flashing through images of last night—the woman's moans, her soaking pussy and the face she made when she came. Fuck, it was like I couldn't get her out of my head. I should've felt guilty, but I didn't. Maybe our paths crossed because she was letting me know that there was life beyond death, beyond love. No one had ever made me feel this way, so maybe I still had a chance to pull away from the grief that was slowly consuming me.

Half an hour later, with a towel around my waist, I stepped back into the living room, still pretty pissed off, wondering how I was supposed to behave around Claire now. I didn't even notice that I wasn't alone anymore. She was sitting on the sofa looking at the pictures in the envelope. She lifted her head and smiled when she saw me.

"I think we've been avoiding each other long enough. It's time, Tobias. Time to start over."

Three

Ellie

Monday morning I was awakened by the sound of my annoying alarm at 6:00 a.m. I lay in bed for some time thinking about Saturday night. The hot, strong, dominant stranger had disappeared from my apartment first thing that morning. The night that we spent together was explosive and I was struggling to erase him from my memory. I hadn't gone out on Sunday at all; I spent all day doing the research for a column that I had been working on, on the side.

This morning I still felt pretty relaxed about what went on between us. The sex had blown my mind and his commanding voice had left me drenched with need. Even now I was having hot flashes, smelling him on my sheets and pillows. I had never had a lover who was so gentle and demanding at the same time. That man without a name, who was passionate, powerful and made me orgasm at least five times. I couldn't stop thinking about his piercing grey eyes. I felt truly and utterly screwed after he was done with me.

Finally I pulled the covers away and got up. I went to the bathroom and looked at my own reflection in the mirror, thinking about the day ahead of me. No one in the office knew who I was and I wanted to stay anonymous for as long as possible. Dad hadn't contacted me since the whole scandal hit the media and I wasn't expecting him to. He made it clear that

I was dead to him, but if I could make it as a reporter, then there was a slim chance that I could turn my luck around.

I knew Dad regretted spending a fortune on my education. I went to the best media school in Scotland, graduated with a first class degree, then managed to secure work experience in a good paper without his help. My father didn't believe that my degree was worth anything. He'd wanted me to become a respectable barrister like him, but I was more excited about writing articles and exposing the truth than his whole legal crap.

When the scandal was leaked to the papers and my life was pulled from beneath my feet, I was forced to spend my last available funds on this property in another city and take a job in a small magazine in Edinburgh.

It'd been weeks since my name was splattered across the papers, but I was still careful, using my fake name whenever I could. I had tried to keep in touch with some friends. Rebecca and Tasha had visited me a few times, but the rest of my friends kept their distance. They were sympathetic but couldn't believe that my father reacted the way he did. I had made a terrible mistake, but I was a human being, believing it was my own judgment that failed me. Now I felt isolated and haunted by the guilt.

After Andrew, I had lost all my confidence in finding real love. It was better to sleep around, not to be tied down. My father made sure that I lost all the privileges and all my memberships to exclusive clubs and societies in Scotland. We were never really close, but he had believed that asshole over me and made the decision to shut me out of his life forever, not letting me explain what actually happened between us.

The scandal crumbled his good reputation and he lost many important clients because of me. He didn't care who had started what; all that mattered to him was that I was involved. Yeah, I was an idiot back then, thinking that Andrew had loved me. I was ready to do anything for him, but he only played with me to get closer to my powerful father.

Now I was managing to scrape by, earning a shitty wage with the magazine. I missed having an unlimited amount of funds. I was never a materialist, although it was nice to be able to buy anything that I needed, but now I was on my own and the bills were slowly piling up, so I had to deal with it.

I brushed my long brown hair, changed into gym clothes, and picked my outfit for today in the bedroom.

Everything was slowly coming together, but I absolutely detested my workplace. All the senior reporters were chauvinist pigs. They had their own established sources around the city and I was stuck with the rest of the crappy stories that no one wanted to touch, just some boring crap that wouldn't help me further my own career at all. I'd never realised how much my father's name could help. I never used it to my advantage, but now I wished I had.

I went down to use the gym, and for the entire workout, I kept wondering who the mystery man was that I'd had sex with Saturday night. I didn't know his name, but I already missed his touch. I imagined being in bed with him again, lost in his touch.

After my workout I returned to my apartment, changed, picked up my briefcase, and then I was ready to conquer another day. I stood outside in the hall for a little while, fiddling with my keys, when I heard someone coming out of the third apartment on my floor. I hadn't had a chance to meet any of my neighbours yet, and for a while I suspected that the two other apartments were empty. Obviously I was wrong.

"I'm telling you, this is the best way," I heard a female voice saying.

Finally finding the right key, I locked the door in a hurry. I glanced up and for a split second I wondered if my vision was fooling me somehow. My heart skipped a beat and then shuddered in my chest. The mystery guy from two nights ago, the one that made me forget about my sorrow and worries, was walking towards me with another woman. There was no doubt that he recognised me. Tingles ravaged my body as his eyes hovered over my face slowly, like he was calculating whether to say anything about the other night. I was just about to ask him what the hell he was doing here, but the woman that was with him erased my question.

"Oh, hello. You must be our new neighbour? I'm Claire McCune and this is my husband, Mack," she said to me. Then two things happened all at once. The door of the apartment next to me opened up, and I dropped all my folders on the floor. I could swear my heart stopped beating for a good several seconds.

No, no, no, no.... This is not happening to me again.

"Let me help you with this," my one-night stand guy offered, going down on his knee and picking up my papers for me. I shot him one of my worst "ready to murder you with my bare hands" glares, trying to breathe at the same time, but my lungs had stopped working. A wife? The perfect hot and gorgeous guy had a wife? And he lived two doors away from me?

"What's going on here, a neighbourhood watch meeting of some sort?" asked the guy who had just come out of the other apartment, flashing us the most brilliant smile.

I thought that I had a brain freeze. People were talking to me, but I was in a daze. Anger boiled inside me like a hot furnace and I thought I was going through a seizure. Mystery guy handed me one of my folders and our fingers brushed accidentally. Electricity shot down to my core, sending waves of piping hot lust down between my legs. I remembered lying on the bed in my apartment with him between my legs, commanding me to keep still. Shit, that was so hot, but then the voice of reason pulled me back to the real world, to the screwed-up reality of the fact that love, honesty and fidelity existed only in fairy tales.

Mack and I looked up. Our new neighbour was tall, slim and quite handsome. Soft or pretty boy-looking, as I would normally describe him to all my girlfriends. He wasn't Scottish either; I detected some sort of foreign accent. He had tanned dark skin and I assumed that one of his parents might have been from the Middle East. Good-looking without a ring on his finger and dressed smart in a pricey blue shirt.

My breathing hadn't come back to normal yet, but somehow I managed to lift myself up. Beads of sweat were running down my back. I was prepared to roar with frustration and fury. How could he not tell me that he had a freaking wife!

"We were just leaving for work when the lady here dropped her folders all over the floor," said the wife, chuckling like this was funny. Her smile was fake and stiff. Besides that, she wasn't very pretty, and that should have made me feel a little better, but the truth was that I was devastated. Her hair was pulled back in a ponytail and she wore a cheap black suit. "I guess we're all new here. Have you just moved in?"

I had to get the hell out of here, fast. My heart pounded in my chest while gorgeous, commanding Mack was eyeing our new neighbour with his sharp grey eyes. I imagined stabbing a knife straight into his heart and then twisting until those eyes popped out of his sockets.

"Yes, I'm in the process of moving in. Do you guys live on this floor?" the new neighbour asked and darted his eyes at me. I was fuming, but I still managed to notice as he checked me out, hovering his dark gaze over my legs.

"My name is Mack McCune and this is my wife, Claire. Unfortunately, we haven't yet had the pleasure to be acquainted with the lady here."

Mack

I said this pointing at the beautiful angel standing in front of me, who looked like she was already plotting how to kill me. I should have told Claire to wait until at least seven to leave, but no, she insisted on leaving early, hoping to find out if Pollock had moved in yet. Panic and shock were colliding with my outburst of sudden desire. When I stared at the woman who had woken me up from my deepest fog, I was ready to forget about my duties and take her away to the place where she belonged—my bed.

The beautiful angel had decided to leave the apartment at the same time as us, ruining our carefully prepared plan. Since losing Charlotte, I had stopped paying attention to women. It was easier to blame it on work, although my father kept telling me that I needed to start dating again. Now, I was experiencing these hidden emotions while she stood close to me, looking shocked, and I had to keep my mouth shut about who I was. That one fucking night would cost me a lot and only in this moment did I begin to realise that.

"Hi, I'm Ellie Frasier, moved in two weeks ago," she said, sounding tense.

What a fucking mess! I wanted to smash my own face with a brick. Ellie—that name alone was making my dick twitch again and this was not the time or place for shit like that.

"Adrian Lurkin."

"Well, it's superb that we all finally know each other," Claire said, laughing. I wished that she would just shut up. We had been forced to get back together and she knew how I felt about her. "How about drinks at our place on Friday night? I hope both of you, Ellie and Adrian, can join us?"

Ellie shot me a bold, surprised look while I nearly lost it. I was ready to explode and drag Claire back to our apartment. Drinks? Was she out of her mind? We were supposed to engage with Lurkin, but not like that, not while another neighbour stood next to him. She was messing up this carefully prepared plan.

"I'm sure they are both very busy, Claire," I said, shooting her an annoyed look. She wasn't getting it. This whole thing wasn't about social interactions anymore. That was the main reason that I stopped trusting women. They had no idea how to follow the rules.

"I would love to, but only if our pretty new neighbour agrees," Adrian said, winking at Ellie, and I instantly wanted to crush his gut with my fists. Fuck. What the hell was wrong with me? I had this woman for one night. We fucked and then I left. That's all there was to it, so why did I care all of a sudden?

We all looked at Ellie, who opened her mouth, then closed it. She looked amazing wearing a white silky blouse and tight black trousers. I liked women that made an effort and she obviously had a good sense of style, but then my internal voice roared at me to get a grip. I had to stop lusting after someone that I couldn't have. My relationship with Claire was much more important than Ellie. We had to put our differences aside. Pollock was dangerous and I had to keep myself in line. Only a few experienced, high-level people knew about this operation and I hoped that one day I would see him rotting in prison.

"I'm kind of busy Friday. I'm sorry. Maybe another time," she replied.

I imagined those lips around my cock, sucking and teasing me.

"Come on, you have to show up. We're all new here," Lurkin insisted.

She glanced at me, swallowing hard and gripping her folders under her breasts. "But I—"

"Oh come on, Ellie. Mack and I insist. It'll be fun to get to know each other. You should have a night off work," Claire said. Then she winked and added, "I've been told I make a mean Sex on the Beach cocktail," putting me in a state of complete unease. Women could be clueless, and of course she had no idea that I'd had the most memorable and euphoric sex with Ellie just two days ago. That was none of her business as she was married herself, but I was putting all the parties involved at risk and that wasn't my style.

I saw curiosity and lust in Lurkin's eyes for Ellie. This wasn't good. I hated that he was looking at her like she was just another easy lay.

The silence stretched for several moments and I was praying for her to say no.

"Okay, I guess you're right," Ellie said and gave us all a fake smile, tossing her brown hair over her shoulder. "Friday night at your place it is, then. I'll make sure to bring something strong. Nice to meet you all. Sorry, but I have to run!"

Then she jumped straight into the lift, leaving me baffled and fucking furious with a semi-hard cock. Claire laughed and Lurkin kept staring at Ellie until the door to the lift shut.

"Friday night, then. Thanks, Claire. I just can't wait to get myself acquainted with Ellie. She seems nice," Lurkin said, then picked up his box and walked inside his apartment, leaving me and Claire alone. It took me a second to realise that I was screwed, completely and utterly, because I had spent the night with a woman that I had expected to never, ever see again.

Four

Ellie

I had no idea how I got to my car without being violently sick. The moment when they both confirmed that Mack was married, I thought I was going to pass out. Not for one second had I suspected that he was seriously involved with another woman or even that he was my neighbour. How could he not tell me when I said that I lived in number thirteen? Well, maybe those were the consequences of having a one-night stand. Men were liars and I had learnt that the hard way when I laid my eyes on Andrew.

My head was vibrating and pulsing with worries. Memories from that night were still pouring into me. Our sticky bodies together, him kissing me and me begging for more. I shouldn't have been feeling guilty about it because he didn't tell me he was married. I was angry that I adored his name, furious with the fact that I was stupid enough to believe that one night with a total stranger could erase all my problems.

My inner voice screamed at me that this wasn't the same as Andrew. He was a mistake, and Mack, well, he was just a scumbag.

Dad had asked me to watch him whenever he was dealing with clients or the press, trying to convince me that I was cut out to be a lawyer, not a reporter. Andrew was one of his clients that I'd decided to help. He had been a married man with three kids.

Then, two days ago, I spent a night with Mack, another married man who had responsibilities and probably kids too. I hadn't asked questions that night; I just wanted to be with someone and figured anyone at that singles party would be free. A moment ago, he pretended that we didn't know each other—bastard. His wife obviously had no idea what had gone on between us, and part of me wished I had said something. Instead, I agreed to a social evening with drinks in their apartment. Geez.

After another ten minutes in the car, I started the engine and got to the office twenty minutes late. Monday morning was important. My perverted misogynistic boss assigned the stories in the morning huddle, but when I arrived the meeting was almost over and I had to take what was left, which, surprisingly, wasn't the usual boring crap. I took the assignment and decided I would turn in a really good article.

In order to forget about Saturday night I had to either kill Mack or move out. Neither of these options was possible. I was broke and alone with absolutely no way of regaining my old life. It was up to me to make it and show my father that I didn't need him in order to be successful.

I put my head down and wiped the tears away, knowing that sooner or later Mack would regret that he used me. For now I had to deal with the consequences of my one-night stand.

***

"So how about we knock together? That way we can all start drinking at the same time. I don't know about you, but I've had a hell of a week," Adrian said when I met him outside my apartment on Friday night. Since that awkward moment when the four of us met in the corridor, I had been asking myself the same question over and over—Was I ready to spend an evening with Mack and his wife, pretending that we hadn't shared the most amazing mind-blowing sex in history? I managed to avoid them all week, but I didn't want to look like a complete coward, so I went. My guilty conscience kept me on my toes, and whenever I closed my eyes, I saw myself burning in hell.

Andrew had seduced me and I had been stupid enough to fall for his charm, for his generosity and tender lovemaking. He had said that he loved me, but once everyone found out about us, he changed his mind, blaming me for inciting the affair, making it sound tawdry and illicit.

Adrian had just given me another signal that he was interested in me. This was our second meeting and he was already flirting. I could use him to get back at Mack. After all, he was single and probably available, but first I needed to be absolutely one hundred percent sure about this.

"Yes, my week was exhausting too. It would be good to have a drinking partner next door." I laughed, sticking to his flirty banter for now. There it was, the excitement for the thrill of the chase in his eyes, the way his jaw twitched when I bit my lip. Okay, so that might have been easier than I wanted, but then I realised that I had a whole awkward evening with Mack ahead of me.

When Adrian knocked, Mack was the one that opened the door. When his eyes found mine I felt like I had just been shocked by a strong electric current. His eyes hovered over my body for a brief second, reclaiming me and reminding me that I was still under his spell.

"Adrian, Ellie, please come on in," he greeted us with a faint smile. Both men shook hands enthusiastically and I forced a bright grin, taking a long, deep breath.

Mack and Claire's apartment had the same set-up as mine. The kitchen was hidden behind a dividing wall, the living room was large and airy, and like me, they were able to enjoy a stunning view of the sea.

I had gone for a simple classic black dress that exposed my long legs, which Mack noticed of course when he asked for our drink preferences. I hated the way his eyes were making me all gooey and weak. Tonight I would make him pay for his lies. Adrian and I sat down on the plain white sofa and several minutes later, the happily-married couple showed up in the living room.

"Sex on the Beach for Ellie and a strong whiskey for you, Adrian," Claire said, smiling at me. God, I wanted to kill myself then. She probably would go mental if she knew that I had slept with her husband. When I glanced at Mack, I caught him watching me, and something inside my stomach twisted. Lust began crawling its way towards my centre, and for a split second I wanted him all over again.

"So, Mack, what do you do for work?" Adrian asked, brushing his knee against mine accidentally on purpose.

Mack noticed and shifted in his chair. One point to me.

Mack

"This and that. I'm doing some driving for an agency at the moment. I have been trying to find something stable since last year," I replied, trying to keep the edge out of my voice. I had been so sure that Ellie wouldn't show up. I nearly had a heart attack when I opened the door and she stood on my doorstep, looking gorgeous and radiant with that twat from next door. "What about you?"

For the last several days I'd been arguing with Claire about who was in charge of this operation. Stephanie would do what I asked her to. She was more cooperative, but Claire, well, she wanted to get promoted this year, so she needed to make an impact.

I had been pissed off all week, but I hadn't brought up this whole social evening with drinks in our apartment. I'd hoped that she had forgotten this, but then tonight she had come home with plenty of buzz, so I had to get ready. I still blamed her for an operation from the past that went terribly wrong. She made a few fatal mistakes, but she was too proud to admit to any of it.

"Yes, Adrian, tell me, what is it that you do? I'm intrigued," Ellie said all of a sudden, placing her hand on that asshole's shoulder. I tensed in my chair, remembering how much she enjoyed my cock the other night.

"I own a few food businesses around Edinburgh. Nothing exciting, Ellie," he said, sliding his eyes down her legs. "What about you?"

"I'm trying to make it as a reporter, but I'm still looking for my breakthrough story," she explained.

"Wow, a reporter. That sounds exciting," Adrian said, sounding like he really did give a fuck.

"It's not as glamorous as it sounds. The magazine that I'm working for is very small. I don't have much say on what I get to write about. Hopefully it will change eventually, but we will see." She shrugged and sank her sexy lips over her glass. So she not only had looks but also a brain. This shouldn't have really bothered me.

"It's probably hard to get established. There's so much competition out there," Claire commented. "I'm a qualified accountant. Mack and I met when I was studying. I tried to set up my own business but found it very challenging."

"Yes, it has been, but I'm determined to succeed. I just need to gain some more experience," Ellie assured Claire. The ice had been kind of broken by now and I had to fucking find some common ground with Lurkin; otherwise, we were going to be stuck here all night. Ellie could be distracting. In any other circumstance maybe I would have been interested, maybe I would've even dated her, but now this seemed like an impossible task.

"There is no doubt about that, Ellie. I think there are many wom–"

"So, Adrian, any unusual hobbies you have?" I asked, cutting off Claire, because I was fed up with her pointless chitchat. We were forced to work together again, and we had a mutual goal: to find common ground with Lurkin. Ellie was a mistake that was probably going to cost me my balls, pissing on my already strained relationship with Claire. My so-called "wife" looked at me, baffled, probably because I had cut her off quite rudely. Lurkin shifted on the sofa, clearing his throat. Okay, so I made this awkward. Nothing was going my way tonight.

"I play cards," he grumbled and took a sip of whiskey.

Cards. I could play poker and let him beat me. Whatever I needed in order to get to his laptop to find out what I could. Ellie started talking to Claire, asking questions about our fucking marriage. There was a reason that I kept away from her since Charlotte died. She needed to make sure not to cross me.

"Well, if it's poker, then we have to play a few hands together one day," I added, trying to sound excited about the whole thing, but I hated that he kept checking Ellie out right in front of me. She was so sexy, with that smooth, glorious tanned skin. Her seductive moans had turned me on the other night. We were just so compatible.

"Sure, why not?" Adrian stated.

"God, I forgot that I had stuff in the oven. Be right back." Claire sprang up and left the room. I hated chitchat and socialising, but I was too invested now to ruin this whole thing just because of some pretty face. Lurkin was tangled in my past and I needed to bring him down.

"So, Ellie, how come you moved into the Grange? Wouldn't it be easier living closer to the city?" Adrian threw her the question. She glanced at me, burning me with her brown sexy eyes, and shifted her weight, moving closer to that scumbag.

"I found an apartment for a very good price. Besides, if I had chosen the city I wouldn't have met you, would I?" she asked, in a low seductive voice that made my cock twitch.

That rat bastard laughed! I was ready to rip his balls out and squash them between my clenched fists.

"So you're single then?" he asked. "No possessive, belligerent boyfriend of any sort?"

Ellie glanced at me and licked her upper lip, sending me a clear signal that she remembered the other night quite clearly.

"No. I'm single, handsome. What about you? How come a guy like you isn't married like our Mack here?"

She was punishing me for the fact that I hadn't mentioned Claire. She had every right to be furious with me. My crotch was burning with discomfort and if I couldn't get hold of myself, I was going to ruin this carefully prepared plan by punching this asshole. That's why I hated getting involved in serious shit with women. I could have taken care of Adrian myself.

"Women don't stick to me at all," Lurkin replied, sending me a wink, and Ellie giggled, running her finger over his arm. It was a good thing that the asshole's phone started ringing, because I couldn't take her game any fucking longer. Lurkin answered, pointing that he was going outside. This would have been the perfect opportunity to record some stuff, but I had a woman that I had fucked senseless pissing on my parade. Claire wasn't in the kitchen; she was probably in the bedroom trying to find the phone bug.

Ellie kept watching Adrian until he disappeared behind the doors, leaving us alone.

"So, when were you supposed to tell me that you were married?" she hissed at me after we were left alone. I dragged my hand through my hair, knowing that what I had done was wrong in every respect, but there was something about her that crushed whatever anger and frustration I held. "And what about that you lived on the same fucking floor as me?"

"This isn't how it looks, Angel," I said, having no idea how to explain myself. I couldn't tell her anything and put her at risk. Lurkin wouldn't hesitate to kill her if he suspected anything. I had already lost the love of my life.

"Don't you dare call me that, you slimy liar. The other night was a massive mistake. I would have never done that with you if I had known that you were my married neighbour," she said, glancing back and forth between the corridor and the bedroom.

She looked so hot when she was pissed like that.

"You enjoyed riding my cock and being under my control, so don't give me that guilty conscience bollocks. Lurkin won't satisfy you the way I did. I don't think anyone will," I snapped.

Her face contracted with anger. This Angel had no idea what else I could do to her. Sex had never felt like it had with her, pushing the boundaries of total surrender. I wanted to tie her up and lick her wet folds until she couldn't take it anymore.

"I guess I'll have to find out, right? At least he isn't tied down, and I wouldn't mind getting to know him a bit better," Ellie said with a sweet smile that twisted my gut. I shifted on the sofa, ready to fuck that idea out of her head, when Claire walked back into the room. I was in some really deep, messy shit. It looked like that one night could not only break me, but also put at risk the other lives that depended on me.

Five

Ellie

Claire walked in with a tray of mini canapés and pizzas, smiling at me, interrupting our bitter exchange. I felt terrible, and I wanted to get out of here as soon as I could. My heart was fluttering. Andrew had seemed kind and loving and he kept telling me that his wife had never satisfied him, that he hadn't slept with her for over a year. I was stupid enough to believe him, lying to my own friends to protect our secret. Now for the first time in my life I was ready to come clean and tell this woman who had invited me into her home and treated me kindly that I had fucked her husband.

Mack was like a wave of new energy. He wasn't Andrew, but I felt so guilty that I still wanted him. I had nearly wrecked one family for what I thought was love. My first lesson in love was harsh enough and I couldn't go through it again.

"So what did I miss?" Adrian asked, walking back to the living room. This whole situation was absurd and I couldn't sit here and pretend that we were all going to be best friends.

"Claire brought food, but I can't stay. I just realised that I have something that I have to take care of. Thank you for drinks," I said and flew off towards the door before anyone could stop me. Adrian looked baffled, and Claire shot Mack a sharp glare, probably blaming him for scaring me off.

I slammed the door behind me, trying to calm my racing heart, and a sudden shot of anxiety attacked. My hands were shaking like crazy. Mack had no right to behave the way he did and I had acted on my emotions again. We had sex; it wasn't supposed to mean anything. Him lying about everything made me his accomplice in the deception, and that didn't sit well with me.

That night I went to bed angry and overwhelmed with guilt. Claire was nice. It was a shame that she had no idea what kind of husband she was married to. The whole thing made me sick because I couldn't deny that I wanted him all over again. My night was ruined. Around midnight I heard Adrian going back to his own apartment. Tears forced their way from my eyes. I knew that I shouldn't have flirted with Adrian to get back at Mack. I had to speak to Claire and tell her the truth.

The next day I arrived at work with a headache. At my desk I took two painkillers and tried to work on an article that my boss so generously assigned to me. It was another boring story, this time about the upcoming strikes in the NHS. My father's voice in my head reminded me that I should have chosen a law degree, because then I wouldn't have this problem.

Deep down I refused to acknowledge that he was right, to accept that my whole life was in shambles.

"Have you read this? The whole damn scandal is so funny." I heard the voice a few desks away from me. Mimi, the tall blond secretary that probably regularly fucked my chauvinistic boss, sounded excited about something. I lifted my head and scanned the room carefully. She was talking to Dean, a handsome reporter who took care of the sports section.

"No, what is it?" he asked.

“That rich daddy’s girl had an affair with a married man. They were caught in her father’s firm by the wife. Apparently the guy denied everything, saying that she seduced him. Can you believe it that people actually follow this shit?”

Mimi laughed, reading snippets of the article from the gossip magazine.

The colour drained from my face and I was ready to dive under the desk and never ever show my face in public again. It’d been weeks since my story filled the papers, and people were still reading about it. I had dyed my hair and wore glasses at work, hoping that I wouldn’t be recognized.

I couldn’t take it anymore. Yes, I was a home wrecker, but Andrew had seduced me to get back at his wife, and to get closer to my powerful father. It was just a game to him, nothing else. My whole life had fallen apart because of that stupid mistake. He sold the story to the papers, pretending that I was the one that initiated it, saying that I craved constant attention.

“People like real-life stories, Mi. Anyway, what’s happened to the girl?”

“Oh, I don’t know. Apparently she’s disappeared.”

I flew off my chair and hurried to the bathroom. I couldn’t listen to this anymore. Remembering how naive and stupid I was then, tears began streaming down my eyes. What was the point getting upset again? This whole thing was behind me now. I took what I could and moved to Edinburgh. My father told me to go to hell, that I should’ve been the one that died, not my younger sister. He always regretted that he was stuck with me after Mum left him.

And now I was proving that my father was right all along. I had barely managed to secure this job. My boss had no idea who I was. I wanted to show my uptight father that I was smart and able to make a name for myself, that I didn't need his money to be respected.

In the ladies' room I wiped the tears away and reapplied my makeup. I had a few small stories that I had to finish by the end of the week. My last conversation with my boss was pathetic. He promised me a column with Jordan, but so far nothing had come of it. All the men on the paper fought over significant stories and I was still a newbie and had no chance.

Worst of all, my head was screwed. Mack had been on my mind all day and every time I thought about his sexy eyes, I lost focus. It looked like my mistake of sleeping with him wasn't going to just go away. I owned the apartment, so I was there to stay. He was off limits and that glorious night with him didn't matter anymore. Everything had been going smoothly until I showed up at that damn party. I should have known that it was a bad idea.

Mack

Last night was a disaster. I wanted to talk to Ellie, but I couldn't leave Claire alone with Lurkin. She could have taken care of herself, but after what had happened in the past, I wasn't willing to risk it. My attempts at arranging a poker night in my place went nowhere. He wasn't too keen, saying that he was busy. My frustration grew when Claire drank too much and started complaining to him that I wasn't interested in doing anything together as a couple. She was starting to look pathetic. The evening was a total disaster. Adrian left around twelve looking slightly tipsy himself.

Scars from that day were opening up again and it was because of Claire. My wife had suffered. I'd had enough of watching scumbags like Lurkin walking free. Since I received his files, I had been looking forward to crushing him slowly and painfully.

Now I was sitting in the kitchen waiting for Claire to get out of the bathroom. Ellie hated me, and she had every right to. She hadn't given me a chance to explain. Besides, what was I supposed to say to her?

This whole thing was too complicated.

"Tequila is a bitch. Can't believe you actually let me drink that much," Claire said when she walked into the living room wearing a white robe. I had stopped counting how many times she tried talk to me about Charlotte. Our conversations about her always ended up in arguments. I still blamed her for Charlotte's death, even to this day.

"You should know your limits," I snapped, boiling inside.

"What's up with you today? Grumpy much?" she asked, walking around me. I should have told her earlier what I was expecting. Many things had changed, but she was delusional enough to believe that I could let go of that shameful scarred past.

I slammed my cup on the worktop, spilling some coffee, and frowned. "Are you fucking kidding me?" I shouted."You shouldn't have invited Lurkin in the first place. We had everything laid out and you've done your own thing as usual."

Okay, I was fucking losing my shit with her, but she had to know her place.

She put the espresso machine on and shook her head. "He seems clean and if we want to get anything out of him, we need to engage on a more personal level. This whole thing would have worked out better if you hadn't interrupted me the whole time," Claire said. "I was trying to have a conversation and you kept barging in. Who does that?"

"The other plan was more reasonable," I argued, feeling frustrated. "And he would have engaged more with me if it wasn't for that girl, Ellie. Why the hell did you have to invite her too?"

"Pull your head out of your ass, Tobias, for God's sake. I'm in this shit with you. You have to start letting go of what happened in the past," she said, raising her voice. "We have to be believable. Besides, that girl can be useful. We can use her to get to him."

Ellie couldn't be involved; no one else could. He preyed on women like her. Lurkin was mine to take care of. Besides that, she was too good for him. Maybe one night of great sex didn't give me a right to lay claim over her, but Lurkin was dangerous and she had to stay away.

"No fucking way. She won't be involved at all. Next time run your ideas by me first before you decide to screw everything up."

Claire pressed her lips into a hard line, and anger flickered in her eyes. All right, maybe I wasn't being fair, but I hated the fact that I was stuck here with her, this woman that I had no feelings for anymore. We had drifted apart years ago.

"You're such an ass. I have explained to you before. She lied to me, told me that she was only going to look around. You can't keep blaming me for what happened. There are things—"

I remembered that day like it was yesterday. Claire and Charlotte were called to the house in a suburb of Glasgow. At the time I was on the streets, attempting to question dealers and a few small-time gang members, away from my own district. Claire had introduced Charlotte to me at university. The two of us had been friends for over a decade, since junior school. Years later, after I married Charlotte, Claire had followed our career path and joined the police force. A year later she became Charlotte's partner. The job came with certain risks, and as a couple we were well aware of it, but never acknowledged it. My wife didn't pick and choose her assignments; she was committed to the job, to the people that she worked with.

I only found out that something was wrong when I switched on the radio several hours later, after I got back to the car. The dispatcher said something about an officer down at the shooting in Milton—that was the area Charlotte was working in that afternoon. A minute later, our surname was mentioned and I panicked. I tried calling, but Claire and Charlotte were both unreachable. I abandoned my duties and drove off, thinking about our upcoming anniversary, about how late our dinner was last night, pointless arguments that we were having recently. Despite the overwhelming anxiety, I knew that she was all right. I kept telling myself that I would be laughing about this tomorrow night.

Charlotte knew how to take care of herself, and we were both aware of the risks that we were putting ourselves in daily. I raced through the streets, filled with tension, until I reached the station. I didn't even get upstairs. One of the officers in the car park told me that something went wrong in Milton, that Claire was in the hospital with Charlotte.

Everything exploded then and I was roaring with unending emotion. My mind was clouded, frantic with shock and unable to focus on a single thought, but somehow I arrived at Glasgow Central half an hour later. Time started moving in slow motion. I argued with the nurses on the front desk for information until they told me where she was being treated, then I raced to the third floor. Claire was sitting in the waiting area with her head down. She was sobbing.

"Where is she, Claire? Charlotte!" I roared, not caring that there were other people there, other patients. I just needed to see my wife. Claire looked at me with her puffy eyes, broken and haunted. She shook her head.

"They just called her death, Tobias. They tried to bring her back for thirty minutes," she whispered. I tangled my hair, feeling like someone had just ripped me apart, kicking me in my gut until I wasn't moving anymore. This was a dream, a prank. Just this morning I had wished her good luck. She wasn't dead —she couldn't be.

I was beside Claire before she had a chance to blink, shaking her.

"What happened? How come you're here and she's somewhere else, away from me?" I yelled at the top of my lungs. Some of the doctors and nurses were trying to pull me away from her, but I was in a rage, ready to kill the woman that had been my wife's partner for as long as I could remember.

"She told me to stay outside, Tobias. I didn't want to listen… oh, God. It all happened so quickly…

"Just shut up, Claire. I can't listen to you. You shouldn't have let her go in alone," I shouted, losing control of myself.

Suddenly I was snapping back to the present. "We aren't getting Ellie involved. I'm going to get something on Lurkin sooner or later."

I hated when Claire brought up the past, like Charlotte meant nothing to her. We had been through this a lot, over and over. She took a deep breath, pretending that these cruel memories weren't affecting her anymore.

"We are going to get something on Lurkin," she corrected me. "You would have to be blind not to see that she was flirting with Lurkin. Think about it—if we get her involved we would have half the work done for us."

"You expect her to fuck him and then give us all the juicy details?" I asked, remembering our erotic moments together. I had no fucking clue what was wrong with me, but I wanted Ellie for myself. Lurkin paid for sex with whores and Ellie was too pure to be tainted with this bullshit. This was wrong and I knew it. She was the first woman that had actually woken me from my mourning in a dreamlike state. No one had managed that since the shooting.

"She might not look like that kind, but she's a reporter. I bet she would do anything for a story," Claire added and then stopped, staring at me with that odd expression on her face, like she just realised something very important. "God, you like her. That's why you're pissed with me right now. You actually like this girl."

"Don't be absurd," I snarled.

"I have known you for over ten years, Mack, and you don't want to work with me and that's okay. You don't need to be ashamed. It's been five years—"

"Shut up, Claire. Shut the fuck up and stay out of my head."

I stormed out of the apartment before I did something that I'd regret later. The moment Claire let my wife go into that building alone, she betrayed me. We hadn't got on since I moved away and now we were expected to be with each other almost twenty-four seven, fixing the painful past.

Ellie had pushed the other side of me that night, the one that I had hidden away. I liked being in control in the bedroom, and with her I aimed to please. She melted my usual coldness and my cock responded in ways I had never expected. I doubt I had ever been that hard before. It was like I was back to myself again, calm and controlled, not impulsive and miserable.

Ellie

By Thursday I'd had enough of writing about dancing dogs and stolen racing pigeons. For at least two nights in a row I heard the guy next door moving furniture, banging and talking at weird hours of the night. He was keeping me awake and my tolerance was waning.

I hadn't seen Mack and Claire since that night in their apartment. The truth of the matter was, I was avoiding them. Even after almost a week, that night with him was still fully alive in my memory. Adrian, on the other hand, wasn't avoiding me and it seemed he remembered how forward I was with him that night. It looked like he finished work the same time as me, and we chatted a few times. Yesterday on my way to the car he asked me out for a drink, saying that his mate opened up a new bar in town and he wanted to take me. I turned the whole thing into a joke, almost panicking, having Mack in my head growling territorially at me the whole time.

Guilt mixed with lust was a really bad combination, because despite how fucked up this whole thing was, I still wanted him and nobody else. Maybe Dad was right—maybe I was just too selfish and self-centred to care about other people's feelings.

After another crappy day at work, I changed into my gym clothes and headed downstairs to use the facilities. Adrian was handsome, single, and he most definitely wasn't married. He ticked all the right boxes and I knew that I should have agreed, but something prevented me. Mack was pissed that I dared to flirt with Adrian. I wasn't looking for a relationship or love, but I wanted to get back at Mack for the hurt his lies had caused, and Adrian gave me the impression that he was only looking for some fun, nothing more.

I signed my name in the concierge, chatted for a little bit with a ginger lad and then left to get on with my workout. After half an hour on the treadmill, I did some pushups and then changed into my swimming costume.

I didn't fancy using the pool tonight, so I headed straight to the sauna. But I saw it was a mistake, because Mack was there lying in the steam. Seeing him punched the air out of my lungs quite suddenly.

Six

Ellie

I stopped at the door, and my whole body vibrated with stupid excitement. I wasn't scared of him; it was the fact that I found myself enclosed in a tiny, steamy, hot box with a gorgeous half-naked Scot who rocked my boat in every single way possible.

The events of that evening when he saved me from that asshole suddenly spun in front of my eyes. I remembered the tantalising heat between us and the wonderful things that my body had experienced during just one night with him. He had an amazing body, perfect in every way.

"Get inside before you let all the heat out."

His strong voice rang in my head and for some reason I complied with his command. My twat of an ex-boyfriend, Andrew, had complemented my body whenever he could, but I never felt that sexy, even when I danced for him. Right now I felt a little too self-conscious in my swimming suit, being so close to this man that had seen me naked.

Mack rose and sat up on the wooden bench, giving me some space next to him, his glorious body shining with moisture. My mouth went dry and I quickly sat down, edging closer to the door to avoid him. I had to get out of here. He was a cheating, lying scumbag and I knew I needed to stay away.

"Just pretend that I'm not here. We aren't exactly on speaking terms," I snarled, folding my arms over my chest. My body was on fire, igniting sparks of lust inside me. I felt his grey eyes on me, but as long as I didn't make eye contact, I would be fine.

"Well, we were on fucking terms only a week ago." Mack chuckled.

I shivered, remembering how good his cock felt inside me. I sighed and looked at him. "How many more women is your wife unaware of? How many were here before me?" I asked, shaking with anger.

He seemed calm, sitting on the bench like everything was perfectly normal, looking at me with his deep grey eyes. "None. I've never had a one-night stand with anyone before you, Angel."

My lungs were on fire and I wanted to scream. What the hell?

Did he just say that I was the first woman that he'd cheated on his wife with? On top of that, he'd called me Angel. I couldn't bloody deny it—I liked it, but I felt pathetic knowing that he was turning me on.

My jaw dropped and small beads of sweat rolled down my back and over my cleavage. The temperature in the sauna must have heated up to about hundred degrees Celsius. I closed my mouth, breathing through my nose. "I don't believe you. Men like you cheat all the time; you were too smooth, too practiced," I said with a small voice. "Plus you knew I lived on the same floor, right? You could have said no."

"This is more complex than you think. That night was supposed to be my last in the apartment. I was planning to be out in the morning," he stated angrily. I frowned, trying to breathe at the same time.

"Last? I don't get it. Were you supposed to move out or sell?" I asked, confused.

"Something like that," he said hesitantly.

Then there was silence. Neither of us said anything for what seemed like a decade. His explanation made some sense, but he was still a cheating bastard who had a wife.

"Adrian asked me out on a date," I blurted out, not even knowing why I needed to justify myself to him. Deep down I was still pissed off and I wanted to make him feel like shit.

"What did you just say?" he asked, shocked and jumping to his feet. Drenching desire shuddered through me like a lightning bolt as his eyes looked right through me.

"I'm going out with Adrian next door. He's nice and—"

I didn't finish my sentence because Mack grabbed my shoulders and pushed me against the wooden bench, his mouth inches away from mine. The moisture in the air made my lungs stop working altogether. I felt the wetness appear between my legs as I started throbbing with intensity, wanting him so badly.

"Stay away from Lurkin. He isn't good for you," he warned me with the same domineering tone of voice that he had used when he fucked me in my apartment.

My crotch was now drenched with the need to have him inside me again. I reminded myself that this was all wrong, the desire and daydreams.

"You can't tell me what to do, Mack," I whispered quietly, trying to smile, but my body failed me.

"You seem to forget, Angel; you loved my orders in the bedroom. You were so turned on when I took control of you and your pleasure."

My nipples were painfully hard, but he hadn't looked down once at my chest. Every part of my body felt like it was on fire, but this had nothing to do with the temperature. His magnificently sculpted chest was right in front of me.

"Go back to your wife. We have nothing to talk about, Mack. I came here to relax," I managed to gasp, although I sounded pathetic. Mack's eyes flickered with mischief and then he did something that I hadn't expected—he kissed me.

His wet lips were on mine, teasing and gently caressing, sensually giving me familiar tingles. That magical feeling pulled and crushed my internal voice of reason. I parted my mouth, and when his tongue began teasing mine I instantly wanted more.

The sticky heavy air made me unable to think clearly. Mack pressed himself against me, pushing me down to recline on the bench. Waves of anticipation scorched my body right down to my core. He began to spread my legs, the touch of his hands causing me to shudder with delight. He pressed his hard erection over my crotch, teasing me.

His possessive kiss turned rough and sensual, each frenzied nip and bite of my mouth melting my defences, every kiss melting my body into a pool of mush. My sex throbbed as he parted my bikini bottoms gently to the side, tickling me with delight and rubbing his hard shaft over my clit. I had never been so turned on.

"You won't be seeing Lurkin. He isn't good for you. Do you understand me? I told you once before, this pussy belongs to me. Do you need a reminder?" Mack asked, pulling away.

I nodded, moving my hands involuntarily over the muscles on his chest, when the door to the sauna opened up.

"Oh, sorry."

We both pulled away, panting, and I wanted to disappear into the ground. Some old random guy was staring at both of us with the most awkward expression on his face. I quickly wriggled myself away from Mack and headed out, not making eye contact with anyone. Mack shouldn't have kissed me, but this was all my fault because I didn't stop him.

Stupid, stupid girl.

Mack

I didn't say anything to the old guy that caught me about to fuck my Angel in the sauna. I hadn't expected to see her there, barely covering up her gorgeous body. Ellie looked stunning in that navy bikini and I was struggling to control my dick when I saw her. It seemed like she had avoided me and Claire all week. We hadn't spoken since she had flirted with Lurkin in front of me, just to piss me off. There wasn't any other explanation for it.

I ran after her, straight inside the ladies' changing room.

"Ellie, listen. I didn't—"

She slapped me. I couldn't fucking believe it. No woman had ever slapped me before. I didn't have a chance to react before she was screaming in my face.

"Get the hell out of here, Mack, before I go to the concierge and make an official complaint that you're harassing me!"

I wanted to drag her over my knee and spank that luscious arse until she learned her lesson and begged me to stop. She had no idea what was going on. Lurkin was a scumbag and she was too pure to get involved with someone like him. I had been forced to lie to her and Claire had already noticed that I liked her. I couldn't afford any drama right now, so I left feeling as though the anger was tearing me apart.

Another moment of weakness and I had nearly thrown away years of working towards this point. I grabbed my stuff and headed upstairs, wondering what the hell was wrong with me.

Ellie was just another woman, one of many.

"Lurkin left while you were downstairs enjoying yourself," Claire snapped at me when I walked through the door. "We should try to get inside his apartment. Get the team in, install the bugs and cameras."

"No, it won't be necessary. That's not how I work these days," I told her, pissed that she was watching my back all the time. Lurkin wouldn't use his apartment to conduct his business. He might be powerful, but he wasn't fucking stupid. She was supposed to be out, reporting our progress to the station. Lurkin was inside most of the day, and I hated waiting around. Some days I really regretted that I was in this line of work. The job could be a tedious waiting game; most of the time I sat on my ass, waiting for other people, for information and evidence processing. Today I had gone to work out for an hour, just to kill time. Five o'clock was my workout routine, but actually I was waiting for Lurkin down in the gym, silently hoping that he would show up. Instead, Ellie appeared out of nowhere in a sexy swimming suit.

She was distracting; I couldn't fucking deny it. Every time I saw her my pulse sped up, reminding me of that night that we shared together.

"And why not?" Claire interrupted my stream of fucked-up thoughts.

"You read the files. We don't have any solid evidence. The superintendent will have my ass on a plate if something goes wrong."

She looked annoyed and raised her left eyebrow, probably thinking that I was telling her a total bullshit story. "You seem to forget that we are a team, Tobias. We both know that he wasn't too keen on your poker night suggestion."

"Claire, I'm fucking serious. You're not thinking clearly. He purchased the apartment legally and we would be wasting time and resources on this. He wouldn't jeopardise a legal enterprise unless he was laundering money, you know this," I told her and left the room, knowing that she was going to be relentless.

When the warm water started running down my spine I relaxed my muscles and started massaging my shaft, attempting to get rid of the distracting image of Ellie down on her knees. That night had awoken a desire that I thought had died during the day of the shooting. The whole operation was pointless. Maybe I should come clean with Claire. There was still time to tell her that I had fucked the civilian because she was helping me to deal with my screwed-up past.

Fuck, I wasn't prepared to waste months of work because I couldn't keep my dick in my pants. Guilt had made me immune to whatever drama was going on in my life. That night with Ellie was one of those moments when I imagined being someone different, when I could pursue a happy moment with a woman that I truly desired.

Ellie

"Would you like a drink?" I asked my colleague, picking up my red mug.

"Coffee would be great, thank you, hon," Susan replied, smiling. I needed to wake up if I was planning on finishing that story about a disabled boxer by three in the afternoon. Maybe I was aiming for too much. After all, the paper was small and my boss already had his favourites. I was no one, just some girl that was working her way through the ranks.

I waited for the water to boil, thinking about my next article and how to impress my boss with it. Phil had hired me last month, while I was still waiting for the sale to go through on my apartment in the Grange. The other day I followed Jordan and Craig, two other reporters, when they went to confirm a statement at the police station. I thought that they would get me involved with whatever article they were working on, but neither of them wanted to talk to me. They joked, trying to humiliate me for being the newbie. The next day Phil told me to focus on the work that I was assigned to, and to stop running around the city after other reporters. Sometimes I wondered if I was really cut out for this job. Maybe my father had been right all along.

Once the water had boiled I was reaching out, ready to pour some into my cup, when I saw a picture of Andrew in the magazine on the table. My heart kicked in my chest and I accidentally tipped the kettle, splashing boiling water all over my hand.

I screamed and jumped away, but it was already too late. The skin on my hand turned bright red. Within moments, painful blisters started appearing all over the front of my forearm. Pain shot through it as I turned on the cold water to try to ease the burning. A few of my colleagues ran into the kitchen, asking me if I was all right. Someone else brought me a first aid kit. My hand was an angry red and the pain was unbearable. I'd made a hell of a mess.

People were nice, trying to help the best they could. I forced the tears away, knowing that I shouldn't show how weak and damaged I was inside. My boss ordered me to go to the hospital and take the rest of the day off.

Susan took me to ER and there I found out that I had a first-degree burn from the scalding. This week couldn't have gotten any worse. Two days ago I slapped Mack, today I had a huge wound, and now it looked like I was going to miss my story deadline. Susan wanted to drive me home, but I insisted that I was all right. My apartment was a mess and on the way I had to do some grocery shopping.

I realised that this was a bad idea as soon as I got back to the Grange. I struggled to carry the two bags all the way to my apartment, my hand throbbing with constant pain. It was Friday night, so I bought wine to get drunk and forget my shitty week. The hospital had given me painkillers that didn't seem to be doing anything. On top of that, the article about Andrew had managed to get me completely down.

After Susan left, I had torn the whole magazine into pieces. It turned out that the bastard had announced his engagement to some high-class solicitor that he met at some conference in Spain. I couldn't believe it—he screwed me promising me the world, divorced his wife in the process, and in the meantime managed to gain another stupid bimbo to warm his bed and boost his reputation.

"Let me get that for you," said a familiar electric voice behind me, taking my grocery bags. I knew that it was Mack the instant that magnetic force shot through me when his fingers brushed over mine. It seemed like he was everywhere, and I couldn't help but wonder how things would have turned out between us if he didn't have a wife.

Seven

Ellie

"Thank you… you don't have to do that," I mumbled, trying to mask the pain and the exhaustion from my voice. Our last meeting had left a sour taste in my mouth and I felt a little ashamed that I'd slapped him. He had no right to kiss me when his wife had probably been upstairs waiting for him. I kind of lost control then, acted impulsively. His short but intense kiss was his weapon. It had pulled me back to my apartment and our night together.

Mack picked up all my shopping bags without saying anything. He looked awesome in a black coat and a red scarf around his neck. I felt worse, knowing that he was never going to be mine, that I had to keep away from him for the sake of his marriage.

"What happened to your hand?" he asked, concern in his voice.

I grimaced when I moved my hand. I wasn't used to this kind of pain. My skin felt like it was literally on fire. "I had a little accident today in the kitchen at work."

We were standing inside the building and his grey eyes were looking through me intensely. My heart skipped several beats, but I plastered Andrew's face in front of me as a reminder that I didn't sleep with married men anymore.

"First or second degree burn?"

"First, but it's all right. It doesn't hurt that much anymore," I assured him, lying through my teeth. Of course it bloody hurt, but I didn't want him to be concerned about me.

"I have something upstairs that should ease the pain and help with the swelling. Let's go," he commanded when the lift arrived. It looked like Mack wasn't angry or even annoyed about that slap from a few days ago. I was clear enough when I'd told him to stay away, but now he was helping me.

Well, great. Now I felt like crap because I'd overreacted and kissed him back.

Oh God, and it felt good.

The dead silence stretched on while we were in the lift. I shifted my weight to the side, biting my lip.

"Mack, listen. I have to apologise," I said. "I shouldn't have slapped you that day, but I was so overwhelmed. We shouldn't have been making out in the sauna. It was wrong."

This was the worst apology that I had ever given, not to mention that I just admitted to him that I was attracted to him. I crumbled when he was around me, but Claire was a nice person. She didn't deserve any of this.

His face was tight and he didn't show any emotion. The tension rose, coursing between us, making me aware that any wrong move would cost more than I'd bargained for. Heat surged down underneath my dress, and all I could think about was him being inside me that night.

My hand throbbed with pain and I couldn't focus properly. Life kept throwing hurdles in front of me. Andrew had achieved what he wanted with his affair with me. He made a deal with my father and forgot about me as soon as I was no longer needed. That was painful, but it made me realise that I never did belong there. Dad always admired my little sister; I was his constant disappointment. The black sheep, as he used to call me.

"Things aren't how they seem, Ellie," Mack said, moving closer to me, placing his mouth next to my ear. "I don't regret anything; I couldn't. That night was so special and I loved how you responded to my touch."

His fresh cologne caressed me. It pushed all the worries away, soothing the discomfort and guilt that shrouded me. I swallowed hard, knowing that we shouldn't be discussing this right now. I had no idea what it meant. Sometimes I imagined what being married to someone that truly loved me would be like, but those dreams were so pointless. I found it hard to believe that love existed in this cruel world.

"I shouldn't have slapped you, but that night was a mistake," I told him. "Don't you love Claire? How could you have done that to her, betrayed her so badly?"

He inhaled sharply, pressing his lips in a hard line. His eyes were filled with frustration and some anger. I didn't know what kind of life he was living. Maybe Claire wasn't making him happy.

"Sometimes people get married for reasons other than love," he replied.

His answer confused the hell out of me. Was he saying that he didn't love Claire? The door to the lift opened up.

"Open the door to your apartment, Ellie."

That strong commanding voice sent a shiver of lust down my spine. My head spun, and that urge to be in his arms grew. I needed to remember that he was taken, even when he fucked me. He probably felt guilty, so he wanted to do me a favour, like all neighbours do. Mack walked inside my apartment, putting the groceries on the worktops.

"Do you want me to help you with putting these away?" he asked, standing way too close to me.

My heartbeat was unsteady but I licked my lips, dismissing whatever the hell was going on inside my body. "No, I'm all right," I assured him.

"Then come with me. I'll give you something for that burn," he commanded. I didn't know why, but I kept hearing the same domineering tone in his voice, the same one he had when he was ordering me to strip.

"Mack, you don't have to do this. The stuff that they gave —"

"This isn't a request, Angel," he stated and walked back to the corridor, heading to his own apartment. Angel… that nickname was like another invitation. I quickly pulled myself together and followed him. Inside his place, I found Claire in the living room, doing something on her laptop. She greeted me in a friendly way and we chatted for a bit. Shortly after that, Mack explained that I'd had an accident at work and that I had burned myself. Claire looked sympathetic and she told Mack to help me with my groceries. We left five minutes later.

"Let's sit down; it's better if I apply the gel myself," Mack stated.

"No, I'm fine. You don't have to do that," I argued, afraid to be so close to his gorgeous scent.

"Why do you always have to defy me? You were so damn obedient in the bedroom," he muttered and dragged me back to the sofa. He smelled amazing, and I instantly wanted to run my lips over his abs. This was getting absurd, to the point where I was no longer thinking rationally. His hand carefully unwrapped my bandage, and goose pimples rose all over my arms.

"If I hadn't been committed, I'd have asked you out on a date," he said after he inspected my wound carefully.

I was so shocked by his words. "Yes, maybe. It was just sex that I needed from you that night, nothing else. I wouldn't really date you."

"And why is that, Ellie? Stay still, please," he asked.

My wound hurt like hell, but I was trying to be brave, forcing myself to stay still. Despite his huge physique, he was very gentle. "I've had some bad experiences with men and it's been a very stressful month," I explained, looking away.

"Did it work?"

"What?"

"Me putting my cock in you, making you mine, fucking you that night? Did I do my job well in de-stressing you?" he asked, with a hint of lust.

I swallowed hard, remembering his touch on my skin. "You were very satisfying, but we shouldn't be talking about this right now and you shouldn't be even be touching me," I told him, feeling heat grow between my legs. "Are you going to tell her about us?"

"I haven't decided yet, Ellie. We've had our ups and downs. I think we should forget about that night for now and try to be friends, or at least cordial neighbours."

Mack's face was telling me that this wasn't what he was thinking about right now. His eyes were hovering over my cleavage.

"I would like that," I said. I was so engrossed by our conversation that I didn't realise when he was done with my new dressing. The skin was still stinging, but the gel was soothing the pain.

"Next time, try to take care of yourself a bit better."

"Thank you."

He smiled, left the tube on the table and left. My heart was speeding, as usual when he was around, and I told myself that his sweet gesture didn't mean anything; he simply didn't like to see me in pain. I'd had butterflies in my belly whenever I was with Andrew, but he had never given me feelings as intense as Mack had. Once I settled back down, I took out my bottle of wine that I bought earlier. The next morning I had to get up early to try to do some work, but hell, things couldn't get any worse. I was ready to empty that bottle tonight, without feeling bad about it.

The guy that I'd had the most amazing sex with was still married. Andrew had gotten away with cheating on his wife and making a lot of money by spreading malicious rumours to the papers about me. And on top of that, I couldn't use the keyboard for the next couple of days until my wound healed.

In the past week I had tried to make a contact with a man inside the police station. I figured that if I had a reliable source, I could convince Phil that I had a reliable enough informant to write a good story. I had spoken to that guy only once, but he said he was willing to help. It was a favour from an old friend. The guy didn't fully trust me yet, but he promised to phone once he had anything new. My phone was dead, so I plugged it into the socket. Suddenly there was a blue flash and all the electricity went off in my apartment. I guess the fuses just blew out. I sat in the darkness for a few seconds, trying to figure out what'd happened and how to fix it.

Frustrated and angry, I phoned downstairs to the concierge and explained what'd happened. They took a while and by the time I could plug the phone back in, I was really pissed off.

An hour later when I checked it, the phone was still dead. Nothing had happened. It looked like the charger must have gotten damaged and stopped working. All that was left for to me do was to sit down and cry. Karma… I knew that it would finally get me. I'd made lots of terrible mistakes, hadn't trusted my instincts, and now I was paying for it.

It looked like I might be missing out on another story. At least my hand had finally stopped throbbing. There were still a lot of unpacked boxes in my bedroom, and there was probably a spare charger somewhere in there, but I just wasn't prepared to go through all that stuff tonight.

Ten minutes later, dressed more casually, I was knocking at Adrian's apartment. I could have gone back to Mack's, but I didn't want to look any more pathetic. It took him a long moment to open the door. I wondered if I had interrupted something important.

"What's up, neighbour?" he asked, lowering his eyes to my cleavage. Okay, I needed to re-think the reasons I thought he was appealing enough to date. Mack had lied, but I didn't think I could date Adrian after all.

"Please tell me that you have an iPhone? My charger just blew up."

"Yes, I think so. Hold on," he said and then disappeared inside. It looked like he wasn't going to invite me in. Maybe he'd changed his mind about me too. I stood in the corridor, praying for my source to call this evening. I needed to write something worthwhile, something with an edge that people could get behind. A few moments later, Adrian came back with the charger for me.

"What do you mean, you don't know? Mack, this is serious. How are we going to pay our bills?" It was Claire's voice coming from next door, shouting pretty loudly.

I looked at Adrian, who lost his smile. I didn't want to listen to Mack and Claire's argument in front of him.

"Get off my case, woman, and stop nagging. I'll get a job!" Mack shouted back.

I took the charger from Adrian. "Right, thank you—"

"Me, nagging? You ungrateful bastard. I have been supporting you all the way with that stupid business of yours. Get a freaking job. It's not difficult. Our debts won't pay themselves!"

Her loud angry voice cut me off. I couldn't believe that they were so loud. Adrian shook his head but didn't say anything. They had seemed all right just half an hour ago. I didn't know that Mack lost his job. During that first evening in his apartment, he mentioned that he was doing some contract work.

"Fuck, I can't take your bullshit, Claire. Life isn't perfect. We wouldn't have to worry about money if you didn't spend a fortune on fucking shoes!"

"I earn money, so I can buy whatever I want. You're useless, Mack. You're just a loser that can't support himself. My father told me not to marry you. He knew."

Her comment set Mack off and he started blaming her for all the things that had gone wrong in his life. Adrian seemed to be enjoying the argument. Me, on the other hand, I couldn't just stand there and pretend that it was okay to listen to their fight.

"All right, thanks. I'll buy a new one tomorrow and get this back to you," I assured Adrian, trying not to pay attention to the screams coming from next door.

"No big deal, Ellie."

Mack

Claire suggested the little show. She wanted Lurkin to hear our argument. I couldn't fucking deny it—the idea was good. Now it all depended on whether Lurkin was ready to take his cleverly prepared act to the next level and actually offer me a job. A guy like Lurkin only cared about his reputation or saving his own skin, and as soon as Claire understood that her plan had failed, we could move on to do things my way.

Claire was determined and she kept me on my toes, but she was too distracting. Memories from the past carried way too many scars and emotional memories. People were making assumptions about me, thinking that working undercover for so long was my way of getting back what I'd lost.

And Claire didn't like the fact that I seemed more worried about Ellie than I was about our operation. That night in the shower I stroked my cock, thinking about Ellie. Fuck, I wanted her so much. We didn't know each other at all, and I simply couldn't get to know her, as much as I wanted to—it just wasn't possible.

None of this mattered. Lurkin was going down either way, and I needed to start by taking really small steps.

Next morning, Claire went back to Glasgow, probably to report our progress, whereas I wasted some time over the next few hours, knowing that I had to show up in the pub about two o'clock—around the time when Lurkin often went there—and it was best if I looked more miserable than usual. People were more sympathetic with losers than confident assholes; that was why I liked playing one. A guy who couldn't keep his job and had problems with his wife definitely seemed like a loser. Ellie and her petite body occupied my mind, however. This whole sitting on my ass all day and waiting for the right moment was taking its toll on me. I liked being out and about. Anticipation, adrenaline and fear of the unknown kept me going. It had taken me a year after the shooting to pick up my gun again. Doctors told me that I had PTSD, but I knew that I was simply grieving.

I threw on some jeans and a jumper and my old leather biker jacket and went out. I liked living in this complex, away from the busy life in the city. The beach was on my doorstep and I had a chance to work out whatever I wanted.

The walk to the local pub was about twenty minutes. Claire knew that she had to leave me alone today. Her comments were slowly grating on my nerves, more than usual.

She also knew that we had to put our issues behind us and work together to fix our rocky relationship. After all, we had always been good friends before I met Charlotte.

The sky was grey and it was pretty damn cold for November.

I went in, ordered a pint of Guinness, and sat down at the corner in front of the TV. It was before kickoff, but the pub was already packed with men and women, all wearing blue and white colours. The Scots were playing the English today, so the atmosphere was pretty good.

"Mind if I join you?"

Fuck me, that was quick. I wasn't expecting him until later, but I guess that I struck a bit of luck. Lurkin was standing in front of me with a pint in his hand. It had taken me a while to figure out where he liked to drink. He was a damn good actor, trying to blend in, staying away from his real occupation.

"Feel free. My wife won't be coming, that's for sure," I said, emphasising the word wife.

"Rough night?" he asked.

I bet he didn't give a damn at all, but at least he was making conversation. "She hates rugby. Besides, I needed a drink. It should be a good game," I muttered.

Lurkin agreed with me until the match started. For the next forty minutes there was a lot of growling, shouting and cursing. Scottish people were very passionate about national sports teams and it wasn't a happy crowd when after the first half we were fucking losing by ten points.

Lurkin chatted to me about banal stuff, asking me about the complex. He had done well for himself. He created his own cover, making sure that no one suspected anything dodgy from a decent citizen like him.

"You know our cute neighbour, Ellie?"

"Yeah, what about her?" I asked, annoyed that he brought her up.

"I asked her out the other day. She seemed hesitant, but I bet I can break her." He laughed and I clenched my fists. This was going to be a hell of an afternoon, and I had thought it was going to be easy.

Eight

Mack

I shifted on my seat, gripping my glass tighter, telling myself that I had to stay calm. Lurkin didn't date; he fucked whatever he wanted and never tied himself to anyone. Alcohol was coursing through my veins, making me angrier and more impulsive than usual. I needed to remember that I was here for one thing only and that thing was Lurkin's trust.

"She's pretty and smart, but I don't think she's the kind that fucks around," I told him, drinking more of my Guinness. He laughed, shaking his head.

"I bet she does, mate," he argued with a wink. Jealous rage rose within me and I didn't know why. I had no right to claim Ellie, but I didn't want this asshole to taint her with his dirty claws. I knew everything about him. He was one twisted son of a bitch.

"At least she doesn't nag like Claire does. They laid me off and she's so panicky, thinking that I won't find anything else," I complained.

Someone at the back started to sing the Scottish national anthem. Some woman told the bloke to shut his mouth.

"Ellie came to borrow a charger last night and we both heard your argument," Lurkin said, not being soft about it at all. Crap, I wasn't expecting Ellie to hear it, and why the fuck did she ask him, not me?

"Sorry, mate, I didn't mean to ruin your pitch, but Claire pissed me off. I'll get a job sooner or later."

"Women, huh," he admitted.

"You should be glad that you're single. Nagging is the worst. All right, so my business didn't take off and I screwed up. I'll do anything for now just to shut her up," I said, sounding down.

"I need drivers, Mack. I'm planning to expand next year. I know that this isn't something that you were probably considering, but I guess it would help you earn some quick cash."

I was ready to slap myself. Lurkin was smart. He didn't piss around the place where he lived and he needed to keep that nice guy persona for people who didn't know about his real business.

"You're offering me a job?" I asked, sounding surprised.

"It might not be long term, but it should sort you out for now until you get back on your feet. And it should get Claire off your back," he added, winking at me, like he understood that I was having a hard time with her.

"Anything, mate. I appreciate it," I said, feeling angry that Claire was right. I didn't believe that Lurkin had enough balls to offer me something like that. I didn't think that he trusted me enough yet, but I guessed I was wrong.

We chatted a bit more, until the second half started. He ordered a few more drinks, showing me what kind of a great neighbour he really was. I bonded with him that afternoon. It was just the beginning, but at least it was progress. Starting Monday, I was done with being stuck indoors all the time. I felt and worked better in the field, where I could make a real difference. Things were moving slowly, but sooner or later Lurkin was going to make an error and I would be ready for it.

Ellie

"I want to write about something meaningful, Phil. I'm a good reporter, but you haven't given me a chance," I argued, standing in my boss's office, trying to fight my corner. I had no idea what had gotten into me. Yesterday had been the worst Sunday in my life. After drinking the whole bottle of wine, a horrific hangover had shut me down. My burn wasn't too bad, though. Mack's gel really helped with the swelling and pain.

My old friend Rebecca cancelled her visit, saying that she just met a guy and he was taking her out. I was having problems adjusting to being on my own. Back in Glasgow I was always surrounded by friends, but since the scandal I had been hearing less and less from them. Deep down I realised that they never truly cared for me; they wanted be seen with me because I was the daughter of one of the most powerful men in Scotland.

"Ellie, you will write whatever it is we need. Crime is for the big boys. Just stick to what you know."

Chauvinistic pig. This wasn't how I imagined my career would be when I got the job here.

"No, Phil. I'm more than capable of writing about murders, gangs and everything else, anything other than some damn cat that went missing two years and finally came back to the owner. I want my name to be on the first page," I said, really fed up with the fact that Phil kept looking at me like I was his next lay. I knew what he wanted, but sleeping with him wouldn't make me feel any better about myself. I had a bloody degree and a master's, spoke two other languages and because of one stupid mistake, I had to work with some pervert that thought women were beneath him.

"Honey, the streets aren't for you and your pretty face. Jordan has people on the inside, his own sources. No one will give you a story for nothing."

"What if I go out and find something interesting?" I snarled in anger, placing my hands on my hips.

"I don't care what you do as long as you bring me what's needed to be written every week—you know, the usual crap."

I pressed my lips in a hard line. The usual crap. So that's what ten years of studies gave me. Some crappy little fluff pieces that weren't relevant to real news and didn't make a difference.

"Fine, I'll do that," I snapped and stormed out of his office. Okay, that wasn't very smart, because, yet again, I let my emotions get in the way. There was no point getting angry. I was simply no one to Phil.

I didn't go back to my desk; instead I headed to the bathroom to change my bandage.

"A private club? With a stripper?"

I stopped in the hallway, hearing Jordan's goofy voice somewhere on the stairs. I hadn't been working at the paper for long, but I had noticed that he was always on his phone.

"Right... yeah... all right, but how do you know that there's something going on up there?"

I moved closer to the wall and waited, chewing my nails. I was done with being a doormat. I bet Jordan was talking to his source. Maybe I could pick up on something interesting.

"Johnny Hodges—wow, that's big. Do you think he's back in the area?"

My heart started beating faster. I knew that surname, Hodges, from somewhere. I had to Google it later.

Jordan was listening and then he said, "Coral. I got it, but we need evidence. Besides, he hasn't been active that much," he added, then laughed out loud. "Thanks, mate, have to go. I have shitloads of work to do."

I backed away quickly, running to the bathroom. I was on my phone then, checking the information about that guy Johnny Hodges. Nothing came up and I bit my lip so hard that I didn't realise it hurt. After some failed searches, I managed to figure out that Coral was the name of a club in a well-known neighbourhood. Something was going on there and Jordan was waiting for information. It took me a moment to calm down. There was no point in getting excited. I had only heard snippets of his conversation, but no one said that I couldn't sniff about in that club to see what else I could find out.

There were only two other girls that worked in the office and they didn't seem to have any ambition. Maybe they were happy writing about the usual crap. I did some polishing and editing until it was time for me to leave.

On the way back to the complex, I made a decision. It was now or never. This kind of opportunity wouldn't present itself again. Phil was going to regret this, because once I had the real story I would sell it to a bigger paper with an editor that bloody well gave a damn.

When I got back to my apartment, I quickly changed into a more provocative outfit, and around seven I drove to Granton. I looked sexy but felt a little less confident when I parked in the dark back street. I was on my own and I needed to be careful. Focus and awareness was the key.

As I stood outside the loud club, I began having second thoughts. But then I reminded myself that this was my career and my new life. Dad wanted nothing to do with me and I needed to prove to him and myself that I was good reporter.

Coral was one of those posh, exclusive clubs filled with rich people and many men that were looking for adventure for a night. I had no idea what I was looking for—something, anything that could take my career to the next level. I needed an article that could get me a job at a real paper.

I used a lot more makeup than usual and wore a short leather mini skirt and high-heeled boots. It was bloody freezing outside and I had to queue for some time before I managed to get inside. My knees were shaking slightly.

The loud music thumped its beat in my head and my stomach churned when I realised how large the club really was. Despite the fact it was Monday night, it was quite busy. There were a few people on the dance floor. I needed to get to the bar.

The bar was less occupied than I thought it would be, but I thought that might be because of some private club downstairs. A few days ago I'd heard Jordan talking about a private club. At the time I hadn't really cared, but now everything was making more sense. I quickly figured out that men needed an invitation to get inside the private section of Coral.

"What would you like?" asked the tall Scot with a friendly manner at the bar. He was young, probably in his early twenties.

"Vodka and Red Bull," I shouted through the loud music. He nodded and I glanced around. A few guys were staring at me. I felt quite intimidated being here on my own, but I was done with playing lost posh girl in the city. It was time to take matters into my own hands.

The barman returned with my drink. I was nervous and my pulse was racing. A few women in tight latex uniforms joined the barman; they were embraced by guys in expensive-looking suits. One of them was that guy from the singles party that I went to in the Grange. If I remembered correctly, his name was Harry.

He had his arms around a pretty redhead with high boots that came over her knees. They ordered a drink and didn't notice me, which was a good thing. I wondered what he was doing here, and when I looked towards the secret door a moment later, I saw Harry sliding through it with the redhead, leaving me burning with raw curiosity.

The handsome barman was now talking to some pretty blonde with big boobs. I had no idea what I was really doing here. My head was screwed by ideas that couldn't really be executed. It would have been good to have a strong man beside me, one who truly cared for me. I sipped a bit of my drink to feel better about myself and glanced around the club.

For a split second I thought that I saw a familiar face, but then I thought, No, he wouldn't be here at this time of the day.

I narrowed my eyes and tossed my hair behind me realising that my eyes weren't misleading me. Adrian, my next-door neighbour, was on the other side of the club talking to some tattooed guy with glasses. They looked engrossed in the conversation. I wondered silently what he was doing in a place like this. Well, I shouldn't really be surprised. First Harry, then Adrian.

I drank more vodka and kept watching them. After some time the tattooed guy looked pissed off, but Adrian turned around and started walking towards the lower part of the club, ignoring him. His face wasn't showing any emotions. The tattooed guy followed him and soon they both vanished behind the doors to the private part of the club.

I didn't waste anymore time. There must be something important behind those doors if all the men were going there. The website of the club hadn't revealed anything specific. I knew that I wouldn't be able to get inside without a code or some sort of invitation. Adrian had said during drinks in Mack's apartment that he had his own business, that it was something to do with food. Half of the time I wasn't listening, trying to deal with the shock I'd experienced when I discovered that Mack was married.

I wandered closer to the door, took out my mobile phone, and waited for someone else to go inside. It took another half hour before a suited and booted guy typed the code in while I pretended that I was on the phone.

Just before the door closed, I slid inside with my heart in my throat. Okay, they were probably going to throw me out of the club, but that was just a small detail. I needed to get used to stuff like this if I wanted to make it as a good reporter.

Once inside, I found myself on a narrow staircase. I hurried down, looking around. In front of me there was a long white corridor filled with stacks of beers crates. I could hear music upstairs, but when I started walking further down the hallway I heard the loud beats of a song coming from the other side, like there was a separate room. Maybe some customers were having their own private party.

Further down, the corridor split in two; there were doors on the right side. All I needed now was to locate Adrian. I had no freaking idea what I was going to say to him. There was a stack of beer pallets and other soft drinks on the right, and when I heard the door, I dropped down, hiding behind them. This was so stupid. I wasn't doing anything wrong. I simply entered the private part of the club reserved for members only.

"How much for a kilo?" asked a rough, deep voice.

"Are you out of your fucking mind?" asked another voice that definitely belonged to Adrian. "There is a time and place for that kind of shit. How many times do I have to bang it into your stupid head? I'm invisible and Stew is the one you should be talking to."

"Sorry, Mr. Lurkin, I had no idea. He only hired me the other week," mumbled the other guy.

"Christ, why do I have to work with so many amateurs? Get the fuck away from me before I fire you, and drop that shit into my car."

"All right, Mr. Lurkin."

I heard footsteps and the door being shut. I couldn't make out anything from this conversation that made sense. It sounded like Adrian was waiting for some sort of package.

"What are you doing here?"

I froze for a second and turned around. There was a tall skinny man standing in front of me. I was so absorbed with what was happening with Adrian that I hadn't seen him approaching.

"Eee… I'm waiting for someone," I blurted out in an uneasy voice, knowing that it was a lame explanation. He looked me up and down like he was checking me out, but I didn't register anything but raw lust in his dark eyes.

"Darren is out of the game and you're late. Come with me; auditions have already started."

"Aahh, okay."

He turned around and started walking away.

"Hurry! I don't have time for any drama," he barked at me, and I followed him, still pretty confused.

He barged through a black door into another large dark room. When my eyes registered the space I nearly lost my balance. In the middle there was a small stage with a pole attached to the ceiling. The lights were illuminating it and flickering. There was a guy sitting at a table with a drink in his hand. At the back there was a small bar.

"I'm sorry, I don't under–"

"Jesus! I told you, I don't want any drama this evening," the tall annoyed guy said, cutting me off. "Get on the stage and show me what you can do. All the other girls weren't very good. We want to see something sinful and erotic."

My stomach dropped, because I realised they were expecting me to dance on the pole; they thought that I was here for some sort of audition. It looked like I had to dive back in my memory and recall all the moves that I so desperately wanted to forget, but unfortunately, the show must go on.

Nine

Ellie

The hugely obese guy was staring at me vacantly, and then he leaned over to speak to the guy who forced me up onto the stage. I felt vulnerable, overly exposed, and quite underdressed in my ridiculously skimpy outfit. I was so scared I could hear my heart thumping in my chest. His black suit was way too tight around his belly, the buttons straining to hold his girth. He looked like an inflated balloon that was ready to burst at any moment.

I needed to pull myself together, focus on the task at hand. They had obviously made a mistake, but I was trapped in this situation. I'd had no idea that they were looking for a dancer. It wouldn't go over too well if I admitted that I snuck in here in hopes of getting some dirt for a news report. I needed to swallow my pride and give it my best shot. What could go wrong? I could feel my stomach clenching with nerves. All I really wanted to do right now was to have a glass of wine on my comfy sofa, watch TV all evening, and forget about this whole mess. Except, if I could dance for them and stay in the club for a bit longer, I might get the story that I had been waiting for since I'd arrived here in Edinburgh.

I knew what my decision was: there was no way I was leaving after the effort I'd made to get this far inside.

Dragging more oxygen into my lungs, I walked towards the pole, telling myself that I was a great dancer, that I had enough talent and charisma to impress them both. They wanted someone who could excite the male audience; well, I was ready to give them the most sensual and sinfully erotic performance of my life. Andrew had loved it when I danced for him, and now I had two jaded men in front of me who wanted to see something special. I grabbed the metal bar and spun around lifting my leg up, showing my toned thighs, keeping my eyes on the fatty in front of me, who finally shifted on his chair. This was just the warm up. All I wanted from them was the connection; once I saw a hint of lust in their eyes I knew I had this in the bag.

After I had fatty's full attention, I positioned myself in front of the pole, facing them. I reached out above my head and gripped the bar tightly. I lifted my legs slowly feeling my stomach muscles tense while I raised my legs and secured them in place around the pole, I smiled seductively, gazing at them from under my lashes, concentrating on my routine. My heart was racing a little, probably because of the adrenaline my nerves jump-started. After a moment I released my hands from the pole and I started sliding down until my hands touched the stage. When I was a child, I went to the best ballet school in Scotland. Dad paid a fortune for private lessons for both me and my sister and we had excelled. We both loved it so much, although the training was hard. I never lost the flexibility or core strength; after I went back to exercising on the pole I was fitter than all my friends.

Slowly, I spread my legs apart showing my leather panties, leaving nothing to the imagination, teasing; I lowered my legs down, until I touched the floor. I winked at fatty and then stood up, keeping my balance. I was improvising now but getting into it, picturing Mack in front of me, wondering how he would react if he saw me on the pole right now.

I walked closer to them, turned around and bent over, showing my firm cheeks, teasing them a little more moving my hips to the rhythm of the soundtrack. I then ran towards the pole and began more complicated spins. By the time the half hour was up, my muscles were burning. I was panting when I finished the performance.

"Excellent, excellent. I like you, girl," said the obese guy, clapping enthusiastically. His piggy face was bright red and he looked like he was having trouble breathing. "We will make you a star of the evening. Nathan, get all her details and start the ball rolling."

I stared at him feeling slightly disorientated. Shit, I didn't expect it to be this easy. They really were expecting me to work for them. My girlfriends knew that I loved pole dancing, but they were never too keen to try it for themselves. Andrew loved it; he got turned on every time I mentioned it to him.

Nathan switched on the lights and the room brightened. The obese guy was speaking to him quickly, waving his sausage fingers at me. After a moment, he said something else and vanished behind the red doors, answering his phone to talk to someone.

"I'm Nathan; sorry I didn't introduce myself earlier. That was Hugo, the main events manager. Dorothy, our housemother, is currently out sick, so I'm taking care of everything. I hope she'll be back soon; otherwise this job is going to kill me. We need someone who can perform mostly on the weekends and for private members of the club. Here are all the details, read it and get back to me if something is not clear," Nathan explained, handing me a white envelope. "Inside there is a pass and my business card. If any of the bouncers give you any trouble, call me immediately."

I was still quite overwhelmed, but I didn't say anything, trying to digest how quickly things were developing. All of a sudden I had a job in the strip club. Nathan kept talking, telling me to follow, showing me around the main bar with the wide stage. He also showed me around a few private rooms, where most of the strippers were performing. My heart was thumping loudly and I tried to take it all in without looking like a complete idiot.

Nathan mentioned that the club was very popular amongst wealthy clients and, as long as I was discreet, I wouldn't have a problem making enough cash. He showed me the changing room and then left when he had a phone call, apologising again.

When I was finally alone, I sat down on the bench going over everything that had just happened in the last hour. My body was pleasantly numb, but my heart kept speeding away. I was absolutely certain I overheard my neighbour Adrian by the entrance. He was angry with that other guy for approaching him here about work. I had no idea what the big deal was. Adrian had his own business, but this whole conversation seemed odd.

Now I was inside the club working as a pole dancer. Jordan had hinted that he had a story here, and if I was lucky enough, I could find out stuff about this guy Johnny

Hodges before Jordan and write the article first. I just had to keep my eyes and ears open.

After I calmed down a little, I looked into the envelope, checking the paperwork and the bright pink pass that came with it. The money was very good: the contract stated that during very busy evenings I could make at least a few hundred pounds in tips each weekend shift. This was crazy. I had no idea that pole dancers could earn that much. The extra cash could help. Living the life of luxury wasn't cheap.

Nathan met up with me again when I was ready to leave. He seemed much less stressed than before my performance.

"Okay, it's all sorted; thank God we finally have the new schedule. We are expecting you on Saturday, so make sure you're here on time," he muttered when I was let back into the main part of the club, through the door that I had sneaked in earlier on. The music was loud and now the dance floor was packed with people.

Suddenly, the idea of being undercover made me excited. I thought that I would get a little drink at the bar to celebrate. I had no idea what was wrong with me. I had danced on the pole before, but never like that and never for this kind of audience. When I lived with my father, I could afford private lessons, now I was on my own. I would need to make up some routines and hope they would be good enough.

I headed to the bar ready to order a shot of tequila. My legs felt a little weak, the adrenaline finally crashing and messing with my equilibrium.

"Ellie, what a surprise. What are you doing here?"

The familiar voice sent a shudder down my spine. I turned around abruptly coming face-to-face with Adrian by the bar with a pint of beer. He shot me his brilliant smile, checking out my cleavage. I hated surprises like that, especially from someone who wasn't supposed to see me here.

"Nothing really. I've arranged to meet a friend, but she hasn't turned up," I lied, telling myself to keep calm.

"What would you like to drink?" he asked, nodding to the waiter. I swallowed hard, plastered a smile on my face and sat down next to him. It looked like this evening wasn't over after all.

Mack

I followed Lurkin all the way from the complex. I saw him visiting a few of his takeaways before he stopped in the city centre. He headed towards that club Coral I had heard about from Claire. I remembered her mentioning a few well- known drug dealers who liked hanging out up there. I doubted that Lurkin wanted to be associated with any of them, but still, it was worth going to see what he was up to. After half an hour, when I found him again, he was at the bar. It took me a moment to recognise that my hot neighbour, Ellie, was with him. This was definitely not what I was expecting. She just didn't strike me as a person that liked places like this.

Ellie was just a stranger and I kept telling myself that I didn't care that she was with him, but the problem was, I did care. I dragged my hand through my hair and decided to watch them for a bit. She was sitting close and they looked like they were enjoying themselves.

Lurkin wanted her because she was pretty and maybe a little naïve. That night in my apartment I knew what he was thinking when he looked at her. It was obvious he wanted to fuck her and toss her away like most of his conquests. I had heard the rumours about his ex-girlfriend: he supposedly beat her to death when he caught her with another man.

Her mother had reported her missing, but the police had no leads, no evidence of foul play and no link to Lurkin, so they dropped the case. Lurkin knew how to be invisible. His criminal records were immaculate. The smarmy bastard had been very careful not to slip up yet.

It looked like Ellie was drinking more than usual. I counted at least four shots since I'd sat down. Lurkin was too comfortable with her. She was so beautiful, I could feel my jealousy rising along with the anxiety of seeing them looking so cosy together. She had no idea what she was getting herself into, especially when it came to man like Lurkin.

Another hour passed, and I sat there watching how he flirted with her, or at least he was attempting to. There was a possibility that he was trying to get her drunk. I wouldn't be surprised if he tried to take advantage of her on the way home or in her apartment. They talked for a bit longer. Then it looked like she finally decided to get going, heading towards the exit. After I made sure that Lurkin was still at the bar, I decided to follow her.

She had on a short skirt and I bet she was driving back to the complex, after definitely being over the limit. Running my hands through my hair, I exhaled deeply. I'd thought that she was a bit smarter than that; obviously I was wrong.

I followed her outside. The streets were busy; taxis and private cars were parked outside the club. I knew that I was wasting valuable time, running after a woman when my suspect was still inside. My priorities hadn't changed, but I couldn't just let her make her way home drunk.

Ellie crossed the street, and a few youths shouted something to her. She showed them the middle finger and carried on walking. I shook my head and caught up with her. After I made sure no one was around, I quietly snuck up on her from behind and dragged her towards the opposite building. She tried to fight, jerking her legs, but I had my palm clasped securely over her sweet mouth. This was too easy. Anyone could attack her here. I was pissed that she didn't realise how dangerous these streets were. I should have placed her over my knee and spanked her so hard she couldn't sit down for a week.

"Shhh, stop struggling. You will get us both into trouble," I hissed at her ear, inhaling her vanilla shampoo. Shit, I recognised that scent—Charlotte had used the same one. Someone upstairs wanted to see us both on the same path.

"Mack?" she mumbled when I pulled away from her.

"What the hell were you doing up there with that idiot?" I demanded, still holding her close to my body, aware that my dick was getting hard. I needed to remember to control myself better. She was just the woman I had fucked.

"I'm not explaining myself to you," she said, trying to pull away, but I held her close, not wanting to let go. "Did you follow me here?"

I exhaled sharply, grabbed her hand and started dragging her towards my car.

"I need you safe in the car first before we talk about this."

She protested, but I was too pissed off to get involved in a serious conversation like this on the street. She needed to grasp that she was in danger. Lurkin was crazy.

"This is absurd. You showed up here asking me why I'm drinking with our neighbour and dragging me to your car expecting me not to ask any questions," she barked as we sat in the car.

"Ellie, be quiet. I need to think for a second," I said, starting the engine and taking a sharp right towards the city. We were going to drive for a while, until my temper cooled and my pulse slowed enough that I wasn't about to have a heart attack. I had to think about how much I needed to conceal from her.

She folded her arms over her chest, glaring at me from the passenger seat. I drove around the dark deserted streets; the air was infused with her perfume and the scent of vanilla shampoo.

"Mack, tell me what the hell is going on. Why were you in the club?" she asked again, when I finally parked up in the road that led to the park. It was late and there was another car close by. People didn't hang around here at this time of night. This area wasn't safe.

I released my seat belt and turned to face her. Ellie's makeup was a little smudged, but she looked beautiful and I was ready to fuck her right here.

Shit, Mack, focus; this isn't the time or the place.

"Lurkin is dangerous and I want you to stay away from him," I said.

"I'm a reporter, Mack, and that explanation is lame. Besides, you shouldn't care what I do; you have no hold over me."

"You have to trust me on this, Angel. Adrian Lurkin is not interested in you. He's not the guy that you think he is," I said, giving her enough to understand that I was being serious. She narrowed her eyes, probably not believing anything I said. "I'm taking you out for a dinner."

"This isn't a good idea, Mack."

"Why is that?"

"Because of Claire. We can't go out for a dinner while your wife is in the apartment, probably waiting for you," she said.

"She won't care. Besides I owe you one," I stated.

I had no idea what I was doing. I should be in the club, tracking Lurkin's every move, taking notes about people he was talking to.

Instead I was taking my neighbour, whom I had fucked every which way from Sunday, to dinner. I was forgetting about my late wife, the woman that I'd loved for years, because Ellie was in my life right now and was accepting me for who I was. This felt wrong, but I couldn't let her get involved with Lurkin. He was too dangerous. The bastard was going to make a mistake soon; it was just a matter of time before I would have something on him.

Ten minutes later I parked outside the small bistro, a place I liked eating at when I was younger. My family was from Glasgow. Dad still lived in the same house, but Mum passed away last year. I spent some time with him right before I moved to the Grange for my assignment. Ellie didn't know any of it, but maybe tonight I was willing to share these real parts of me that were hidden. I needed to gain her trust, but at what cost?

Ten

Ellie

Mack was secretive; he was trying to confuse me by talking in some kind of cryptic code. He crossed the line attacking me like that on the street. For me, it was too much of a coincidence that he was here, straight after I met Adrian for a drink. I agreed to go to dinner because I didn't want to tell him about my job in the club.

For some reason Mack knew that I was in the Coral tonight, but how?

He took me to a small bistro and asked for the table at the back, demanding but charming, as usual. The waitress was swooning over him and I couldn't help but roll my eyes. Yes, I knew that he was hot, but I wanted to scream into her ear that he was also married.

I wasn't leaving this table until I had some real answers.

"I'm still waiting, Mack," I said, after the waitress brought our menus. I'd had a couple of shots so I felt much braver than usual. He didn't care that he just crept away from my bed after our night together, sneaking out on me like that. We weren't together, God, we weren't even friends. He couldn't just follow me around.

"I was in the area, Ellie, and when I saw you with him, I got worried," he explained, staring down at the menu. I tapped my fingers over the table, glaring at him, annoyed. My palms were sweaty and I was having trouble deciding which question to ask first. Mack's alluring confidence reminded so much of Andrew, but Mack was much more skilled in bed. Crap, I needed to get a grip and forget about that night.

"Right, so you have just admitted that you've been stalking me?"

"No, I had no idea that you were in the club."

"Yeah, right," I muttered and leaned over the table. "I'm not stupid, Mack. I want to know everything and you have five seconds; otherwise I'm going to walk out of here."

I wasn't taking any more bullshit from him. He was hiding something important, and I knew for a fact that he didn't like Adrian.

He ran his hand through his hair, staring at me with frustration.

"Fine; my marriage is falling apart. Claire and I ... well, we haven't been getting on with each other really, since last year."

The waitress interrupted us again. Mack cleared his throat and ordered food and wine for us. I couldn't believe that he had just revealed to me that he and Claire were having problems; I wasn't ready to hear it. Andrew had used the same line; he started by saying that his wife was expecting too much, that he wasn't happy.

"I don't need to know about your marriage, Mack. Just tell me, what do you know about Adrian and how come he is so off limits?" I asked, letting him know that I wasn't prepared to discuss his issues with Claire. I'd been so naïve and foolish back then, believing Andrew's emotional confession. That was his way of convincing me that he was ready to leave his wife for me. I wondered how many times he had used that line on other girls.

Mack's eyes drifted down to my lips, and a sudden dose of heat scorched through me, flushing my cheeks. I shifted on the chair, recognising that look. This was the second time that Mack had warned me to stay away from Adrian. It was like he held some sort of grudge against him, but that wasn't possible. We all only just met each other.

"He's involved in dodgy business, Ellie, and he doesn't date women. He plays with them, and once he gets bored he tosses them away like garbage."

Like all men, I thought. Mack should have known I wasn't looking for a relationship, and I didn't think I liked Adrian that much to let him fuck me. For a moment I considered telling him about what I had overheard in the club, but I held my tongue. This was nothing to do with Mack, and I didn't want to share that I had gone to Coral and managed to get a job as a pole dancer. This would only send him over the edge.

"Whatever, I don't care. You already know that I'm not planning to get involved with anyone. My career is much more important. There is a story in that club, a story worth writing about," I said, and drank some more wine. I didn't like that Mack was leading me to believe no one was good enough for me. "One of the reporters from the office has an inside source in that club."

"You don't even know what you're doing," he said, shaking his head.

"Don't treat me like an idiot. I'm fully aware that this is dangerous, but I have aspirations of doing more than begging for scraps of stories and trying to make them newsworthy. I want to write about crime on the streets, not fucking dancing cats or some vapid celebrity and their latest affair."

"I'll put you in contact with some people. I can find you an unnamed source," he said with irritation. "If that will keep you away from trouble I will do it. I'm telling you, Adrian is dangerous. He may not look like it, but he is. Stay away, dammit!"

I glared at him, wondering why he was so adamant about his theory. Mack was a driver, and he had just moved into the complex. None of us knew anything about each other, and to me, Adrian was a regular guy. I wanted to hear solid facts, not Mack's personal opinions about someone that may only be based on jealousy.

"I can't promise you that, Mack. This is my life and my career."

Mack put his knife and fork aside and clasped his hands together, looking at me intensely.

"You're putting yourself in danger, Ellie. I know that I haven't been honest with you, but trust me, Adrian is lethal and clever. If you get in too deep, I won't be able to protect you," he said. A shiver crawled over my spine, igniting desire in my belly. That bossy, dominant side of Mack drew me closer and I wanted him to have his way with me.

"I shouldn't concern you. I'm a reporter and this is my career," I told him, finishing my wine, pissed off that he was trying to tell me what to do. "And you shouldn't care about my safety. I am no one to you."

"Ellie, my Angel, you have no idea who you are to me. You have reached into my chest and restarted my dead, lifeless heart. You have pulled me out of my misery, made me want to start living again. But you're right—I shouldn't talk like that, because of Claire and because of the fact that she's my wife. Come on, let's get you home," he said, getting up and throwing some cash on the table. My heart stuttered in my chest when I finally understood the meaning of his words.

Was he saying that after such a short time he was falling for me?

I didn't think I could get anything out of him this evening. We were leaving and in the car he was back to his moody, withdrawn self. Andrew had acted the same, telling me that with me life made more sense, promising that his wife wouldn't be a problem.

The drive to the complex was tense and we didn't speak a word. I felt the zooming pressure that kept growing between us. I was fighting with myself and my own morals. I shouldn't desire him, but I did. I shouldn't want to be with him, but my heart reacted every time he was close.

It was pitch black when we arrived at the car park. My stomach made a funny jolt when I realised that I had to go back to my apartment and Mack would slide into his bed where his wife was waiting for him.

The overwhelming sadness hit me, and I needed to get away from the car, from him.

"Ellie, look at me."

My heart skipped a beat when I recognised that voice. Husky and demanding.

"What do…?"

He didn't let me finish what I wanted to say; his lips were on mine in an instant, kissing me deeply. He felt so good, the heat from his body filling me with unexpected desire. Instead of pushing him away, I moaned when he sucked in on my bottom lip, dragging me on top of him.

The steering wheel was digging into my back, and it was almost impossible to move, but I stopped caring and worrying about any consequences of this glorious moment. I felt his cock press against my core where I needed him most. I was caught up in a moment of weakness, aching for his demanding mouth.

"Fuck, you're so sweet, Angel," he rasped, pulling my dress up around my waist, his hands burning into my skin as they trailed my flesh, that demanding mouth kissing my neck. He nibbled on my clavicle letting me feel his teeth.

I moaned and leaned into him and he let out a guttural growl from the back of his throat. His hands roamed over my back and up to my shoulders, pulling my body down to feel his majestic cock, grinding his hips and nudging my clit with his movement. I called out his name at the sensations, only to have them enhanced by his fingers tracing the curve of my spine gently. Kissing back up to my jaw, his lips were rough, teasing and tasting every inch of my neck, then travelling to my mouth where he claimed me once again. I felt like I needed every inch of him, to experience the same passionate night again.

Pulling back from me so we were millimetres apart, he inhaled the scent of my hair and whispered into my throat, "Do you need me, Angel? Do you need the release that only I can give you? You know that perfect pussy belongs to me, don't you?"

I couldn't answer him. I could only moan my response; he did something to me, made me compliant and needy.

"Angel, do you want me to make you come?" he asked in hushed tone.

"Yes. Please, Mack, please just touch me."

Sliding his right hand down my body, over the wrinkled dress, he found my belly button, dipping his finger in and around. It was torturous. I needed his touch so badly I felt pained at his teasing. "This isn't your pussy is it?" he murmured. Sliding his fingers lower, he drew circles on my inner thigh. "This isn't your pussy either, but I can feel your heat. Your desire has already soaked through my jeans and your thighs are sticky with need," he growled out as he walked his fingers to my underwear, his hand cupping my sex. He pressed the heel of his palm against my clit, and I thought I could orgasm from that one touch. I moaned loudly.

"Now, now, Angel, not yet. All good things come to those who wait, and you will wait till I tell you to come. Do you understand?" I was so busy trying to grind against his hand to cause some friction I couldn't answer him. He moved his hand away and I mewled at the loss. "Answer me, Angel. Do you understand?"

"Yes, Mack, I understand. I'll be good, but I need you. Please, Mack, please."

He nodded his agreement and pulled at the side of my thong. Tearing it from my body, he lifted his hips and shoved it in his pocket. The connection of our bodies was heavenly. I moved my hips against him and he hissed through his teeth. Seating himself back down, he tutted and wagged his finger at me, and for a moment I worried he would leave me unfulfilled, but he leaned forward and bit my sensitive nipple. It was such a shock that I gasped, which turned into a yelp, and felt my body gush its response. "No, Angel, I am always in charge."

The voice of reason was long gone. I just wanted to rip my clothes off and tell him to take control and fuck me in the car or on the dashboard. Whatever, I didn't care anymore. I turned into someone else, a woman that only fucked married men, a woman that wasn't Ellie Grant anymore.

Mack

She was waking me up again and I couldn't stop myself. I had to have her in my arms, taste her lips and feel that sweet wet spot between her legs.

Her soft pussy was drenched; she was beyond turned on. I could smell her arousal, a heavenly musk that hung in the air. The only thing that separated me from her aching pussy was the thick material of my jeans.

The space in the car was cramped and awkward, yet she made me lose control like this so quickly. I bit her neck and suckled on the pulse point behind her ear. I loved hearing her sexy moans. I hated the fact that we had to hide like this, but right then I didn't have any other option.

I thrust my fingers inside her, then turned my hand slightly and used the heel of my palm to push against her clit whilst curling my fingers against the front wall of her entrance, adjusting myself, so I had access to her upper body. I pulled down her dress so I could see those magnificent breasts.

"You have to be quiet, Angel. We can't get caught," I said, using the tone of voice I knew would get her wetter. She bit her lip, her long dark hair falling behind her. Her beautiful face flushed, her lips swollen from our kisses and the way she was biting on the corner of her lip—she unraveled me. She was stunning, and I wanted to see her coming undone, all over me.

Ellie whimpered when I continued to fuck her with my fingers, kissing her small breasts, lapping at her nipples, pulling the tip with my upper lip and tongue one at the time. Every time she made a sound I pulled away, reminding her about the rules. I felt her pussy muscles clenching around my finger. She was so close, but it was up to me if I would allow her to climax.

I wanted to bend her over the car and fuck her until she screamed, until I didn't feel the pressure in my balls anymore.

My breath hissed out as she rode my fingers searching for her release. She shook and gasped as her orgasm left her. I felt the evidence of it on my wrist and I felt satisfied, calmed. Making her come apart in my arms was the best part of this terrible day, seeing her struggling for breath as the orgasm shook her core muscles.

I was painfully hard, I felt pre cum in my boxers, and my cock ached for her. I imagined her tied up to the bed, waiting with that anticipation in her eyes. She had no idea how much pleasure I could give her, how much I wanted to bury my cock in her tight pussy.

Any other woman I'd ever slept with couldn't compare. Ellie was the woman that I wanted to possess and own.

"Mack, why? Why do you keep punishing me like that? Claire is a nice person and she doesn't deserve this betrayal," Ellie said, suddenly moving back to the passenger seat. My cock was throbbing and it was going to take countless hours of masturbation to get any kind of release, to erase this scene from my memory.

"I can't stay away. I'm losing control around you, and Claire… she's not important," I said, wanting more, needing to get rid of these hopeless emotions that were wreaking havoc in my body.

"No, Mack, this has happened before. I've ruined somebody else's family because I slept with a married man. This has to stop, please," she cried.

I frowned staring at the distress on her face, wondering if she was telling the truth. Had she fucked someone just for the sake of it? After all, I had no idea who she was, who she was running away from. Fuck, I couldn't even tell her that I wasn't married to Claire. Boiling guilt poured into my stomach all of a sudden. I should have known that I needed to respect the memory of my dead wife and stop jeopardising this operation by pursing Ellie.

"What happened to the guy?" I asked. This wasn't normal or healthy the way I hung on for her answer. She looked at me with tears in her eyes. I was a pathetic motherfucker asking her about an affair. It was none of my business. I didn't even know her when it happened, but I couldn't stand the thought of anyone touching my Angel. "He must have been a moron if he let you go," I said to deflect my true feelings on the matter.

"Nothing. I don't want to talk about it. Just stay away from me; otherwise I'm telling Claire," she hissed at me and hurried out of the car.

Why did I have to make my life so difficult? I had never wanted anyone more than I wanted her right now, but she was off limits. This fucking operation and Lurkin was more important than anyone. I needed to get a grip and put this in perspective; my priority was to put Lurkin away.

I watched her as she walked home. I waited ten minutes and then got out of the car. That was it; my limit had been reached. This was going to be my final undercover operation. Once this whole thing was over I would talk to the superintendent and resign.

Ellie probably wouldn't want to have anything to do with me once she found out who I was and the fact that I had lied to her.

My phone started ringing; it was an unknown number. I didn't want to talk to anyone, but the past few days hadn't been productive at all.

"Hello."

Lurkin talked. "Mack, it's Adrian. We need to postpone the meeting until next week. Something has come up."

"Anything I can help you with?" I asked, knowing that something must have happened. Maybe his recent shipment had been delayed. Fuck! I wanted to speed things up, but this operation kept hitting wall after wall, and there it was, another fucking roadblock. Was this operation doomed to fail?

"No, it's a problem that I need to take care of myself. I hope that won't complicate your situation with Claire?"

Bastard. He was laughing at me, making sure I knew he deemed me emasculated and pussy whipped, as if that made me less of a man. I gripped my phone tighter, feeling like the bones in my knuckles were going to snap at any moment. I was impulsive and that was my greatest flaw. Sometimes I made decisions that had negative consequences due to my impatience.

"Don't worry about it. I can deal with her. I'll be waiting for your phone call. Just let me know when, and I'll pop over to see you," I assured him, doing everything I could in my power to keep myself in line. We had some evidence, but nowhere near enough to put him away for a significant amount of time. We wanted real justice for his crimes, not a slap on the wrist and a fine. We needed something more concrete: the list of his distributors and the business that he was laundering his money in, names of his trusted advisors and inner circle of henchmen.

Things like that took weeks, months, sometimes even years, but I wasn't anticipating living this life for that long. I wanted to bust him for drugs and move on. I had wasted so much time planning my retribution for this scumbag, and then I met Ellie and it changed my priorities. At some point I had to tell her how much she meant to me.

The question remained. Could I move away from what I had been doing for over ten years?I didn't think I could.

Eleven

Ellie

Mack had consumed my thoughts since that night in the car. While I was supposed to concentrate in the office, my skin tingled remembering his touch; my heart raced when I thought about how it felt to have him control my pleasure. If it wasn't for the fact that we were in the car park, we would have had sex in the car. We were all over each other, squashed in the car seat. The whole experience felt incredibly intimate and somehow liberating. I wanted him badly and couldn't even think about Claire and the fact that I was making another mistake.

I was attempting to finish an article about skyrocketing immigration in certain parts of Scotland, but so far I'd written only two sentences. Phil had finally given me something more ambitious this time around, well, according to him, but I still felt undervalued. I forced myself not to comment on his kind gesture. The truth was that I needed a job. Bills wouldn't pay themselves.

This time last year I was in love, thinking that Andrew was the only man that could ever make me happy, but it was a lie. He only pretended I meant something to him. I had always believed in karma, and I knew that things would turn around for me. Andrew would eventually get his just desserts for using me, making what I felt for him a lie. Now Mack was in the picture and everything felt different. Last night proved that I couldn't help myself when I was around him, married or not. Whenever he was around I felt like I was burning, finally coming to life. His words stripped away the layers of misery that my soul had been carrying since I left home and the scandal that had alienated me from my father.

I couldn't help but wonder how to deal with the sizzling attraction that sparked between us. I could only blame myself for that night at Harry's party when I thought that sex could solve all my problems.

I shook my head and told myself to get on with the article. Mimi had been all over Jordan today, bringing him coffee and flirting openly in front of everyone. I noticed that he had been taking phone calls in the boardroom, and I knew that it was probably about the Johnny Hodges case, but I knew that I was a step ahead of him and he couldn't have more information than me.

Several hours later, after not getting much done, I headed straight home. It was Friday. I hadn't seen Mack for the whole week, since our steamy encounter in the car. I was aware that he most probably was trying to avoid talking to me again. I kept bumping into Claire, who seemed overly friendly, at times too curious about what I had been up to. She probably knew that Mack wasn't faithful to her and now she was trying to get information out of me.

Mack was convinced that Adrian was bad news and I shouldn't be getting involved with him. I purposely didn't tell him about that secret conversation that I overheard in the corridor just before my audition. Adrian had his own food distribution business, and as far as I was aware, he was probably talking about his stock or something like that.

I kept playing Jordan's conversation in my head over and over again, trying to research about that guy he'd mentioned, but I wasn't getting anywhere. I looked online and in the archives, but in both it seemed that Johnny Hodges never existed.

At least the gossip sites weren't writing about me anymore. Now and again, I read about a case in which my father was involved. He still had enough credibility to attract media coverage.

Couple of days ago, when I was on the way to work, I bumped into Adrian in the corridor. He invited me up for another drink. I just told him that I'd get back to him, pretending like I was late. I couldn't stop thinking about Mack and his warning.

At a quarter to nine, my phone rang. Nathan wanted me to perform tonight. I said yes in panic, but deep down I was questioning if I was really ready for it. We hadn't discussed the fact that I wasn't a stripper but a dancer; I was waiting to see what he expected. I could dance on the pole, but taking my clothes off for men was an entirely different thing. During my audition, everything went so quickly, and before I knew it I was hired. Now I was having cold feet.

My heart raced when I was getting ready. My moment in Mack's car flooded my mind like a tsunami. I didn't fight him—one kiss and I was in his arms, melting away. Seeing Claire and speaking to her about her husband was agonising. Women always knew and I was aware that she was keeping an eye on me. Maybe Mack was right; maybe they were having problems, but this was none of my business. I couldn't expect him to leave her for me. We were using sex to push away our demons, our troubled past.

I reached the centre of Edinburgh with my pink pass in my hand. The club was busy on Friday night, and the bar was packed. My heart stuttered between my ribs when I thought about tonight, their expectations and the clients that they had. I'd danced for Andrew, and we had a laugh, but this wasn't a game. Nathan was expecting me to dance to seduce the audience.

"Right, there you are. How long before you can get out on the stage?" Nathan asked, appearing in front of me out of nowhere. He looked really smart tonight dressed in a black fitted suit and red tie.

"Err … I don't have an outfit. I haven't had a chance to —"

"No problem, Bella. We will have something for you. Come with me," he cut me off, waving his hand to follow him.

The private part of the club was busy too, and I had no idea where to look as a few very handsome men passed us on the way. Nathan didn't waste much time. He was walking fast until we reached what seemed to be a private room.

"Pick something sexy and revealing. We have a few VIP clients here tonight, and they want to be entertained," Nathan said, opening a huge walk-in wardrobe filled with hundreds of costumes.

"Oh right," I muttered, running my fingers over the skimpy see-through and figure-hugging pieces. My confidence was slowly shrinking. I had worn sexy underwear for Andrew, but that was for his eyes only. Was I really ready for this?

"You have half an hour. Just don't be too long; everyone is waiting. I have already announced you," Nathan said and left muttering to himself something about professionalism.

I walked inside, my gut clenching with nerves. I started searching for something sexy but tasteful. I was hoping to speak to other strippers, trying to find out if they knew anything about Johnny Hodges. I started going through the black leather costumes, running my fingers over a few sparkling bodices, when I heard slamming doors. It was probably Nathan again. I was just about to ask him if he had forgotten his head, when a familiar voice rang out through the room making me stay where I was in the wardrobe closet.

"How many more trucks do we need for this month?"

Adrian, my neighbour was in the room. I recognised his voice again. This was the second time. I stayed hidden, not wanting him to see me here. I started to wonder if he was a member of the club. It seemed that he liked hanging out here quite a lot.

"Four more, but I don't know if that's enough. There is a high demand for white powder, and some guys are getting impatient with the amount of time they need to wait for the deliveries," said another voice that I didn't recognise. I stopped breathing, trying to catch every word.

"There have been spot checks on the motorways. We are losing money. I'm trying to deal with it, search for alternative routes, but it's getting tougher out there," continued the voice.

"They just have to be patient. Talk to the heads and reassure them they will get their stuff. I need a bit more time."

"Our distribution network is strong, but we have too many dealers that are becoming sloppy. I've spoken to a few heads and they are trying to handle the problem."

"The cash keeps rolling; that's the main thing. I'll supply stock. There will always be enough smack heads out there that need to get high." Adrian laughed and my stomach sank. The sudden realisation hit me like a giant avalanche. Drugs—they were talking about distributing drugs. How could I be so stupid not to grasp it?

They obviously had no idea that I was here and I didn't want to find out what they would do if they discovered me listening in.

"Yeah, you're right. Johnny isn't happy though. He keeps reminding us to be careful. He heard there's an undercover operation in the city, but we're not sure who is involved. They have learned to keep their mouths shut and no one wants to talk."

"It's been years and so far we haven't been caught. I don't believe that we have a problem. The money aspect, that's what I'm mainly conscious about. We need to be vigilant. Report anyone suspicious, anyone who seems untrustworthy."

"Maybe we should pull the new transport and wait. Hodges won't be happy if someone fucks up."

"No, everything is going ahead as planned," Adrian said sharply. "I've arranged to meet up with a new driver. I don't think that we need to worry about any shitheads being undercover. Now I've a few things that I need to take care of. Just talk to them and reassure them that everything goes as planned."

"Will do."

I waited for them to leave, my heart pounding loudly in my chest. Adrian had just moved in and he wasn't an ordinary businessman after all. He supplied drugs, possibly all over Scotland.

Was it possible that Mack knew who he really was and that was why he was trying to warn me to stay away from him? Now his warnings were loud and clear, and I finally had a story. I needed to decide how to proceed, because for sure Phil would never let me write about this stuff. I had to focus and find someone who would talk. How hard would that be?

Mack

I was following Charlotte, making sure that she was safe. She had a gun in her hand, and she was keeping her posture low, sneaking around the old bungalow as the sun was disappearing behind the horizon. I remembered us sitting in front of the TV, watching the news a night before, relaxing. I remembered how the weatherman forecasted some heavy showers. He was wrong, again.

I felt her pounding heart, her speeding pulse, and the rush of adrenaline. Claire was somewhere else, and I wondered why she let her go in alone.

Charlotte's bright brown eyes registered the voices coming from the cracked window. She stopped instantly, listening in.

She had a clear objective: to secure the premises and arrest one of the guys who was involved in a burglary earlier on, in another area. Someone had given her a lead and now she was pursuing it.

I was behind her, but she couldn't see me. She continued to walk slowly around the house until she reached the door.

I liked that dream, I liked that I could look at her and appreciate her beauty. Her black hair was tied up in a ponytail.

I remembered telling her that she looked sexy when she left with Claire early in the morning.

She couldn't see the guy that appeared behind her. I screamed, but no one heard me. That skinny asshole knocked her out. I couldn't do anything. It was my dream, but I was helpless, standing there hearing him call to someone else to help him.

I witnessed how another guy appeared in the doorway. After that everything went black.

Next thing I knew I was inside the house, in the bedroom. My wife was handcuffed to the bed. Someone had stripped her clothes off, and she was lying there in her underwear, looking peaceful. Fear and dread shot through me like I had just been stunned. She was in danger.

A man appeared at the door holding a brown leather belt. He had a cigarette in his mouth, and his arms were covered in tattoos. Jeans hung low on his hips and his white vest was smudged with stains of blood. He was unshaven, with dark hair and dark eyes.

"Wake up, sleeping beauty," he said and spat on the floor. Charlotte blinked rapidly, trying to get up, quickly realising that she was chained to the bed.

"Other officers will be here in a moment. You better watch it, asshole!" she barked, trying to hide the panic in her voice. The guy laughed and was on top of her before she could blink.

"They will be a while. Don't worry, we'll have fun here. By the time I'm finished with you, it will be too late," he snarled and slapped her, then ripped her bra off. She screamed, trying to get him off her, but he held her face in place, laughing.

"Who would have thought it? I never thought I'd have a chance to do a police pussy," he laughed and hit her with the belt. Charlotte was kicking and screaming until the very end, until she had no more strength left in her. Her face was puffy, swollen, tears were dripping down, mixed with blood. I roared when he unzipped his trousers. I wanted to rip his face off, witnessing as he parted her legs and shoved himself inside her.

I turned to see his face, to remember the bastard that hurt my wife. When I looked, his face shifted and I was staring at Adrian Lurkin. He fucked my wife until she wasn't moving anymore, then laughed, stabbing her with a long sharp knife.

I let go of a loud growl and leapt forward clenching my fingers around Adrian's neck. That was not enough. I couldn't let him die without experiencing real suffering. My body was drenched with sweat and I was stuck in my hatred, choking him.

"Tobias… it's me… stop pl—"

It took me a second to realise that it wasn't Adrian that I was choking, but Claire.

Twelve

Mack

I pulled away from her, shaking like I was having a seizure. The room was dark, and for a moment I only heard my own heavy breaths. I felt like I was drowning in black waters, unable to get back to the surface. Slowly and steadily I started recognising my bedroom, my clothes on the floor, and Claire. Sweat drenched my face; my T-shirt was stuck to my back. It was just a nightmare. I was dreaming about that day when Charlotte made a decision to leave Claire and check out that damned bungalow. I cursed a few times, trying to lift myself off the floor, desperate for more air.

Claire was lying on her back staring at me with shock and fear. She was so fucking pale.

"Are you okay? What happened?" I asked, not recognising my own voice. Cold chills shivered through me. Destructive images from the past flooded back into me, reminding me that I had no one in this world, that I was so fucking lost.

"You woke me up. I heard you screaming. I just came here to check on you, and when I shook you, I don't know, you must've still been in your nightmare because you started choking me like you were trying to kill me." She dragged herself back to a sitting position.

My body was shaking. Sweat, there was so much sweat covering me. I'd had nightmares before, nightmares about the day of the shooting, dreams about Charlotte burning alive, but this was one of the worst. I could have killed Claire. When I looked at my hands I was fucking shaking. Shit, I had to pull myself together.

"What the hell is happening to me?" I asked myself, hiding my face in my palms. I was dreaming about Lurkin fucking my wife, raping her, but he wasn't there, he wasn't involved, so why? Why him?

My subconscious had started playing tricks on me. The prick that had hurt her was a twisted son of a bitch. Lucky for him I had never laid my hands on him. I couldn't keep reliving this. It was one poor judgment call, and she got trapped. Claire couldn't help her, but she shouldn't have let her go in on her own, no matter how safe it looked out there.

I was falling apart, slowly, and now it had gotten to the point where I couldn't function.

"You dreamed about her, didn't you?" Claire asked quietly, and moved towards me. "I heard her name a couple of times." She grabbed my hand. I didn't want to fight with her right now, in these early hours of the morning when I was a total wreck. There was no point in lying. She knew that I had never really come to terms with what happened. She knew that I never accepted that my wife had to die.

I nodded. "I was there with her when she was sneaking into that bungalow, when that scum was hurting her. His face … hell, his face, it turned into fucking Lurkin and I watched as he raped her and I was helpless, Claire! I couldn't help Charlotte," I roared and Claire squeezed my hand tighter, saying something to me. She was whispering calming words that were supposed to make me feel better.

"Don't think about this," she said. "That motherfucker was shot and now this whole thing is over; it has been for years. This operation is different. We are playing our parts. You're dreaming about her because of stress and probably because we're working together again."

My muscles were tense and I couldn't relax, but my breathing was slowing down. I needed Ellie now, not Claire. Ellie was the only woman that could wake me up from that nightmare. She could touch me and I would forget about my wounded soul.

I knew that it was impossible though. I couldn't let myself believe she would be the answer to soothe the savage beast that screamed in my chest. She let me control her body and bring her pleasure and that was the only distraction that helped me forget the past, to lose the pain for that brief moment.

"I'm sorry … I'm sorry that I tried to hurt you. I think I'll go outside to get some fresh air," I said, pushing myself up on my feet. There was no way I could continue letting Claire see me like that, so fucked up. Fine, after years of struggling I accepted that I shouldn't keep blaming her anymore, that I should let it go. They were partners and Charlotte trusted her. It wasn't Claire's decision, but my wife's.

She couldn't help her, she moved on, married a guy and now she was after a promotion. I was stuck in the cycle of taking assignment after assignment, hiding in my work. Not seeing my family, not caring for anything but feeding my psyche of my fucked up self, reliving my faults and mistakes—until that night with Ellie.

"Maybe you should talk to someone, Tobias, a doctor. You know that there is a suppo–"

"I'll take care of this by myself, once I see Lurkin behind bars."

"Tobias, I'm not your enemy. We are in this together," she reminded me.

"I know, Claire. I realise that, but I'm fed up sitting around and waiting. I'll be right back," I called to her and left the bedroom. My legs were shaking; my hands, everything felt like I was in someone else's body.

I was a wreck. Maybe Claire was right; maybe I needed to see a shrink. Charlotte didn't enjoy being dominated in the bedroom and I accepted it. Back then, I was happy, satisfied with the love that we felt for each other. When she died I became a different man.

Ellie had agreed and she was a willing participant. It took only a second to realise that she wasn't like anyone else. Sex with her kept the demons at bay. She was a woman that I took advantage of, a woman that shouldn't have crossed my path.

I put my jacket on and slid through the door, trying to calm down. My head was spinning. Thoughts and memories were punishing me and I wanted to bury myself in her, forgetting about my responsibilities and the criminals that were out there.

It was dawn, just after 5:00 a.m. as I walked to the front, trying to catch the first glimpses of the sunrise. I took out my phone and scrolled through my contacts. Dad was up, despite the early hour. He wasn't a very good sleeper, since Mum had passed away.

"Tobias, is that you?" Dad asked when he picked up the phone. He had the tendency to always make sure he knew who he was speaking with.

"Yes, Dad, it's me. I'm in Scotland, near Edinburgh," I explained, feeling utterly drained. I should have made this phone call sooner. My sister had been looking after him for a while now, but Dad missed me a hell of a lot. I always made excuses not to come home, blaming work for lack of time. This had been the longest time away from home since I started this job.

"Does that mean you will be home soon, Son?" he asked, sounding hopeful.

"Possibly, but I'm not done with this case yet. This is my last operation. I think I'm done with this lifestyle," I groaned into the phone, wondering if Ellie would agree to move away with me. Maybe I was getting ahead of myself, but she was perfect for me and we both wanted the same thing: acceptance. Love—maybe this was too much to ask, but friendship and sex. Yes, that was more than we both asked for.

"What's changed? Have you met someone?"

"Claire is here with me. We are working together again. After three years," I explained.

"You're avoiding the question, Son. Rita misses you and so do the kids. If there is someone there that can heal-—"

"No one can heal me, Dad. You know that, but this woman. She doesn't know who I am. It's so damned complicated."

"You will find a way. Before Charlotte you always knew what to do. I would like to meet the woman that has you in knots, so bear that in mind, Tobias." Dad chuckled, pushing me to the edge. Of course, in normal relationships people go for family dinners and stuff like that, but this wasn't a normal situation.

I had a long way to go before I could approach something like that. Dad gave me some updates about Rita and the kids. I fucking missed them, but I had unfinished business here. I couldn't just abandon this operation.

Ellie

Last night I was quite shaken by the whole conversation between Adrian and some other guy. Maybe it was a good thing that I didn't go out with him on a proper date. Mack had warned me, but how did he know that Adrian wasn't just an ordinary businessman?

Nathan had to come over to remind me that I had to get out on the stage eventually. I was so distracted that I had completely forgotten that I had to perform. I picked up a red slutty thing, which was supposed to be a costume, and I headed out on the stage. I met a few strippers that paraded around the changing room topless; some of them knew how to seduce men until they threw money at them. The whole thing went so fast that I didn't have a chance to talk to anyone. I danced, using the routines that I knew, and all the men seemed to love it.

Then on Sunday I was resting, trying to research more about that mysterious guy, Johnny Hodges, hoping a search of social media might bear some fruit. I heard Mack and Claire in the corridor arguing that he hadn't found a job yet. They were loud, but my heart stuttered every time I heard his voice. He had this strange paralysing effect on me that clouded my better judgment.

Monday was uneventful, and on Tuesday morning I overheard Jordan talking about the club again with Phil. He thought that there was something going on up there. Well, too bad. I was sitting quietly minding my own business knowing that sooner or later I would have a story. I'd tried to talk to Phil about it, but as usual he didn't care about opinions. To him I was still just a pretty face with great legs.

I'd been anxious during my performance at the club, thinking that maybe men would recognise me from the papers. I knew it was silly, but I couldn't let my father know what I was doing. He had frequently reminded me of the disappointment I was to him, and I had to be careful. Dad probably still wanted to keep an eye on me, so he would be ready to humiliate me when I messed up again. I hated the way he wanted to control everyone.

By lunchtime I was so distracted that I decided to get some fresh air. I still had no idea what to do with this new information. If Adrian was really a dangerous drug supplier, then I had an even bigger story than I realised. I had to be sure, which meant I needed to start hunting for real evidence.

In the coffee shop while I was eating a baguette, I got a text from the club, asking me to be there tonight. I was ready to text back that I wasn't available, but after thinking about it for some time, I decided to go. This was my opportunity. I needed to talk to the other girls, find out if they at least suspected what was going on.

After weeks of not hearing from anyone, I was still waiting for any kind of contact from my friends. I still considered them my good friends. Dad was probably too busy to care if I was still alive or not. It was like my other life had never existed before and now I was no one.

Shivers crawled over my spine when I thought about Mack and Adrian. I considered telling him about what I had overheard, but I kind of already knew what he would say.

I quickly changed into jeans, put an old hoodie on, and drove to the club. I worried that this was getting out of control. I wasn't a stripper. I would be all right as long as Nathan respected that.

If anyone recognised me now, anyone from the media or my old crew, then I wouldn't have a shitty job to go back to. I would have nothing left in my life. I was determined to get this story to prove my self-worth to the world, to myself, and to my Dad. My father had defended murderers, gangsters, people involved in sex crimes, and other clients that no other solicitor wanted to represent, and he was still loved and revered for his ability. I was just his spoiled, crappy daughter that broke a perfectly loving happy family.

I wanted to have this all behind me, but I never thought that starting over somewhere else was going to be this hard.

When I arrived at the club, I decided there was no point dwelling on what I had done. I fucked a married man, broke his happy family, and now I was just paying for it. I did say I believed in karma.

At the door I nearly crashed into Nathan, who looked stressed.

"Right, you're finally here. I need you in one of the private rooms," he said, running his hand through his hair.

"Private rooms?" I questioned, getting a bad feeling about this.

"We have certain clients that want a private performance. It's absolute havoc in here. I need you to cover for me," he explained.

"All right. I can dance, but I'm not stripping," I stated.

"What?" Nathan heaved a sighed. "It's a strip club, Bella. Everyone strips here, but fair enough. This client wasn't specific; he just wanted to see someone on the pole in some kind of mask."

"Mask?" I questioned him.

"Yeah, he wants you to cover your face. Come on … don't look at me like that. I'm just the messenger; Hugh is paying my wage too."

"But what if he asks me to, you know … to strip?" I whispered. What the hell was I thinking, getting a job in a strip club and expecting not to take my clothes off?

Nathan smiled confidently, trying to hide his exhaustion.

"You will be behind glass, so don't stress. Prude pole dancer. Who would have thought it?" He laughed, shaking his head. He took me to the changing room and one of the girls showed me the free lockers. I made a mental note to speak to her after this whole thing was over.

I changed into a long see-though black silky dress and put a sparkly mask on. I noticed that many strippers were dressed up in all sorts of costumes, so I wasn't the only one. My legs were a bit shaky when Joan left me by the entrance, telling me that I was going to be all right.

I went inside the stage enclosure and hopped on the pole, knowing that I needed to get a grip and just get on with it. The space was large enough to dance but only just. I glanced at my client, ready to give him my flirtatious smile, but then I froze. The man behind the glass door wasn't just an ordinary client. I was staring straight at Andrew. The guy who had ripped my heart out of my chest, then stamped on it whilst ruining my reputation and my life.

Thirteen

Ellie

I nearly lost my balance. Andrew smiled at me and gestured for me to carry on. He sat on a comfortable leather sofa, looking relaxed. His eyes hovered over my body, stopping at my legs, then my thighs, as my heartbeat accelerated. Fury overwhelmed me, riding through me like a storm, weakening my knees.

It took me only a few seconds to notice that he didn't recognise me. I had dyed my hair since he last saw me and I was wearing a mask. He never paid attention to small details. He was too self-absorbed to recognise the small dimple on my shoulder that he used to like kissing during sex.

I remembered that I had to breathe, and if I wanted to carry on working in the club, I needed to calm down. My hands were shaking when I gripped the pole. I reminded myself that he came here for entertainment, and as far as I knew I was just another girl.

My heart was thumping in my chest, pumping adrenaline into my veins.

He was here, but why?

The media had lynched me, made out that I was a poisonous flower that destroyed his perfectly loving family, whereas Andrew's reputation hadn't been affected. A few papers mentioned him, but it was always with reference to my name. I forced my body to spin around the pole, pushing my muscles to work in time to the rhythm of the music. He never loved me, but he used those three words like a weapon to manipulate me so he could get what he wanted. He'd taken part of my soul and ripped it to pieces and then set it on fire publicly.

Andrew was very good looking. Tall, slim, always well dressed, with that cute dark hair and strong jaw. Here in the strip club, he wore a blue suit—and the shirt I had given him on his birthday. Our last exchange was sour and devastating. My father was there, reprimanding me like I was still a little girl, like I didn't even deserve to talk to him in private. Andrew stood there, looking handsome and perfect, not even trying to defend me. He didn't react when my father called me a whore, a stupid bitch that was destroying his career. It was the worst day of my life.

If I had known in the beginning that he was using me, then maybe I could have avoided all the drama.

Now, he was sitting behind the glass, eager and excited to see my moves. I had no choice; I wasn't ready to confront him, so I started dancing. With my story I could help clean my reputation and show my father that I was after all his daughter.

I danced, spun around, showing him my best moves, determined to be seductive, sinful and provocative. He shifted on the sofa a few times, staring at me with absolute desire. I knew that look on his face when he was turned on, the way his eyes flickered with excitement as I bent down, teasing him. Andrew had the dark sensual looks of his Italian heritage. He was also rich and successful, and within days he had me wrapped around his little finger.

It took a while to get into a rhythm. I was a little unfocused, aware of every move. I had loved him—well, I'd thought I had. After his wife caught us, the whole truth came out. I learned that he started sleeping with me because he wanted to get back at his wife and he needed to get closer to my father. He didn't love me or care what happened to me afterward or that I had to leave Glasgow.

Dark, haunting emotions were mounting inside me, forcing me to do this, to dance. I knew that I shouldn't have slept with him; I admitted that the whole thing went too far, but that cold bastard told my father that I was the one that seduced him, that he was going through a rough time and was easily swayed by my charms.

Panting, I steadied myself on my feet when I was done. I bowed slightly and vanished behind the doors as soon as he started clapping. Nauseous and lost, I ran through the corridor. I barged into the changing room, ripping the mask from my eyes. The stripper that had lent me a hair clip earlier on was there, changing. Aimee, that was her name.

"Are you all right?"

I shut my eyes, trying to steady my pounding heart, telling myself this whole thing was only a bad dream. Andrew Hamilton wasn't in the club tonight. He was supposed to be abroad, far, far away from me.

"Yes … well, no. I don't know," I said. My body was shaking and my thoughts racing.

"It's always hard the first time, but don't worry, you will get used to it," she assured me, smiling. She was about my height, maybe even shorter, pretty with lots of freckles all over her nose. "I hope the client wasn't inappropriate. Some of them are real pigs!"

"Oh no, I wasn't stripping. I danced on the pole," I explained, feeling like an idiot.

"Well, you're lucky then. I'm only good at taking my clothes off." She chuckled. "Which room did you go to? The club is mental tonight; Nathan is stressed out."

"Err … I'm not sure … the third one on the corner."

"The third one? Wow that's strange. He normally likes a lap dance, nothing so dry."

I stilled and looked at her.

"What did you just say?" I asked.

"Well, Johnny normally likes strippers or a lap dancer. He's here once a month at least," she explained, walking around the room and picking up stuff for her outfit.

I told myself to keep breathing, but I couldn't take enough oxygen into my lungs.

"Do you know him, the client? Tall, smoky eyes, dark hair, beard? I thought his name was—"

"Hot, right? Johnny Hodges. He's the guest of Mr. Lurkin, who partly owns this club. Don't say anything to anyone. We aren't supposed to talk about him," she said with serious expression.

I blinked rapidly, staring at her like she just slapped me. "That client out there? Did you say that his name was Johnny Hodges?"

"Shhh. Don't be so loud. I wasn't supposed to use his name!"

Mack

Lurkin had called me again, after a week. He gave me the address to one of his warehouses on the outskirts of Edinburgh and told me to show up. He was short staffed tonight, so I jumped at the opportunity like any good neighbour would.

I sat in his office for about half an hour, working through the pointless paperwork, trying to remember who Mack McCune was. All my documents were impeccable, the guys in Glasgow had done a great job in faking my identity. Lurkin couldn't be taken for granted. He was careful and I had to play a dumb ass.

"I have five trucks that need to go out tonight. Raj will give you the delivery schedule. If you don't mess anything up, I want you here tomorrow at the same time." Lurkin chuckled, trying to be funny.

"There won't be any mess-up. I can assure you," I stated. "Thanks for this, Adrian. I appreciate it."

"Don't sweat it. We're neighbours; we should be helping each other. Besides, your woman will have your balls if you screw up." He said that loud enough for the other guys to hear him. They all laughed, and I laughed too, but deep down I imagined him in the interrogation room, terrified and not so confident.

I needed to remind myself that this was part of my act, that Mack McCune had to make his wife happy, regardless. "How about I organise a boys' night one evening? A couple of beers, a good cigar, a few hands of poker and maybe food. What do you say?"

"Good idea, but you should include Claire, so then I can invite Ellie. She finally agreed to go out with me."

Rage washed through to me like a giant storm. What the fuck? Did he think that he was dating her?

"Okay, sounds good. Guess I was wrong. You managed to break her, then?"

"Believe it or not I bumped into her in the club the other night and we had a drink. I'll speak to her. I'm sure she will be up for it," Lurkin added, with a wink.

I told myself to stay calm. This wasn't the time to screw up this whole operation. After I was done with the paperwork, he started introducing me around. Raj was his right-hand guy. He was Indian, with a Sikh turban on his head and a very thick accent. I was making mental notes, counting the number of people that worked in the warehouse tonight.

I left the depot around seven that night and came back at five a.m. The deliveries were straight forward, and Raj had given me enough details so I wouldn't mess anything up.

I went to bed just after seven in the morning, exhausted, but glad that I made some kind of progress. Claire was taking care of all the reports for the superintendent. I slept until three, for the first time not dreaming about Charlotte, but Ellie. I woke up with a hard dick, remembering our last steamy moment in the car. Fuck, she was so responsive and wet.

The apartment was empty. Things between me and Claire were still quite strained, but we were getting along. At least we were trying. That incident when I woke up strangling her must have shaken her up a little. She probably thought I was losing my mind. Claire had been Charlotte's friend and her death had shaken her up too. All these years I had been blaming Claire for what happened and now I felt guilty about it. She was just doing her job and Charlotte was stubborn, even I knew that. My father had been telling me that I had to control myself better, that being impulsive wasn't helping my case.

I went to the gym and worked out, trying not thinking about Ellie. Lurkin had a few more shifts for me later on in the week. I didn't want to be stuck in the apartment all day today and I wasn't too keen on the paperwork. There was another option—I could knock on Ellie's door and find out if she was all right. She was pissed off with me and I owed her an apology.

I decided against this idea, and instead, I headed out and drove to the city. The drive took over half an hour. The traffic was slow moving today, but I didn't mind. I didn't have to be anywhere. I was driving around, killing time and thinking about the case.

After not being able to figure out what to do, I ended up in Coral. I had plenty of women that I could have called, but I couldn't get Ellie out of my head. Her long smooth skin made my dick hard and I had no idea how to deal with this fucked up situation. She was so infuriating, doing exactly what I asked her not to do, fucking dating Lurkin.

Dad wanted to see me, from our short and to the point conversation he had figured out that I finally found a woman that pulled me away from my unhappy past, a woman who could put my grieving soul back together. I shook my head, knowing that he was wrong. Ellie couldn't heal my grief.

The bouncer gave me a nod when I slipped through. Women were eyeing me up. I couldn't deny I saw them looking. I wanted to have a quiet drink, avoid talking to anyone. Tonight, I wasn't Mack McCune, but Tobias Stanley. He was a guy who couldn't stop thinking about his unattainable neighbour. How pathetic.

The first thing that hit me in the club was the amount of people on the dance floor and at the bar. Earlier in the day I had read that a famous rock band was going to play tonight. I was probably too old for the company in here, but I needed some time out, a break.

I had my pass to the private part of the club. Maybe I was violating the fucking rules, but whatever, this case was going to take longer than I anticipated. It was late evening, I felt lonely and sexually frustrated. Tonight I needed a woman that could understand that I wanted to possess her, physically and mentally. Thoughts about Ellie were overwhelming. I had to forget about her.

My mood shifted when I noticed that the bar was packed too. A few long-legged strippers were hanging over clients. I knew that Lurkin was a member, he liked hanging around here, but he was very careful. He kept a low profile, avoided trouble.

I'd always had a pretty high sex drive, and when I married Charlotte, we were all over each other. During our honeymoon we barely left the bedroom. I was fed up with reminding myself that Ellie wasn't her. After Charlotte's death I got this notion that if I could control a woman's orgasm, then I could control my grief. The only time that I managed to accomplish it was with Ellie, the night that we met and that time in my car.

She mentioned that she had been involved with a married man before. I understood. She didn't want to repeat patterns from the past. She was anxious not to make the same mistake again.

I ordered some whiskey, watching other customers, and half an hour later, I requested a private dance. A pretty long-legged brunette walked me to one of the rooms, chatting with me all the way.

I just had to blow off some steam, get it together and get focused.

The room was spacious, with red carpet and red walls. The lighting seemed over the top. When the dancer showed up I realized my plan had failed. Ellie, my sexy, submissive neighbour stood in front of me.

It looked like this wasn't a joke. She was here to dance for me when I wanted to erase her from my mind forever.

Fourteen

Ellie

"Is this a joke?" I asked Mack, who was supposed to be my next client. Nathan was having a laugh. He asked me to cover for someone in an open performing room. I was a little anxious, worried that maybe it was Andrew again asking for another round, this time with physical contact.

Unfortunately this was much worse, because I was standing face-to-face with Mack.

"I could ask you the same question, Angel. What the hell are you doing in here?"

He'd given me a clear warning to stay away from the club, and I ignored it. I stood in front of him, feeling completely vulnerable and shocked he was here. Mack's eyes were on me, moving down over my black leather stripper costume. There was very little to it, but it still covered the essentials. I had on the tiniest pair of leather shorts; they covered my pubic bone and rode high up the back exposing most of my cheeks. I suppose they were a little better than a leather G-string. The top consisted of a black leather push-up bra. On my feet I wore six-inch platform heels with black ribbons crisscrossed up my calves fastening just under my knee. I was still recovering from the shock, after what I had heard from Cora, one of the other girls, finding out that

Adrian owned the club. Not to mention Aimee telling me that Andrew was Johnny Hodges.

I was treading on very thin ice here, because technically I was working for Adrian and he was somehow connected to my ex. I needed to remember that I wasn't anonymous. My pictures had been in the papers, and it was just a matter of time before anyone would recognise me. I needed to think fast, give Mack something, a believable story, but I wasn't sure what to say or do.

"Sit down. I'm going to dance for you," I stated, improvising, placing my hands on my hips. I thought that I could use my body to distract him, so he wouldn't ask questions. Heat crawled its way up my thighs. Part of me was ready to throw myself at him, the other part was afraid to be the other woman once again.

"Ellie, what the fuck are you doing here?" he demanded, grabbing my shoulders and yanking me towards his chest. Okay, so he wasn't up to having fun with me. He wanted answers.

"I'm quite good on the pole and when one of the reporters was talking about this club I decided to check it out. Before I knew it, one thing led to another and I was hired."

"As a fucking stripper?" he repeated with disbelief. "Why didn't you say anything earlier on?"

"No, I don't strip. I dance on the pole and I didn't tell you because I wasn't sure if I was really up for this," I explained, annoyed that he demanded to know what was going on, even after I told him to stay away from me. "Anyway, don't turn this around. What the hell are you doing here? I thought that you didn't do this kind of thing?"

I was pissed off all of a sudden. I didn't know why I was so stupid, thinking that Mack was misunderstood and unhappy. He was just like any other man.

"That isn't relevant, Ellie. Tell me how the hell you managed to get a job here in the first place."

He was too distracting, holding me so close. I couldn't think straight, aware of his cologne, his strong hands around my body.

"Let go of me. This is none of your business. I'm not your concern," I hissed, trying to pull away, but he brought me closer, our faces only inches apart.

I wanted to feel his cock inside me, fucking me hard and taking control like before. Since that night in my apartment, I couldn't stop thinking about his sweet tortures, about the mark that he left on my soul. Another married man and already he was feeding on my emotions, on my damaged heart. I didn't need a repeat, but I wanted him.

"You know how much I've missed you, Angel?" he asked, loosening up his grip and brushing his lips over mine gently, tasting. My voice of reason screamed at me to push him away, but my body was drawn to his like a moth to a flame, wanting to be tormented by his dominance.

"I'm at work, Mack, and we shouldn't be doing this."

It was my reasonable side that was speaking now. I was here for a story, nothing else. I didn't want love, and I didn't want to sleep with married men, but that attraction between us was intense and so overbearing. All of a sudden I didn't know what to do.

"Dance for me, Angel. I'm here now and I'm not leaving until I get what I want," he said with mischief in his eyes, speaking to me softly. My heart skipped a beat, then began racing away faster and faster. "Tonight, you will please me."

My throat went dry when he released me and sat on the leather sofa looking at me. Those hungry eyes began tracing my lips, my breasts, his gaze moving downwards slowly, admiring the parts of me that he'd owned. I was so turned on, instantly becoming aware of that tone in his voice that he used only when we were alone. I was still apprehensive, still unsure that this was the way to go.

"Mack, please. We have crossed the line, not once or twice, but many times. You should leave," I mumbled, fighting to throw away his proposition.

I liked it when he took control over me, when he pleasured me and I screamed, asking for more. I didn't feel ashamed or lost with him. My playing a submissive to his sexual dominance allowed me to let go of everything in my life but those moments with him. He helped me forget about my father, any money worries, being overlooked at work—everything. It was him and I was locked in passion and lust. I was his for the taking. I felt like I finally connected with another human being.

Mack was calm, his eyes filled with warmth.

"My marriage is almost nonexistent, Ellie. I have been having nightmares for years and you're waking me from them. I want you to feel pleasure and not feel guilty about it. I want you, not Claire. Every day I wonder if there is an easy way out of this complicated situation. All I know is you and I won't end. You must trust me."

My reasonable side told me that I should go back to the changing room and ask someone else to cover for me, but I couldn't move, my skin itched for his touch. Warm desire poured low into my stomach. The rhythmical throbbing between my legs reminded me how much we both enjoyed that role-play in the bedroom. How much I wanted to be dominated by him, and no one else.

I ran my tongue over my lips, imagining him moaning while I held his dick in my mouth.

I stopped thinking about what was wrong or right, and instead I took a step back and bent my knees. He came here to enjoy a performance, and I was ready to give him one.

He parted his lips and inhaled sharply. I could get him off, just moving and teasing him. I felt confident, maybe a bit scared that he gave me the control back.

I bent my knees a little more, then straightened my posture swaying my hips from side to side. There was a pole in the room, but I was a little apprehensive dancing for Mack. Previously I had only danced for Andrew. I wanted to please him because I was in love, now I was just about to do that for Mack. I couldn't fool myself. We were just lovers; his words were empty and I needed to remember that I didn't believe in love anymore.

I decided to ignore whatever emotions I was experiencing and have fun. Show him what I could do.

Mack's stormy grey eyes were heavy, tracing my every movement. He shifted, leaning closer with a sharp intake of breath. I wanted him so much. I didn't even realise how much I missed his touch in the past week.

Without thinking much about this, I approached the pole. I used my right hand to sway myself on the metal bar a few times, smiling at him. Mack was looking at me like I was a sexual object for his pleasure, his eyes large and his jaw tight as he gritted his teeth.

"Come here, Angel," he commanded all of a sudden. I obeyed instantly, jumping off the pole and standing right in from of him. Heat clouded my mind. His lips looked delicious, inviting, and I leaned down wanting to taste them.

He grabbed my face and pulled me closer to him, teasing me, letting me know how much his mouth had missed me. I moaned, and my pussy throbbed wanting him to touch it, caress it.

Light-headed, I pulled away and knelt down between his legs, knowing what I wanted to do. He was rock hard and I smiled to myself, thinking that my pole routine had worked. My nipples were tight and my breasts felt heavy, ready for him to play with.

"Angel," he purred low in his throat whispering huskily so that I was forced to lean in to hear him properly. "The last time we were together I gave your pretty pussy some attention and now it's my turn for pleasure. What would you like to do to me?"

Wrapping my hair around his fist, he pulled gently backwards so my body leaned away from him and I was forced to look into his beautiful eyes. I saw his arm move but didn't know its destination until he popped my right breast out, pinching my nipple and pulling it, teasing. I just couldn't find words to answer him.

"Don't mash those lips together; I have a better use for them. I want you to suck my cock." He enunciated each of the last words with a sharp pinch of my nipple.

It was all too much. I was so aroused by this man and needy for him. I unbuckled his belt and undid his jeans as fast as I possibly could; he lifted his hips so I could move the pants down to his ankles to give me full access to him.

I leaned down and flicked my tongue over the slit on the glans and he groaned deep in his chest. Holding the base and squeezing gently, I wrapped my mouth around the head and licked at that sensitive spot just underneath with the flat of my tongue. Sucking harder, I took more of him into my mouth, sliding down slowly and humming my pleasure. I spread my saliva using the hand wrapped around him to lubricate his shaft.

"Sweet Jesus, Angel!" he hissed and I grinned, sliding back up his shaft and releasing him with an audible pop. I leaned forward again revelling in having some control, when Mack suddenly stood up. He thrust slowly into my mouth and when he reached the back I gulped, allowing him to go deeper. He growled as he withdrew and pushed in again. I lifted my free hand and cupped his balls, gently massaging them in my palm. He jumped ever so slightly at the shock of it. His face began to redden and a slight sheen appeared on his top lip. I let go of his cock and pulled my other breast free and pinched my nipples for him, humming my pleasure.

"Angel I am close, so close," he spat through gritted teeth. I put both my hands on his arse cheeks, gripping gently with my nails and pulling his cheeks apart. He put both hands on my head and gently fucked my face. "Oh God, Oh fuck. Oh, Angel, yes!" he cried as his shot his salty load in my mouth, and I took all he had to give me.

Mack

My balls just exploded. I had never come so hard in my life. Ellie's blow job skills outnumbered all my recent encounters with other women. Collapsing in my seat, I panted, completely out of breath and unable to form a thought or say any words.

I picked up her small body and brought her to my chest, still panting like an animal. My breathing slowed and I came back to myself and knew I had to return the favour.

"Good God, Ellie, I want to devour your pussy until you are unable to move," I said, not caring for the fucking world that I was breaking the rules, but I wanted to have her again, just for me, somewhere where we wouldn't be disturbed.

Her pupils dilated with surprise, and her cheeks were flushed, probably from the effort that she put into blowing me with such skill.

"Mack, it's not for me. I'm not going to go through this again. Claire… she-–"

"Forget about Claire or anyone else. I want you, so give me a chance. What time are you getting out of here?"

"Another hour," she replied.

"I won't stand waiting, knowing that you're going to perform for someone else," I said, gritting my teeth again, bringing her closer to my face. I could read her eyes; the apprehension and worry was close to the surface.

"I have a complicated past and I want to concentrate on moving in a positive direction in my life. I want to build my career and become a better person. I don't know what are you expecting from me. You're tied up. I was involved with a married man before and it ruined my whole life. We can't risk it. I like Claire. She shouldn't suffer because things between you two are rough at the moment," she said, shaking her head.

I kept breathing. Frustration raged inside me like a sudden avalanche. This small creature picked me up and made it clear that she didn't want to lie. I couldn't let her go.

"I'll wait for you outside. I'm leaving Claire, Ellie. She doesn't mean anything to me anymore. You're the person that I want to be with."

She wiggled away, standing up. I zipped my trousers and left.

I could see she had many doubts and wished I could give her the truth. I had been working in this field for a long time and I knew that I would be out of the game if I told her anything.

She reminded me a little bit of Charlotte, with her stubborn determination and drive to succeed. Maybe after what happened I became paranoid, but Ellie was putting herself in danger. She looked incredible in that little outfit. The sooner she quit, the better I would be sleeping at night.

An hour later, she appeared at the door, looking wary, and my cock twisted remembering her fucking me with her mouth. She didn't want me to wait for her, but I was too pissed off to even consider letting her go home alone. I hated reporters; they always dug for answers when they weren't supposed to, putting themselves in danger.

"Tell me, why are you so adamant about working there?" I asked after we started walking along the busy street.

"My boss at the magazine is a chauvinistic pig and a complete arse. He thinks that all women are beneath him. I came here to prove to someone that I could be a real journalist—that I had some value in the world—to someone who doesn't believe in me," she explained, looking away.

"Someone?" I questioned.

"My father. He never believed in me or that I could achieve anything. I have been picturing him seeing my name on a byline, seeing my article on the first page of his morning paper," she continued, her voice hard. "I didn't get the job in the club because I was bored and wanted lecherous men ogling me. I overheard another reporter talking about Johnny Hodges, so I decided to check it out."

"Come again? Did you say Johnny Hodges?" I repeated, losing my breath for good few seconds.

Fifteen

Mack

I was waiting for Ellie's response, holding my breath. Johnny Hodges was the guy behind scenes, the person that my unit had been trying to track down since it turned out that Lurkin was connected to him. I knew when I saw her in the club that she was getting too close to that asshole.

She couldn't have known about Johnny Hodges. He was invisible and only certain people knew who he really was. He used that name as a cover. Lurkin was using his connections in Spain to bring pricey products into the UK. My priority was to figure out how he was doing that, without getting caught.

"I don't think I can explain this to you here. It's complicated," she mumbled, staring down at her nails. She was beautiful and at times naive. I didn't want other men to take advantage of her.

I dragged my hand through my hair, trying to breathe. She knew too much already and I didn't want us to be overheard by anyone. We needed to find a better place. I was aware that this conversation was going to be difficult.

"We need to go back to your apartment, Ellie," I said, wanting her to know that I was serious. The guys from intelligence hadn't had anything new on Hodges for a while. Maybe it was my lucky day tonight.

"The complex? You want to talk when your wife is next door?" she asked, looking at me like I was crazy. Okay, that was bad idea. Her apartment was out of the question.

"You're right. I have a better idea. Let's go."

I grabbed her hand and started walking towards a tall red building. The Marriott hotel was just around the corner. Claire had been right. Ellie was a reporter and I had underestimated her, thinking that she had no idea what was going on with Lurkin. I didn't believe in coincidences, but any information about Johnny Hodges was valuable. Claire had been studying the files from a couple of months ago. It was when Lurkin had nearly been busted for drugs, but we couldn't prosecute him because of lack of evidence. She wasn't too happy about our recent setback. We had been stuck together for weeks now and she was probably missing her husband. After that incident in my bedroom I was determined to keep myself in line, to avoid any conflicts. I was losing control, but I didn't want to see another shrink. Therapy didn't quite work.

Ellie was too quiet; she kept glancing behind her back from time to time. I was feeling on edge and was annoyed that I found her in the club, frustrated that I couldn't get away from her alluring spell.

We walked inside the building and I asked for a room with a double bed. I was going to have her tonight, but I needed answers first. Ellie wasn't stupid and I had no idea how long I'd be able to keep the truth about me from her, including the fact that my real name was Tobias Stanley.

I was expecting Ellie to be difficult or to throw a fit, but she didn't say anything. We were both tense. The ride in the lift was long and all the way to the room I needed to remind myself to stay calm. Ellie was nothing more than a woman that craved my company. She wanted to escape and, like everyone else, she was running away from something in her past. I sensed that she had been hurt by a man, and now she was hiding. Some selfish bastard probably broke her trust.

"We should talk about this, Mack," she finally said when we got inside the room and I shut the door behind me. Her eyes fell on the large bed in the middle of the room. The decor was purple and white. I liked it. I wanted to bring her into my arms and assure her that she had nothing to worry about, that Claire was just my partner, not a woman that I loved.

"That's why we are here, Ellie, so we can talk without being interrupted," I said, hoping that she would at least relax. "Tell me, when did you hear the name Johnny Hodges?"

She circled around the room trailing her fingers over the furniture, obviously playing for time before she sat down on the chair. Her eyes were wary, hiding a myriad of emotions. I needed to know if I was the reason she was so worried.

"Nathan, the assistant manager, asked me to cover for someone yesterday. When I showed up, the guy … oh God, I—" she stammered, hiding her face in her hands. "It was Andrew, the married guy that I'd had an affair with."

I was slightly confused and amazed that this would have ever happened. I didn't want to know about her past lovers, but I couldn't avoid this conversation any longer.

"Did he recognise you?" I asked.

"No, I was wearing a mask with the costume, but I can't be sure," she said. "I was shocked that he was there, surprised. I couldn't just turn around and leave, so I danced for him, like he was any other regular client."

"I'm sorry, but what does your ex have to do with Johnny Hodges?"

She took a deep breath and looked at me with distant, like she was still fighting with herself. I didn't push before, didn't ask questions about where she was from and if she had any family, but it was time to change that. This operation was crucial, and it was time to pull Lurkin down.

"My surname isn't Frasier, Mack, it's Grant. My father is Jonathan Grant."

"Grant … Jonathan Grant. Where have I heard that name before?" I asked myself, thinking out loud. That surname had been in the papers recently. It took me a moment to realise that this Grant was a well-known barrister who had won a number of well-publicised high-profile cases in the UK. He was a defence solicitor and wasn't afraid to fight with even the toughest prosecutors. He had various clients, from scumbags to high-class businessmen. It seemed that he could get anyone out of trouble.

A few months ago, there was another story in the paper. His beloved daughter was caught sleeping with one of his clients, Andrew Hamilton. Grant offered to take his case.

"Hold on, Ellie Grant … the recent case. I heard about that story," I said, knowing how everyone had lynched her. That guy Hamilton kept giving these absurd interviews, insisting that she was the one that seduced him. Not the other way around.

"His wife caught us in their bed, in his house. Oh God, this is so embarrassing. I went through with it, knowing that he was married, that he had kids. This went on for months and months. He wanted to leave his wife, he told me that he loved me, that I was the one, but in the end all of it was just lies," she said, sitting down on the bed, looking so broken.

Now I understood why she felt so guilty about us getting involved. I couldn't let this affect me, whatever happened between us. I was forgetting my role in this. The media had written all sorts of stories about her. I didn't quite follow the story, but I did realise that many people had.

"So you ended up in The Grange?"

"My father disowned me. I had twenty-four hours to pack my bags and leave the house that had I spent most of my life in. We didn't get on, even before the scandal hit the media—I went to study journalism when he insisted on law. The scandal gave him an excuse to cut all ties with me."

"It was a mistake, one error. I think your father overreacted," I insisted, not quite sure what the big deal was. Okay, so she screwed up with one of her daddy's clients. These stories were common and, judging from what she said, it appeared to me that her father was an asshole.

She shook her head.

"No, he lost many important clients because of what happened. He didn't want to listen; he just told me to get out. We'd had our differences, but what hurt the most was the fact that he believed that asshole, not me. Andrew had told him that I instigated the affair, that it was my idea, when it was Andrew who seduced me, led me on and lied to me."

Bastard. Grant was known for being harsh, but Ellie was his daughter. She made a simple mistake.

"I was so angry, so disappointed that he used me like that. I have lost everything because I fell in love. When I went to the club, I saw him there."

"Don't worry about it, Angel, he ob–"

"He's Johnny Hodges, Mack," she cut me off all of a sudden. "One of the dancers said that he is there regularly. Adrian owns shares in the club and apparently Andrew is his partner."

"What are you talking about, Ellie?" I demanded, trying to process what she was saying. That was impossible. That asshole couldn't be Johnny Hodges. He wouldn't just use that name in the club around other people.

"The stripper was convinced that Adrian had connections to Andrew. She kept calling him Mr. Hodges. I spoke to Nathan tonight, before I went to dance for you, and he confirmed that Hodges had always been a special guest in the club," she said getting agitated with me, probably because she had to repeat herself. Andrew Hamilton…that surname didn't tell me anything. He was a nobody, then suddenly became a somebody. For years Hodges had always been the silent partner, the guy behind the scenes. His name was mentioned at times, but the unit could never find anything. They couldn't link him to anyone around Lurkin.

"What else do you know, Angel?" I said, tucking her hair behind her ear.

"There is something going on in the club. You were right about Adrian. He can't be trusted."

"He offered me a job as a driver; he wants to help me to keep Claire off my back."

Ellie chewed on her lips; that name hung between us like a dead bird. I couldn't stand that she was so deeply involved with this case.

"You shouldn't be working with him, Mack."

I went down on my knees and grabbed her hands.

"Tell me everything. I need to know what's going on out there."

"More than I wanted to know. Adrian has been talking about some shipments and I think it's about drugs. I overheard him when I was in the changing room."

"What? You were listening in?"

"I had no choice; I was getting ready and they came in."

"Fuck, I don't want to think what could have happened if Lurkin caught you eavesdropping," I snarled, tensing my muscles. She was so reckless, putting her life in jeopardy.

"He didn't. I'm fine. I think you're overreacting," she said.

"Ellie, I don't overreact and you're making me so mad. I might not know much about your family, but I know for a fact that your father wouldn't give a fuck about you if you suddenly became queen."

"This isn't all because of my father. It's also about my reputation and self-respect. My father has never supported me in anything I wanted to do for myself, and Andrew used me, just to get closer to him. After all that, he still became his client. No one knew about the affair and what followed, but the press seemed to have every scrap of information. I suspect that he was the one that's been selling information to the papers to make himself look good before his hearing."

I wrapped my arm around her, knowing that she had gone through a lot.

"So I guess he didn't leave his wife for you?"

"He ended it as soon as she found out. It was a nightmare; I didn't sleep for days. Paparazzi were following me everywhere I went. My career was over. That's when I left and saw an apartment advertised in the Grange in the middle of nowhere. Died my hair and started using my mother's maiden name as my surname. After a month passed, I finally got a job in that shitty paper."

Ellie

I felt like a coward, I didn't want to hide anymore from him, but I still couldn't quite comprehend that Andrew knew Adrian and they were involved in some sort of dodgy business together. An icy chill crept down my spine when I thought about how little I actually knew about my ex-lover.

From the file that my father had on his desk, it turned out that Andrew had some financial problems. He was accused of fraud among other things. My father didn't want to work for him. He didn't like cases like that. Andrew was turned away, and then, a few weeks later, Dad asked me to speak to him, find out if he was worth his time. My father was disappointed that I didn't pursue law, but he kept trying to spark my interest. He encouraged me to speak to his clients. I felt important to him when we discussed his business, so I said yes. Andrew charmed me straight away. He was charismatic and flirtatious. I lost my head over him.

Yesterday, I couldn't sleep, thinking about the amount of information that I had. Adrian, the handsome neighbour next door, was supplying drugs. Andrew had assured me that he was innocent and that someone was trying to destroy his career. He had me wrapped around his little finger. He got what he wanted and then got rid of me.

"Angel, you don't need to prove anything to anyone. You're putting yourself at risk and I can't allow that," Mack said, tightening his jaw.

"It's not your decision to make. I have already started working on the article. This is my own way of seeking redemption. When the scandal hit the media, I was ruined. All my life, I had been trying to gain some kind of recognition or acknowledgment from my father. I have never succeeded. I know you probably won't understand, but this is something that I have to do," I stated, wanting to bury myself in his chest and forget about the past few months.

I didn't want to fight with him anymore or weigh up the pros and cons of a relationship with him. It was foolish, but Mack didn't turn away. He wasn't even shocked when I revealed my real name.

We talked for a bit longer, about my life back in Glasgow. Mack was trying hard to cheer me up. He wasn't judgmental like everyone else. He moved on the bed next to me and slowly I became aware that we were alone in the hotel room. My skin prickled with waves of heat, and when I glanced in his eyes, I saw that he noticed it too. We were sitting on the bed, staring at each other, and both calculating the next move.

"Angel, I can't sit here and pretend that I don't want you. Let's forget about Lurkin and your ex," he rasped, leaning close to my ear. I tossed my hair behind me, inhaling in a sharp breath. I recognised his tone of voice. He wanted me to play submissive, like during our first night together. I deserved a break, and maybe I was making another mistake, but I felt connected to him. He knew how to control me, how to own me.

I nodded, and my throat tightened when I realised that Mack cared about me.

"Move further up the bed," he said, and muscles inside my stomach clenched in anticipation. It was easy to forget being with him, when he was so ready to please me and himself. I lay on the bed, and Mack began taking my clothes off. I whimpered when he spread my legs and ran his thumb over my folds.

"I'm going to lick your wet tight pussy until you come hard for me," he said, pulling on my underwear, ripping the lace on the side. I was still wearing my top, but nothing else.

"Tell me, Angel, do you want me to make you come?" he asked, his eyes wide and dangerous.

"Yes, Mack … I want to escape, please."

"Yes, Angel, you will, but not just yet. I want to play with you first. I haven't played with this pussy for a while now, Angel, and I've missed it."

Sixteen

Ellie

Mack traced his fingers over my stomach. His eyes were on me, hard and heavy with desire. Then he crawled up and kissed me, slipping his tongue inside my mouth and tangling it with mine. I grabbed his face eagerly, feeling his hard cock rubbing against my wet sex. I needed more, wanted to feel his skin caressing mine. I lifted my hips to get more friction. I was so needy for him.

He was so good with helping to ease the tension, letting me forget about everything else. In that moment we were together and that was all that mattered. His mouth was hard devouring mine, his lips teased and sucked. He moaned my name, gripping my hips in his palms, sliding his finger back to my sex. I cried out as he stroked the lips of my sex spreading my arousal. He moved his head to my neck and inhaled deeply. He bit my shoulder, marking me, claiming me as his and then his lips were feasting on my neck, showering me with kisses and nips and licks.

"Let's get rid of that, shall we? I need to see you naked," he said, and helped me to remove my T-shirt and bra. Within moments I was lying naked on the bed shivering in anticipation. I frowned as I realised he was still fully clothed, staring straight into my eyes. He slapped my hand when I reached out to touch the bulge his dick made in his pants, growling out, "I am in control here, Angel. Everything is when I say and on my terms." He stood from the bed and watched me lie there naked and ready for him. "Open your legs for me, Angel. Show yourself to me."

I bent my knees and moved my legs apart so he could see me. I was nervous about being laid bare for him, hoping I pleased him. "Touch yourself; let me see how you like to please yourself." He took his shirt off and toed his shoes off, kicking them to the side. He leaned back against the TV unit and folded his arms across his chest. "Show me, Angel, I'm waiting."

I was mortified; I had never masturbated for anyone else before. I screwed my eyes shut and started to cup my breast with my left hand, trailing down my tummy with my right, stroking the flesh on my lower abdomen just above my pubic bone. Pinching my nipple until it was a hard bud.

"Angel, I need to see your eyes. Open them for me." Opening my eyes, I flushed red. This seemed so personal and I felt so exposed by his request. "I always give you pleasure, Angel. I always make sure you are taken care of. I just want to see how you take care of yourself. Nothing to be ashamed of. You are beautiful."

He smiled a lazy grin at me and it gave me courage. Widening my legs, I slid my hand down and into my folds spreading my cream around my hardened clit, I sighed at the pleasure in the contact and started to gently circle my clit, my other hand continuing to tease my sensitive nipples. I could feel my orgasm building and I arched my back slightly, my breath becoming shorter. Pushing two fingers of my left hand into my opening, wishing it were Mack there instead, I ground my hips against my hand trying to find my release. Looking at Mack, I could see I was affecting him. His hand was rubbing his dick through his jeans and his eyes were almost black with desire. I could feel my orgasm getting closer; I was almost there.

"Stop, Angel, hands by your sides. Do not touch."

"What? Are you kidding me? I need to come. Please don't make me stop," I begged him. Leaning between my thighs, he inserted two fingers into me. The joy of having him stimulate me when I was so close made me call out.

"You forget, Angel, this is my pussy. I decide the pleasure you receive."

I was so close, just one more stroke and I would burst into bliss, but he removed his fingers. I felt the loss of him keenly and pressed my thighs together for some relief. " No, Angel, don't forget the rules. When I say you can come you will come." I was desperate, panting—my body on fire. I started to shake with the need to release.

"You can't do this to me, Mack. I need to come. You can't torture me like this," I begged, almost in tears. I was delirious with need.

"Turn over, Angel. Lie on your tummy." I did as he asked, hoping that it would get me closer to release.

"My beautiful impatient girl," he said, picking something up from the floor. He knelt on the bed next to me and leaned over to place kisses on my shoulders. "I need to teach you a lesson; there is an old saying: all good things come to those who wait. Have you heard that before?"

He straddled my thighs and slid his hand down my arm and placed it behind my back. Doing the same with the other arm, he fastened them together with what I assumed was my bra. He slid from the bed and pulled my legs so I moved towards the edge where he picked me up by my waist so I was face down, arse up. "Oh, my beautiful Angel, that is some view," he growled out, sounding close to losing his cool. I waited to see what would happen next. Hearing the unmistakable sound of his zipper, I wiggled my hips in anticipation. I could hear the movement of clothes but nothing else for what seemed ten minutes but was more like twenty seconds. Then a breath of cool air blew against my hot sex, making me cry out at the attention.

Mack waited to the count of ten, and then he licked my clit with the flat of his tongue moving up to my entrance. He gripped my thighs keeping me in place and thrust his tongue deeper. I couldn't keep myself from moaning. My orgasm started to build once more and I was desperate to find my release. Mack suckled on my clit, humming and grazing me with his teeth, sliding a finger in and out. The way he fucked me with it was absolute bliss. I couldn't keep still. I ground my hips against his face needing this more than the air in my lungs. Pressure started to build low in my belly.

"Oh, Mack, I'm going to come, oh god, Mack!" I yelled.

Then he was gone. I had been teetering on the edge and he left me hanging. I gasped air into my body, unable to find the words of frustration when I felt his cock ram home. He held my waist and buried himself into me over and over, my channel squeezing him tight sucking him into my body, his balls stimulating my clit with every thrust.

"Angel, let me hear you, tell me who owns this pussy!" he yelled hitting that magic spot inside me.

"Oh fuck, Mack," I sobbed, "you own my pussy. It's yours," I screamed as my orgasm finally washed over me, making me lose my vision behind a blur of bliss, my body tightening and sucking Mack in further as he reached his release too. Mack collapsed next to me on the bed, both of us heaving for breath. I was vaguely aware of Mack removing my bra from my wrists and covering us both with the duvet.

Mack

The morning light blinded me as I awoke in a strange room with a hot body in my arms. I was dreaming about Charlotte again, her soft skin caressing mine, her smile. After a moment I recognised the space around me. Last night was unexpected. Yet again Ellie made me lose control. She consumed me slowly. She was unlike anyone else I'd ever met before. I fucked her last night and I didn't feel guilty about it at all.

My desire burned for her. My dead cells were reawakened; the need to be close to her was back. Every time she whimpered I was overwhelmed with euphoria and need of full control.

I had no idea how long this could last, maybe a few more weeks. I wasn't delusional. I was working undercover, trying to catch a notorious drug smuggler. Ellie wasn't my future. Yes, she pulled me away from the misery I carried, but this wouldn't last. We were both too damaged.

She turned around, blinked a few times, and smiled at me.

"Morning."

"Morning, Angel," I said, knowing that I shouldn't get too attached. No one could replace my wife, and Ellie would hate me once she learned the truth about me. "I need to be in work in an hour. Plenty of time to enjoy myself for a bit longer."

I winked at her and she smiled. I liked looking at her so relaxed and happy. She reached out and traced her fingers over my chest, licking her lips. Fuck, I was hard within seconds. She had no idea how sexy she was. How come this woman had such a profound effect on me?

I needed to get back to the apartment and relay all I had learned to Claire about Johnny Hodges, but I didn't want to think about my duties yet.

"Why do you have this scar? What happened?" she asked.

I looked at where her fingers were and I stilled. Two years ago, I had a call out to one of the areas in East Glasgow. I wasn't ready; it was a year after Charlotte's death. My shrink had given me the all clear only because I was telling him what he wanted to hear. I was lying to everyone then, Dad, my sister, and my new partner.

"I was shot. There was a robbery in the house," I explained. I felt like a scumbag, misleading her about who I was, about this scar. She couldn't know that she was in danger.

She lifted herself on her elbows, staring at me with disbelief. One of the guys was supposed to cover me, but his gun jammed and he didn't fire in time. I lay on the pavement in my own blood for a good ten minutes before any other unit could get to me. It was the scariest moment in my life. I was ready to die then, but for some reason God spared my pathetic life.

"Were you with Claire then?" she asked, staring at me intensely, her fingers gently brushing the thin scar on my skin.

I remembered waking up in the hospital several hours later, crying like a fucking baby. It was then I realised that I had to keep living, breathing the air that Charlotte had once breathed, tasting the food that she liked. I knew that I couldn't cope. I didn't want to. Dad came to visit me and he knew that I wasn't right. After the operation, the surgeon had given the go ahead. I was transferred to a private psychiatric ward to help me work through my guilt and my grief. Dad was with me the whole time, trying to tether me to the living world.

"Luckily she was away, so she didn't have to deal with it," I said, and sat on the bed. Maybe I had taken this whole thing with her too far. I was losing my focus, but at least Ellie had given me crucial information, something that could finally push the whole operation forward.

"Maybe it was better that she wasn't there when it happened. I remember when one of my friends was burgled a couple of years ago. At that time I was away in Shetland Islands and she was supposed to look after the house. It was —"

"Shetland Islands? Why did you go there?" I asked, bewildered.

"I was with this guy at the time and we wanted to have a short break away, somewhere quiet and picturesque, and he picked the Shetland Islands. Don't get me wrong, I wouldn't ever choose to go there, but I was smitten with him and when he suggested it I cringed," she explained, smiling to herself like she was bringing back good, playful memories from the past. "And I never regretted that I traveled there. I've discovered the most idyllic and perfect location in the whole universe, and the best part—the islands were still in Scotland."

My pulse speeded up instantly and I wondered if she was messing with my head. We couldn't possibly have that in common. This simply sounded too good to be true. Shetland Islands were Charlotte's and my favorite destination. It was expensive to get there, but we always liked pursuing unknown places. One day Charlotte told me that she wanted to visit Lerwick and an hour later we were heading to the airport. We lived on an impulse, making plans as we were going along. Lerwick port turned out to be one of the most fascinating places that I ever visited. When we were at the Island, we weren't rushing anywhere; life was slow and we were happier than ever before. After that one trip, we kept going back, to be closer with nature and all the great people that we'd met out there.

"Okay, this will sound very strange, but Shetland Islands is one of these places that I kept visiting over and over again. Every time I'm there I keep falling in love with it more and more," I said, clearing my throat, letting her know that I was absolutely serious. She gasped, widening her eyes, shaking her head. "It looks like our life just keeps throwing surprises at us. I would love to take you there one day, Ellie."

I was imagining visiting the same places with Ellie where I took Charlotte all those years ago, eating in the same pubs and restaurants, making love in the beautiful stone cottage by the fire. Not many people appreciated the islands and I had a hard time believing that Ellie had been there too.

"God, Mack, I'm in love with Lerwick and all the other islands. I stay in the cottage in the port … this sounds so crazy."

"Yes, I'm shocked too," I admitted, thinking that maybe I was reading too much into this. Yes, we both enjoyed the same beautiful destination, that raw part of Scotland, but that didn't mean we had a future together, that we were made for each other. I cleared my throat, ready to end this conversation. "Anyways, I have to get ready for work. It's late and I want to avoid morning traffic if I can help it."

She nodded, still staring at me like she was seeing me for the first time in her life. I headed to the bathroom, and once there I started taking a few deep breaths to calm my racing pulse. I thought that I could never go back to Shetland Islands, because of Charlotte, but now I wasn't so sure that I could simply forget about it, knowing that Ellie not only understood me, but also that she was in love in Lerwick just like Charlotte was. I had an urge to get back to the room, slip back into bed and make love to her. Instead I forced myself to take a shower, remembering that I was still an undercover detective that was pursing another case. This was real life and I was too fucked up to believe in fairy tales. This was just one hell of a coincidence.

Ellie was dressed when I came out of the bathroom. She sensed the distance that I put between us but didn't press me to talk. We said our goodbyes and an hour later I was driving to the depot feeling conflicted. My Angel didn't expect anything from me or ask me to give up my life for her. She didn't trust me yet, and that was understandable after what happened with that asshole and Jonathan Grant.

Raj briefed me quickly and I was back on the road, faster than I planned. The other guys worked in the afternoons. Claire didn't ask any questions of me when I came back to the complex in the evening. I hadn't learned anything new. Lurkin wasn't in the office and Raj wasn't too keen on talking to me. He just wanted to do his job and go home. She fucking knew that her questions would put me on edge, and besides that, she was tracking my phone. I briefed her with everything I knew from Ellie, and we discussed the plan for the next week without arguments this time.

From then on, I slipped back into a routine. I woke up in the morning, drove to the depot and then started my shift. I was losing days and nothing was happening. Slowly the frustration started to show. I wasn't picking up anything suspicious on Lurkin's stock. Claire kept telling me to be patient, but I was on edge, trying not to think about Ellie and her beautiful skin. Each day I wondered if I was doing the right thing, getting close to her or even thinking about her. She was avoiding me again, and I couldn't keep an eye on her because I was on the road most of the time.

I fucking missed her, and I was jeopardising the progress that Claire and I made. My sex with her was impulsive. Everything I had done so far seemed focused on her. Charlotte often pointed out that I needed to try harder; my impulsive personality was holding me back.

Then, a week later after arriving at work, I noticed that the depot was much busier than usual. I spotted new guys loading trucks and some youngsters by the door. Raj saw me and approached me as soon as I walked in.

"You will be driving with Marvin tonight. He's part of the old crew. Mr. Lurkin thinks that you're ready for more challenging work," he said. I nodded and followed him towards the group of guys that stood at the back. Raj introduced me around and explained that I was to join them.

Marvin turned out to be a young Scottish lad who smelled like he had been smoking weed for years. I was also introduced to Greg, Dan and Leigh.

"So you're the new guy, huh? Fuck, I thought you would be younger." Marvin laughed.

"Well, I thought that your balls would have dropped. Looks like we're both shit out of luck, mate," I shot back and the rest of the guys laughed. Marvin laughed too, and then gave me a brief overview of the crew. Greg was forty-three and had been working for Lurkin for over a year. Dan and Leigh were new like me. I chatted with them, waiting for Marvin to get on with things, keeping an eye on the stock. Lurkin was clever, but I knew that he was smuggling coke in some of the trucks. The problem was that I couldn't fucking prove it, and until I could, I had to keep playing my role.

"Lurkin is loaded. It looks like I should be into the food business. That's where the money is," muttered Greg, playing some stupid game on his iPhone.

"I have no idea. It sounds to me like he got lucky," I responded.

"Nah, he just knows the right people," he added and then smiled like he knew more than he was prepared to say. I wanted to ask him what he meant, but that fucking Marvin was calling me to get into the truck because he wanted to head out earlier.

Marvin was just a kid, a very mouthy kid who had a tendency to talk over me. Halfway through our delivery schedule, I learned that he grew up on a council estate along with seven other siblings. His father wasn't around much and his mother worked two jobs to keep paying the bills.

His cousin worked for Lurkin, so he managed to get him a job too. I was nodding, trying to figure out if Lurkin trusted him enough to get him involved with the drugs. The job was simple: we were delivering some Asian food products around most of Edinburgh and Marvin's job was to introduce me to all the other clients.

I kept my story to myself and told him what he needed to hear, about Claire and how nagging she had been at times. When we stopped for lunch and Marvin relaxed a bit more, he began telling me about his time on the streets when he was part of a gang.

"My Ma was trying to keep us all out of trouble, you know, but my cousin introduced me to some people. Couple of years ago he got stuck in one of the houses when two police chicks invaded the house. Someone from the gang managed to let the others know and they were quickly surrounded," Marvin was saying.

"Yeah, and what happened then?"

"Man, you should have seen it. One of them got inside, but then she got cornered. Apparently there was some dude there who was directly linked to Johnny Hodges. That chick had no chance. He got ordered to make an example out of her."

"Where was this, in Edinburgh?" I questioned, the hairs on the back of my neck rising at the way-too-familiar sound of this story.

"Near Glasgow. Well, that guy was psycho. He fucked her so bad that he killed her, but the boss was happy. You know what they say about Johnny Hodges, right?"

I lost my bearings then and nearly cut off the circulation to my hands gripping the wheel so hard, knowing what woman Marvin was talking about.

Seventeen

Ellie

I was sure that I already had my breakthrough story. There was something going on in that club, something big, and on top of that Adrian was smuggling drugs for money. Mack was fobbing me off, but he knew more than he was prepared to say. He was hiding stuff from me, and probably from Claire too for some reason. I had to stay focused and find more evidence. Nathan had asked me to dance, but I texted back saying that I was sick. I needed a break and work had been manic. The magazine was celebrating a special issue and Phil had given me more work. My job as a pole dancer needed to wait. Jordan was out in the field, chasing another story, keeping me out of the loop, along with everyone else.

I knew that I had to go back to Coral on the weekend, ask more questions about Andrew, and find out if anyone knew anything else about Adrian. I hated the fact that Andrew was now connected to my father, that he had the best defence solicitor in Scotland. Now I understood everything—he used me to get to him, probably sensing that he was going to be in trouble soon.

My father used to be different, kind and loving. After Katie's death he transformed, became bitter and unpleasant. That was his way of dealing with my sister's death. I knew he cared for her, more than he ever cared for me.

When I got home, it was just after six. Once I had some food, I sat on the sofa and focused on the information that was in front of me. Wealthy small business owner who leads a double life is connected to a drug smuggler with no real criminal past. All I needed to know was how Adrian knew Andrew and what kind of business they were both into.

I was trying to work, but thoughts about Mack and our latest night together were distracting. On top of that he was fascinated by Shetland Islands, just like I was. God, why did I keep doing this to myself? We had the chemistry, and we were both in love with that rural, raw part of Scotland, Lerwick. I couldn't deny that there was something about him that drew me deeper and further into wanting to be with him. A relationship was out of the question and I didn't need to be tangled up with another affair. Love wasn't for me. Yes, Mack was handsome, kind, caring and protective. The kind of man that I could see myself being with, but was he the kind of man who tired of a woman and went on to another? Was that what happened with Claire? Or did they merely find out they weren't suited to each other? Either way, I didn't want to be the one to break another marriage.

All of a sudden my phone started vibrating, and I snapped out of daydreaming about Mack and our perfect life together. I glanced at the screen noticing that it was an unknown number. Not many people knew what was going on with me these days. My friends were keeping their distance and my father, well, he wanted nothing to do with me. I sent the phone to voicemail and went back to typing.

After a while I received a text message saying that I had a voicemail. I dialled the number to listen.

"I know who you are and I know where you're hiding. I want five thousand pounds or I'm going to the press. Jonathan Grant will be pleased to know that his daughter is using fake papers while working as a reporter. I'll call again tomorrow. Answer this time; otherwise your face will be all over the news again."

Blocks of ice cascaded down to my stomach. I stared at the phone for several minutes thinking that this was some kind of mistake. No one knew that I was using a different surname. I'd chatted with some of my girlfriends, but they wouldn't do that, they wouldn't sell me out, and so far no one had visited me to know where I lived. The voice … I had no idea who it could belong to. Someone must have talked about me. Or had I been recognised? Maybe it was someone at work, or on the street?

All of a sudden the article didn't seem important anymore. This guy, whoever he was, wanted money in exchange for his silence. I really didn't need this right now.

Mum had left us when I was young. I never remembered her, but right then, I wished that I could see her, talk to her. I suddenly felt so lonely and abandoned. For as long as I could remember there had always been me, Katie and Dad, until that tragic accident years ago. Katie, my little sister, had died in a fire and that was the reason that Dad hated me.

Now, some psycho was trying to blackmail me for money, when I was trying so hard to redeem myself, to make people forget that I was a home wrecker.

I closed the laptop and got up, wondering if it was wise to call my father. He made it clear that he didn't want anything to do with me, but this was about him too. Surely, he wouldn't want another scandal. This could crush his already wounded reputation forever.

I picked up my jacket with the car keys and decided to go out for a drive to clear my head. Maybe it was Andrew. Maybe he recognised me when I was dancing for him in the club. He had proven to me that he was capable of destroying me.

It was dark when I left my apartment, and I instantly felt depressed. I couldn't imagine spending Christmas here alone, without any friends. I thought about Mack, wondered if he had plans already, but I quickly pushed away these thoughts. He had a wife that he needed to look after.

I sat in the car for five minutes thinking about what to do, weighing my options. Dad was too furious with me and he wouldn't take my phone call. My father had angered many people, but I couldn't think of anyone who would have known about my plans.

I listened to the voicemail again, trying to pick up on anything, the accent, the tone, but nothing came to my mind. I was just about to switch on my engine and drive off when I spotted Mack with Adrian walking side by side towards the car park.

I frowned, watching as Mack was laughing from something that Adrian had said. I couldn't quite believe what I was seeing. All this time Mack had been telling me to stay away and now they were leaving together. Adrian was kind enough to offer Mack a job, so maybe this was none of my business. I had enough problems that I needed to take care of, but something about this didn't seem right.

I made a split second decision: I decided to follow Adrian's swanky car. Maybe I was being paranoid. They were probably only discussing work, but I didn't like the fact that Mack had been so critical about Adrian and now he was hanging out with him, like they were the best buddies. I kept driving after them, certain that Mack wouldn't do anything illegal. He knew that Adrian was smuggling drugs and that he was using his business as cover up. It was odd that he was going somewhere with him, especially so late at night. My thoughts were racing while I tried to keep a safe distance so they wouldn't notice me.

I followed them through to the city centre, rolling through the busy traffic. Adrian's car was gorgeous and it was easy to keep an eye on it amongst the other cars. He obviously liked bringing attention to himself.

They passed through the city, heading towards the outskirts. When they finally stopped, I didn't recognise the area at all. It was an old industrial park, filled with burned-out cars, dumped rubbish, and a few ruins of abandoned buildings. They didn't leave the car, and I started to get worried. Suspicions heightened my senses and my heart skipped a beat when a black BMW arrived. Three burly well-built men stepped out of the car. They started talking, and it looked like Adrian was introducing Mack to them. It was dark and some of the street-lamps weren't working. I managed to see that one of the guys passed some kind of package to Mack.

I couldn't breathe, my pulse was speeding. I had no idea what was in that package, but I suspected that it wasn't good. When the large guys had driven off, Mack shook hands with Adrian.

This wasn't any kind of social meeting and I was truly convinced that there were drugs in that package. Whatever it was, it wasn't legal. I had my own theory about what went down in isolated places like that. I shook my head trying to get a grip on the whole situation, not wanting to believe that Mack was involved with anything illegal.

I sat there watching them until they jumped back in Adrian's car and vanished. All the things that I had shared with him the other night didn't matter anymore. Mack had lied to me. Adrian offered him money and he jumped at the opportunity. I had no idea what to think or who to trust anymore. It was time to fight back, time to start taking control of my life and write this damned story.

Mack

The evening that Marvin had told me about his cousin and Johnny Hodges, I didn't think I was going to make it to the end of the shift. Darkness had shrouded me. Marvin kept talking, but I fell into despair; the world around was crushing me.

"Hey, mate … mate, are you all right?" Marvin asked, snapping his fingers in front of my face. "You went a bit pale. Don't fucking tell me that you get travel sick."

"I'm fine, bad heartburn," I snapped back, trying to breathe, but the air wasn't getting into my lungs. I knew the psycho Marvin was talking about; I knew him well, as I had been seeing his face in my nightmare for quite some time now. He was dead, shot during riots. He was lucky that I didn't get my hands on him first; otherwise he would've suffered a long and very painful death. For months after

Charlotte's funeral, I imagined how much she had to suffer that day, how much that psycho had hurt her.

Marvin kept talking and I struggled to pull away from the shattering grief. For years everyone was certain that this guy just wanted to have some fun, that he went too far because Charlotte was a police officer. He caught her off guard, he was high, and lost control. I believed them, tried to let it go, but something in the back of my mind told me that this wasn't it.

Johnny fucking Hodges—he was behind this all along and no one had known. Marvin liked to big himself up pretending to be in the know, but I knew that he wasn't bullshitting me. Charlotte made a decision to go in there alone, Hodges didn't like that she got inside, so he told one of his guys to make an example out of her. Rage was filling me up slowly and I was having trouble keeping still. Finally, everything made sense: the recording from that day, the noises that were coming out of that room. Yeah, I made myself listen to it, because I wanted to remember that voice. And now the truth came to light.

When we arrived back at the depot, I pushed myself to pretend that I was fine. Lurkin had waited for me. I wasn't ready to talk, I was ready to wreck him, but my objectives had changed. I didn't care about Lurkin anymore; I had to get closer to Johnny Hodges, the man who was responsible for my wife's death.

"Can I have a quick word with you, Mack?" he asked. I nodded mechanically.

"I might have something better for you tomorrow, a job that can earn you shit loads of money; just let me know if you're interested," he said once I was inside his office. He looked serious and I knew that I just hit the jackpot, but I didn't care. Yesterday, I'd have been ecstatic; right now I was seriously pissed off.

"Whatever, as long as I'll make enough cash and keep my woman off my back," I said, knowing that I needed that lead, needed to know if he could take me right to the top.

"Good, I'm glad to hear it. I'll give you more details tomorrow. Remember, keep this between you and me," he said, patting me on the back.

"Will do."

I nodded. I had no fucking idea how I managed to get through that conversation. I didn't remember getting back to the car, but I remembered throwing up on the side street, my stomach heaving. When I finally stopped, I smashed my fists into the wall until my knuckles bled. Charlotte had died because she was just in the wrong place at the wrong time.

My breathing was raspy and shallow, my head was spinning. I sobbed, hanging on the wheel, remembering what that bastard had done to her. Johnny fucking Hodges. I hadn't even realised how important he was after all.

The pain was spreading into my bones, coursing through my veins like a poison. After all these years I was so close and I was going to kill that motherfucker with my own bare hands.

Hours later, I drove back to the complex, still shaking. When I walked through the door, I didn't know if it was day or night. I had no idea who I was anymore.

"Tobias, you're late. Why … God, what happened?" Claire asked when I slid down on the floor, closing my eyes.

"Johnny Hodges is Lurkin's silent partner; they own Coral together in the city. His real name is Andrew Hamilton," I explained, barely recognising my own fucking voice. The grief overshadowed everything; it kept slipping in, crushing me deeper and driving me further away from sanity.

"Mack, what happened? You're shaking."

She was asking questions again, so many fucking probing questions. It wasn't her fault. Only now I began to realise that I had been wrong all these years for blaming her.

I carried on talking. "Lurkin wants me to be part of his naughty boys squad. Tomorrow is the day."

"I don't care about that scumbag; just tell me what happened, Tobias?"

"Johnny Hodges asked that piece of shit Nate to make an example of Charlotte. What he did to her, this wasn't a spontaneous decision—it was an order."

Claire sat down next to me and stared at me with horror in her eyes.

"How do you know all this?" she asked.

"I had a chat with someone, a lad that works for Lurkin. He grew up on the streets and he liked to talk, sharing his little stories."

Claire was asking me lots of stuff about Marvin, but I wasn't in the room. I knew that Ellie had been involved with that piece of shit. Andrew, her ex that made Ellie his. Everything was spinning and I questioned my own judgment, wondering why I had to be there that night at the party.

This whole thing was bigger than I thought, but I was overcome with grief, my soul ripped away from my body. Claire started pulling info on that garbage Hamilton. She helped to get me on my feet, saying nice words, calming words.

I couldn't break again. I couldn't go through another round of therapy. I had a job to do and we finally had some real progress. Lurkin was mine and we were close. I shut my eyes in the dark bedroom and distracted myself with thoughts of Ellie. That night that we spent together she had made me a man again. She had pulled me away from my grief, but now that I knew who she was, this thing was over, forever.

Eighteen

Ellie

I went to the office the next day, feeling like I had been run over by a truck. My head was hurting and my body was aching. In one night everything had fallen apart. Mack had been playing me, probably since the moment he saw me. He knew all along who Adrian was and what kind of business he was into. I felt sick to my stomach, knowing that I let myself believe there was something special going on between us.

There was a possibility that he was discussing work with Adrian and I was making the wrong assumptions. After all, he seemed decent, so caring and protective. I didn't want to be fooled by his handsome face and amazing body. He was meeting with very dodgy people in the middle of the night in an abandoned lot, which didn't look good. We had great sex, fooled around, but that was it. I wasn't planning to keep up with his nonsense.

After the morning meeting, I took some painkillers and finally switched on my phone. I didn't want to think about that creepy voicemail, but I had to eventually deal with it. I was scared to get tangled up with another scandal, but Phil wouldn't have hired me if he had known who I was. He didn't even look at my paperwork when I came in for my interview. I heard him once saying to Jordan that he only wanted sexy women working at the paper, which made him a complete wanker.

I switched on my desktop and went on Google. Now, I was just about to do something that I promised myself that I would never do: spy on Andrew again. I typed his name into a search engine trying to breathe at the same time. Several new pictures popped up and I couldn't believe that I waited this long to find out what he had been up to. His new woman was five foot nine and looked like a model. There were several pictures of him and my father at some parties, posing together, looking very cosy together.

It looked like Andrew had officially become my father's client. They'd started working together as soon as I left Glasgow. There were some snippets of information about me, but nothing important. One of the gossip sites suggested that I moved abroad. Andrew was divorced, his ex-wife kept the house, and he had to spend a fortune on the child maintenance. I was taking all the information in slowly, while my heart fluttered between my ribs.

None of this was fair. Andrew was happy and he got everything he wanted, whereas I was sad and alone, patching up my shattered heart.

Mack didn't mean anything anymore. Now I finally began to understand why he wanted me to stay away from Adrian, why he kept following me. Adrian had money and Mack was under pressure. He just lost his job and he and Claire were probably in financial trouble. It was clear that Adrian offered him an opportunity to make quick cash and Mack took it.

I stayed at my desk thinking about all the possibilities, trying to get on with my work. Whoever was blackmailing me, knew my every step and I needed to deal with it fast. I thought about all the people that turned their backs on me, and I knew that eventually they were going to pay. Eventually my father would see for himself that Andrew was using him, but then it would be too late. Nice and polite Ellie was gone, but she still remembered that day when everything imploded. The day when I became a home wrecker.

Andrew was kissing me, his wet mouth moving down my neck. We were in his enormous house, in his bedroom. I felt thrilled that his wife had moved out and I had him all to myself. The lonely days were over. I moaned when he bit the sensitive skin on my arm gently, then kissed me, moving his tongue inside my mouth.

"Ellie … do you know how much it turns me on having you here, in my bed?" he pulled away and asked. Those dark eyes were hypnotic and I was lost in him as he looked down at me. He started tracing his hand down my side, smiling wickedly and slipping his fingers under the hem of my knickers. I sucked in a breath; tingles ravaged my body.

I groaned with approval when his thumb massaged my sex. I was in my bra, and he was still fully dressed. I picked out my best underwear, especially for him. Today he promised that we would celebrate that he was finally free. I was beaming with love, and I couldn't wait to tell all my friends about him. Andrew stopped driving me insane with his touch, jumped off the bed and got rid of his clothes. I had never seen anyone undress so fast.

Andrew Hamilton was a handsome man, tall and broad in his shoulders. There'd been a spark between us instantly, but at first I didn't allow myself to even think about him that way. He was my father's potential client. A year later, I was in his house, his bedroom.

"What the fuck is going on here, Andrew?"

The voice startled both of us. I turned around, my heart nearly stopping. Andrew covered his crotch. The blood drained from his face. Theresa, his ex-wife stood in the doorway with her hands on her hips, looking from me to Andrew.

"Darling, she's no one to me," he started saying, and I looked at him in disbelief, wondering why he insisted on lying now, when she was standing right here looking at us. She didn't care for him anymore, so he might as well tell her the truth.

I brought the sheet over my chest, fighting for the last bit of modesty. I had never met up with her face-to-face before, but looking at her that day, I couldn't deny that she was stunning,

"Andrew, this is your chance. Tell her what you have been telling me, you know, about the court case, about the divorce papers, about why she won't let you see the kids," I said, narrowing my eyes at her with anger. From all his previous stories I understood that she had treated him like shit and apparently married him for his money.

"Shut up, Ellie, and stop talking rubbish," he snapped at me. My jaw dropped and for a second I thought that he was joking. "What are you doing here, Theresa? You were supposed to be in Berlin. What? Are you spying on me now?"

"This is unbelievable. I thought you'd changed. I thought that I could give you another chance, but this … this is just so beyond."

"Oh, shut up. Don't be so dramatic. It's just sex. She doesn't mean anything to me. Ellie is Jonathan Grant daughter, Theresa. You know that this whole thing was about business," he said walking up to her all of a sudden.

My jaw dropped. I couldn't bloody believe it. Surely, he was playing a role; he didn't mean any of this. For months he had been saying that he would be getting divorced and today was the start of it.

"Andrew, what are you talking about? Just tell her everything you told me," I said, getting upset, my voice vibrating.

"See? She's even doing it now, trying to get my attention." He laughed, pointing at me. "You and the kids, you guys mean everything to me. I'll change; I promise you."

Theresa darted her eyes at me, shaking her head. She didn't even look that surprised.

"I'm sorry to break this to you, sweetie, but Andrew has been doing this for years, promising other women that he'll leave me for them. He doesn't love you and he never will. It's sad, but that's the truth," she said. Surely, she was just spiteful that she caught us. Andrew wouldn't do that to me, not after all the promises.

"I love my wife, Ellie," he said then and those words were hurtful. I told myself that he was still playing a game, that he was pretending.

"See? Don't hope for anything," Theresa said to me. "He has always been like that. You were probably his fourth woman on the side this year. Our marriage has been dead since the moment I found out that he fucked my best friend a couple of years ago, but I kept it between us, for the sake of our kids. Now I guess I'm finally over it, ready to divorce him."

Mack

"Are you all right?" Claire asked me for the fourth time while we were going through the files on Johnny Hodges. I couldn't answer her, because deep down I knew that I wasn't all right. The past twenty-four hours were difficult. Yeah, I was making progress in the case, but my whole life felt like it was falling apart all over again.

"I can't believe that we missed him all this time," I shouted, getting up, feeling exhausted all of a sudden. Claire sighed and put her palm on my shoulder.

"Don't stress about it. We have him; we just need concrete proof. You need to dig deeper, establish links and the connection between Lurkin and Hodges," she said.

My heart hadn't stopped banging since I came back from that meeting with Lurkin. After days of discussing it, he finally introduced me to people that he trusted. I learnt that he was hiding drugs in meat products and using standard delivery vans to distribute it. Lurkin used his food business as a cover up.

Lurkin was careful, though. He didn't share all his secrets with me, but I managed to figure out enough from his instructions and by speaking to others. Whatever I did during my probation had worked out pretty good, because now he trusted me.

He was playing a game with me trying to impress me, hoping that maybe I would become more obedient if he could intimidate me. I wasn't expecting to see three Irish brothers in this part of Scotland. I knew them well, from the police files, but I was stunned to learn that they were involved in business with him.

During that short and very abrupt meeting, Lurkin laid out the rules. The three Irish brothers were there to demonstrate to me what would happen if I broke any of these rules. Inside the package that they handed to me was someone's hand.

"Here on these streets, I'm no longer your neighbour, Mack. I'm offering you something spectacular, because I see potential in you. This package was necessary," Lurkin said after I managed to recover from shock, shaking away the nausea.

"Mack, you have to stop being like that. You're scaring me. We are halfway there." Claire's voice pulled me back into the real world. I couldn't stop thinking about that package and the Irish brothers. Lurkin was more dangerous than Claire and I suspected.

I shoved aside the picture of Andrew Hamilton, dragging my hand through my hair and trying to breathe steadily. On top of that, his being Ellie's ex-lover was bothering me. We hadn't spoken since that night in the hotel. I should have recognised her from the papers. Fuck, I had been so foolish, thinking that it was all right to fuck a stranger.

"Sorry, I lost focus for a second," I replied.

"You know … I think that maybe we should speak to Ellie, get her involved. After all, she was close to Hamilton."

"No way. This is the last thing that I need right now," I shouted, losing my temper again. Ellie had managed to make me forget about my wounds; she managed to do something that other women could not. There was no way that I was leading Ellie back to that asshole Hamilton. She had been through enough.

"You care for her, don't you? That's why you don't want her in this, right?"

I was on my feet before I knew it, pacing around the room to keep myself in line, but the darkness was creeping in.

"She's no one to me, Claire. I lost the only woman that I ever loved and that's the bottom line," I said, raising my voice.

Claire exhaled, shoving paperwork together. For years no one had ever gotten close to Hodges. The ex-wife, the kids, they were his protection, but it looked like he couldn't keep them either. He was in danger of fucking up his cover.

Claire chewed on her lips, looking at me with resentment. She wasn't happy with me and the way I worked, but she had no idea that I was taking this very personally. I wanted to get my hands on Hodges before anyone could touch him. She had no idea what I was planning.

"All right. We will do this your way, but I'm not covering for you, Tobias. If you fuck up, don't come crawling back," she said, probably because she was sensing that I wanted to do things my way, and Claire liked procedures and always followed the rules.

Ellie was the key to everything, but I couldn't tell her the truth. This was my war, my way of doing things. I needed to keep her out of it, for now.

"Fine, fine, don't nag. Everything is ready for tonight. The boys upstairs will get the updates once I get on the road," I assured her. She wasn't too happy with me. We both went through a lot and tonight we'd be right in the middle of a large drop. Lurkin was getting greedy and Claire knew that all it took was one mistake and we would be found out.

"Charlotte will get justice. Don't worry about that. Just stay focused," she added quietly before she left the room. A tingle of shame crawled up my back when I realised that she was right. My wife's memory was with me forever and everyone that was involved in her death was already dead. It was just a matter of time.

Nineteen

Ellie

I didn't want to believe that Mack was involved with drugs, so after tossing and turning for most of the night, I decided to confront him. After all, I felt connected to him and couldn't just forget about our amazing moments together. I woke up early, just after five, knowing that I needed to see if he was hiding something. The stranger who was blackmailing me didn't call again and that was worrying. I didn't want to be surprised with another scandal. Phil would fire me straight away and I wouldn't be able to afford to live in the complex, not without steady income.

I drove through the empty roads to the location that I set up on my iPhone yesterday. It was an industrial part of the city, located close to the docks. I parked my car on the side street, in front of semidetached run-down houses. I had learnt that this location wasn't particularly safe, but Mack would be just finishing his night shift and I needed to speak to him.

This morning the depot looked busy. There were trucks coming in and out. A few dodgy-looking guys were smoking outside. I yawned, dreaming about strong coffee, hoping that Mack would tell me the truth. We had been through this conversation many times. Now he needed to come clean.

For about ten minutes I sat in the car, using my phone to make notes about cars that were arriving and leaving. If Adrian was really supplying drugs, then I had something. On top of that he knew Andrew, and that didn't make much sense. After all, I didn't really know my ex. Obviously everyone here knew him as Johnny Hodges. Jordan was interested in him. We hadn't spoken since that night when my father had confronted me in front of him. I wondered how he would react if I told him that I discovered his little secret.

In a few minutes I had enough photos that would go well with my article. I was already imagining police raiding the warehouse. As long as my name was on the first page, I didn't care. A knock at my window startled me. I lifted my head up, seeing some old guy asking me if I had a cigarette.

"I don't smoke," I said, pointing out to leave me alone. He seemed about fifty with an old worn leather jacket and long shaggy beard. He was smiling, and I noticed that he was missing half of his teeth. A few of minutes later, he was gone and I exhaled with relief. I rolled my window down and opened the door, thinking that maybe it was a good idea to look around. Suddenly someone shoved me towards the door. I gagged at the strong odour of cigarettes and alcohol.

"This isn't a very good place for such a pretty lady like you," the attacker growled, moving his face close to mine. He was much younger than the first guy. He had a pale face and a gold front tooth. Fear scorched through me. I didn't want to move in case he was planning to be violent towards me.

"Let go of me," I shouted, but his grip was tight around my wrists.

"What's in your handbag?" he demanded.

"Nothing. I don't have anything there, just some notes and makeup," I mumbled.

"Van, check it, and make sure you take her phone," barked the tattooed guy to the older one, who opened the car from the passenger side. I tried to push him away shouting, aware that I would lose all my notes and my phone. The youngster slammed me over the car, and sharp pain shot down my back. I was so fucking stupid, sitting here and pretending that I was some fancy reporter, working undercover. Now I couldn't even fight back.

"eReader and an iPhone. Darren, she's loaded," croaked the other guy.

"We need cash, pretty girl. Have you got any?"

"No, I've nothing on me," I said and spat all over his face, trying to push him away, but I didn't get far. A few steps and he was on me again. My heart kicked in my chest when he wiped his face and squeezed my arm tighter, nearly breaking my bones.

"I'll show you how to behave in a moment, you bitch," he shouted and then slapped me. I didn't have a chance to react. In one moment I was by my car and the next I was on the pavement. My cheek was burning and my vision was blurry.

"Put that fucking bag back on the seat; otherwise I'll break his scrawny neck, you old bastard."

A loud, deep voice startled me. I pushed my hair away from my damp skin and saw Mack. He had his finger clenched around the youngster's neck and it looked like he was slowly suffocating him. I scrambled off the floor, taking sharp deep breaths, my heart racing away.

"All right, mate, fine, no problem. Let him go. We don't want no trouble," mumbled the greasy older guy who'd approached me first, dropping my handbag on the seat. Mack's face was tense, focused on me. The youngster was waving his hand, his eyes bulging out of his sockets. I looked around; the sun was slowly rising. I couldn't bring any attention to myself, not right here. When Mack finally let go of his grip, the youngster crashed on the ground, taking long rough breaths.

"Now get the fuck out of here before I lose my temper and fuck you up!"

I had never seen anyone pick themselves up so fast. That young guy couldn't be any older than eighteen, but he cursed and stumbled away. The old guy followed him, glaring at us from time to time.

"Ellie! Are you all right?" Mack asked. He was beside me within a moment. I didn't want him to touch me and I didn't want to look at him. I needed to talk to him first, confront him about what I saw the other night.

"I'm fine. I don't need your help, thank you very much," I snapped back, trying to pick my stuff up off the floor. His touch sent tingles of awareness down my spine, but I told my reasonable side to dismiss it.

"What the hell are you doing here at this time in the morning?" he demanded and squatted down to help me with my paperwork.

"This is none of your business. I saw you with Lurkin last night and now I understand everything," I said, snatching the papers away from his hand.

He looked surprised, astonished even, but I didn't give a fuck anymore. I saw the package and I heard Adrian in the club; he was a drug supplier. Mack shook his head, exhaling. He was in casual clothes, wearing old jeans and a dark jacket. He worked for Adrian. Maybe I was making a big deal out of nothing, but I knew what I saw. He was protecting Adrian, thinking that I wouldn't guess that he was one of the bad guys.

"I'm mad, Ellie, furious, and right now I want to punish you," he growled. "But it's not safe here. That's why you're coming with me. We are not talking here."

He grabbed my elbow and started pushing me inside the passenger door. I was trying to resist, but he looked like he was going to explode.

"Stop manhandling me, I'm not doing—"

"Shhh, Angel. I'm literally on the verge of losing control and taking you right here and right now. Put your seat belt on; you're risking your life exposing yourself like that," he cut me off, shutting the door and walking around the car. I stopped breathing when he got in the driver's side, overwhelming the space with his anger. His sharp eyes were looking around. Goose pimples shot down my arm and I swallowed hard. I was pretty shaken up, slightly apprehensive about what happened.

I couldn't fight with him even if I wanted to and right now he looked like he was ready to smack me.

"Keys," he ordered with that domineering tone that I recognised instantly. My heart was skipping beats while I looked for them. Tension zoomed through the air, and I felt beads of sweat running down my spine.

"Take me home right now," I said, when I finally handed him the ring of keys. The engine roared to life and he drove off, pretending like he didn't hear me.

"Fuck, Ellie! How could you be so foolish? Anyone could have seen you there," he shouted, pressing his lips in a hard line. Mack had lost his mind. He was driving like he was crazy, passing cars on a double line. It was very early morning, and the streets weren't busy, but still. I wasn't ready to die.

"Me foolish? You're selling drugs and helping Adrian. You're a hypocrite!"

"You don't understand anything. We need to talk, but I'm done with your bullshit. I have tolerated it long enough."

"You tolerating me? Ha!" I said, not believing what I just heard. "You're lucky that I didn't go straight to the police!"

He didn't say anything to that, but that vein on his neck was pulsing dangerously fast. The awkward silence stretched until we reached the city centre. Mack didn't take me home. He put his foot down and stopped in front of the Hilton hotel. His face was tight, muscles tense, and I was going crazy, wondering what he was planning.

"You have two options, Ellie: I either carry you to the room or you go yourself like a good girl," he said, pausing and looking directly into my eyes. "So what's it going to be?"

Mack

I left the depot just before six. Lurkin was running a distribution network around Edinburgh and he had his people around the area, watching and letting him know if the police came sniffing around. I was heading straight to my car when I saw Ellie with some tattooed youngster on the street. It looked like she was just about to get mugged. I lost my head. Anger took over my body and I was ready to strangle him.

I had no idea what on earth she was doing here, but then she mentioned that she saw me and Lurkin here. She was relentless, determined to carry on investigating when I clearly told her to stay away. Fuck, now I had no choice but to explain myself to her.

"You won't dare to carry me inside the hotel. I'll tell them that you kidnapped me."

"Well, then I'll tell them that you're sick, that you have taken some LSD and I'm here to take care of you," I said putting on a concerned voice. Ellie folded her arms over her chest, glaring at me with fury. Oh yes, I wasn't letting her go anywhere, until she told me what she knew and saw.

"Don't fight with me, Angel. I want to talk. I promise that I'll let you go once I explain everything."

"You're so twisted. I can't believe I didn't see it earlier," she spat and I smiled to myself. Yeah, I had issues, but right now I was ready to kill someone. She was making me crazy.

"We are wasting time. Let's go. The sooner we get on with this the better."

Ellie was obedient in the bedroom, but she didn't like to be told what to do on the street. She fought with me when I tried to take her hand, and then, pleaded for me to take her home again. I couldn't just let her go, not now. We had been playing this cat and mouse game for a while, but now she put herself in real danger. The reception was slow, so checking in took a bit longer than necessary. I was anxious, wondering if anyone had followed us. She didn't look at me or talk to me in the lift.

On top of that, my dick realised she was near and woke up. I was thinking about punishment, about how much I wanted to take her again. I didn't care about her fucking job. She put herself at risk, and not for the first time.

I unlocked the door to the stylish room. We both walked in, and the images from the other night started floating back to me again.

"I'm still waiting, Mack. Explain how come you don't think that you're one fucked up son of a bitch," she said, dropping her handbag on the bed and unzipping her coat. Hell, this whole thing was going to end badly and I was getting turned on.

I was beside her before she could take another breath, slamming her into my chest. It was my anger and impulsive nature that took over.

"You have pissed me off being so reckless and stupid and I'll punish you for it," I growled, my lips inches away from her. Her perfume was intoxicating, her lovely skin wanted to be caressed. She trembled under my hands, but the anger didn't fade, her eyes were focused and sharp.

"Let go of me. I'm not playing this game. You're just like Lurkin."

I wanted to laugh. Lurkin was a piece of shit and her voice was low and hoarse. She couldn't fool me. I bet she was so wet for me that her pussy was throbbing with want and need. Instead of arguments and explanations, I pressed my lips over hers and kissed her. She fought with me, trying to pull away, but her skin felt amazing.

"Stop it, Angel. I know you want me to punish you," I said and held her in my arms. Her body slowly began to relax and finally she was kissing me back, moaning into my mouth. I fucking loved that sound, and I was soon in a daze, kissing and pulling her mouth.

Ellie was still trying to fight, but we both knew that she was mine and I wanted to be inside her tight wetness.

"Mack, oh please, I want you," she mumbled. I took my jacket off, kissing her neck. When I was free from my heavy clothes, I grabbed her hips and pulled her closer, nibbling her skin. She groaned, but I was still furious, still afraid that someone could have snapped her neck.

I pulled away, breathing hard, my cock painfully hard. Ellie was flustered, lips swollen and she looked fuckable.

"You put yourself in danger, made me mad and fought with me. You can't even imagine how much I'm going to enjoy punishing you," I stated. "Take your clothes off, but leave the underwear on."

I was slipping into my old self and this wasn't a request, it was command. She obeyed me straight away. I waited, watching with fascination how she took her clothes off. I needed to remember that she was the only person that could pull me away from my misery, but right then I was so fucking furious with her that all I wanted was to possess her, hurt her, all because she disobeyed me.

Twenty

Ellie

My head spun, desire drenched my core as I lay spread on the bed in my underwear, taking long shallow breaths, not knowing what to expect from the angry man that stood in front of me.

Mack had taken control over me, ceasing the explosive demands for answers and making me forget about why we came to the room in the first place. I had been so angry all the way to the hotel and now I was lost in my need to be dominated by him.

This sudden outburst of passion was my new addiction. I needed him now and I wanted him always. Another bolt of liquid heat shot through me when he climbed on top of me, pushing my wrists up. His touch was rough, and for a long while my heavy breaths interrupted the silence. I hissed when he squeezed my wrists so tight that it hurt. The pain was quickly replaced by heat, and his touch was almost too much to resist.

"Now you're at my mercy, Angel," he warned and pulled a pair of handcuffs out of his pocket. I widened my eyes, wondering why he carried handcuffs in his pocket, and why I was getting so turned on by this act, his power. The plan was to talk, to find out why he had been lying to me all this time. Now, I could barely keep up with the excitement, panting with anticipation as he unhooked my bra first, then he handcuffed me to the bed, his gaze on me heavy with desire, gleaming with control.

Mack lifted the corners of his lips, his smile dark and taunting. I had no idea what he was planning. When he checked that I couldn't move, he got off the bed and started undressing. My mouth was dry as I watched him, feeling a deep ache between my legs. He left his pants on and climbed back on the bed. When his lips found mine again, I moaned into his mouth, and his fingertips lightly brushed the apex of my thighs. He didn't let me enjoy him much, breaking up the kiss, moving on the side next to me, resting his head on his hand.

"Tell me, Angel, why do you make me so mad?" he asked and began tracing his finger over my stomach. God, I wanted to touch him so much, but the handcuffs restrained me and wriggling made them dig into my skin. I would just have to wait. I attempted to gather my thoughts, concentrating, fighting with my own desires.

"Don't know. I wanted answers and you were so secretive," I hissed, wanting to feel his stiff cock between my legs.

"Wrong answer," he growled, twisting my body to the side and slapping my ass. It wasn't a light slap, but hard and sharp. The sound echoed through the room. I felt it sizzle my skin as the secondary burn of the slap resounded in my muscles, the glorious heat making me more aroused. When I was on my back again, Mack pulled my knickers down. His mouth attacked my nipples first, licking and sucking each one to hard pointed studs. I moaned, arching my hips up, needing contact, and stretching my arms until my muscles felt numb.

"Oh please, I need—"

"Be quiet, this is your punishment. You put yourself at risk and now you won't gain any pleasure from me," he barked, cutting me off.

I cried out when I felt him moving down between my legs, down to my wet sex, massaging and flicking my clit. A hot burst of pleasure spread through me, and tension clenched my abdomen. I felt the buildup deep in my core, the warmth from my stinging ass, the delight in my aroused nipples, and the tingles on my clit. All these amazing sensations pushed my body ever closer to orgasm. He was making me crazy torturing and teasing me with his skilled fingers. I was so close, my body was straining, flushed with the need of release. Just when I thought I would climax, he stilled all motions of his hand and didn't let me come.

"Arrggg, Mack, oh please … please, I need this," I begged, jerking my hands, but I was only hurting myself. I heard his deep laugh, then felt his fingers on my stomach, tracing the line of my body. Within seconds he was rubbing my sex with his thumb again, over and over, until I thought that I would come, until I couldn't take it anymore. Then he stopped again and I cursed with frustration. Sweat was dripping down my face, my nipples were hard, sensitive, and my whole body was on fire.

I lost count of how many times he kept teasing me and teasing me, bringing me right to the edge, but he always stopped just before I could come. When I called him a bastard, he turned around and slapped me, much harder than the last time. He really was punishing me.

"This is for putting yourself in danger, for not listening," he said. He put two fingers inside me and I felt my muscles tightening, the fullness overwhelming. In that moment I hated him that he left me hanging. I couldn't make my mouth work correctly, feeling the pressure in every cell, every vein. My head was throbbing when I felt that he wasn't lying next to me anymore. He left me on the bed, wet and drenched with desire. I had no idea how much time had passed, seconds, minutes. My arousal kept pulsing, my breathing long and laboured.

I was mildly aware that Mack was in the bathroom. The doors were shut. After it felt like another hour passed, I heard the shower. My body ached for his, and when he finally came out, he was dripping wet, naked and perfect. I swallowed hard, wondering what he was going to do next, admiring the toned muscles on his chest. I drank all of him in, watching and praying that the punishment was over.

When he was on top of me again, I tried to relax, not daring to say anything in case I angered him.

"You're mine, Angel. I need you to remember that when I'm fucking you hard," he whispered, looking down at me. I nodded, waiting. Mack pushed my legs apart with his knee and then shoved his hard cock inside me.

I screamed and my body quivered as I took him in, fighting to hold on for a bit longer. He clearly wasn't planning to be slow or gentle. He started fucking me hard, pulling my legs up, so he was penetrating me so deep it was almost painful as his cock touched the back of my cervix. Sweat broke over the nape of my neck and my eyes rolled to the back of my head as he pounded himself inside me.

"Fuck, you feel so good, this will be quick."

I couldn't feel my arms anymore. I cried out when my legs trembled from the sensations. My muscles contracted, clenching and welcoming the approaching orgasm. The air was thick and then I was coming hard, more intensely than ever before, when we both heard the loud bang. All of a sudden someone had barged through the door and Mack stilled, cursing loudly. He was on his feet, naked, standing in the middle of the room.

When I finally lifted my head, I thought that I was having a hallucination. Claire was standing in the room with a gun in her hands, staring at both of us with her eyes wide open.

It was deja vu all over again.

Twenty-One

Mack

Claire kicked open the door and charged through it holding her gun level, ready to shoot, stopping dead in her tracks as she cased the room for her target. Her eyes met mine, and her jaw dropped open. She froze, seeing me on the bed, naked, nestled between Ellie's legs. I cursed loudly, shifted my position and picked up my boxers off the floor, covering my rapidly shrinking dick.

"Jesus fucking Christ, are you okay, Mack?" Claire asked, lowering the gun, shaking her head in disbelief. She looked over at Ellie, who was handcuffed to the bed, flushed red, looking mortified and probably equally as shocked as I was. I quickly covered her naked body and moved to release her, thinking of how I was going to get the hell out of this clusterfuck.

"For fuck's sake, Claire, you couldn't have chosen a worse moment to interrupt," I snapped at her, wondering what the hell she had been thinking, storming into the room like that, taking the door out. Ellie was hiding behind the sheets with her mouth wide open, moving her gaze from me to Claire. This was bad; so bad that I had no idea how to react.

"What in God's name is going on in here?" Claire asked, recovering her normal high-pitched voice. She was trying to come off that she wasn't all right with this situation, and the truth was she was probably freaking out. The awkward silence grew heavy around us.

"No, I'm the one that's going to ask any questions. What the hell are you doing here and how did you find me in the first fucking place?"

"The boys at base put tracking on your phone. The SI told me that we needed something like that, just to feel safe. We discussed it—don't tell me that you don't remember," she said, irritated, wiping the sweat beading on her forehead and shutting the busted door as best she could. "I thought that you were in trouble. Your phone was off and I started to worry when I didn't hear from you."

"Does base know about this?"

"No, I haven't had a chance to speak to them yet. I got here as soon as I could, because, as I said, I thought you were in trouble."

Now the hazy conversation about tracking apps from weeks ago slowly filtered into my conscious mind coming back to me. The superintendent wanted to make sure there were no screw-ups, so Claire came up with the idea of activating tracking devices on our phones, but as usual she overreacted. She didn't need to follow me all the way here, walking in on me when I was fucking Ellie.

"Claire," Ellie whimpered. "I'm so sorry. I didn't want you to find out like this…Mack and I—"

"Ellie, don't talk for a moment," I said, cutting her off sharply, knowing that whatever she was going to say wouldn't mitigate the fact that Claire had caught us. I didn't want to play this pathetic game anymore. Claire wasn't my wife and I didn't answer to her. My heart was fucking racing like a thoroughbred and I was still semi-hard from my session with Ellie.

Claire flopped down into a chair, looking like she could do with a stiff drink. This whole thing was so fucked up and I had no idea where to begin unravelling it. "I cannot believe you didn't tell me that you were sleeping with her! I asked you if you liked her and you denied it, Tobias. You lied to my face," she said, shaking her head.

Ellie hissed a breath, looking mortified. I wanted to comfort her, take her into my arms and let her know that she had nothing to worry about, but Claire was here and this was already very awkward.

"We met the night before you arrived at the complex. There was a party going on in one of the apartments. I didn't say anything, because at the time this was supposed to be only one night," I said, dragging my hand through my hair. "Soon one night turned into two and, before I knew it, I was losing control of the situation."

Claire raised her left eyebrow, looking like she didn't want to believe me. Since Charlotte's death, she hadn't seen me with any other women, so I understood her astonishment and disbelief.

"You should have called, Tobias. I was freaking out, thinking that someone had talked. You were supposed to brief me this morning," Claire continued, while Ellie was latching onto every word. "Tobias, tell her what is going on. I don't think you can keep lying about this any longer. It's your fault that I barged in here."

I clenched my fists, realising that she was right. The moment I started sleeping with Ellie I was no longer Mack McCune, but Tobias Stanley. Ellie kept staring at both of us, looking confused. She looked so fuckable right then. Hell, I needed to get a grip and stop thinking about shit like that.

"Mack? What are you two talking about and why does she keep calling you Tobias?"

Claire snorted, shaking her head. I wanted to snap at her that she wasn't helping. I cursed loudly thinking that I should just get it over with. Ellie deserved to know the truth. I had been feeding her lie after lie, and nothing good could come of it.

"Claire isn't my real wife, Ellie, and my real name isn't Mack McCune," I said.

Ellie shifted on the bed, swallowing hard, looking at me like I may have lost my fucking mind. "Is this some kind of a sick joke?"

"No, it's not a joke. My real name is Tobias Stanley and I'm a police detective, so is Claire. We are currently assigned to investigate Adrian Lurkin, who, as you already know, is a dangerous drug smuggler," I explained as slowly and calmly as I could, emphasising the words 'drug smuggler'. Ellie looked stunned, her gaze shifting from me to Claire. I could tell she didn't believe me.

Claire came to my aid. "He's telling you the truth, Ellie. I wasn't supposed to be here at all. Tobias was working with another partner, but a day before her arrival, she broke her leg, so they sent me instead. Our boss insisted that a married couple would be more believable."

I started putting my clothes on, giving Ellie a bit of time to digest all she had been told so far. She was shaking her head, taking long cleansing breaths. Yeah, it was a lot to take in.

"That first night that we met, I was scheduled to leave in the morning," I said, wanting to let her know I was certain at that time that it would be just one night, but things changed. She became something much more than a one-night stand. The moment I met her I transformed, shifting from a moody, miserable fuck to a real man. "Our boss wasn't sure if Lurkin was going to move in after all. There had been some problems with his documents, but all of a sudden everything had been sorted out. Lurkin paid for the apartment outright, and we had a go ahead."

Ellie brought the sheet up closer to her chin and I started to wonder what she was thinking. I understood that she must be confused. This whole story sounded unbelievable. She probably hated me right now, hated that she had gotten involved with me in the first place.

"Then you're not actually married?" she asked, almost choking on that last word.

"We needed to act like we were," Claire explained. "But in a real life, no, we are not married. We have a forged marriage certificate, a complete fake life, and we sleep in separate bedrooms. This whole thing had been set up in order to get closer to Lurkin. We shouldn't even be telling you this, but I don't think we can afford to lie about it any longer, due to the circumstances."

"Oh my God! All this time…all this time I have been torturing myself over being with yet another married man. How could you, Mack...er, Tobias, whoever the hell you are?" she shouted, shaking her head in disbelief.

"I couldn't say anything, Angel, not even when I realised that you lived next door. At the party we both wanted only one night. I thought that was it, that I would never see you again. I was supposed to be on a plane the next morning, but none of this worked out the way I planned," I explained, hoping that she would understand, yet feeling like a total coward. "Then he finally moved in and I had to play along."

"Jesus, Tobias, you're unbelievable," Claire said. "Get a grip. We need to plan what happens now. I understand why you didn't want her involved, but we're past that. I know that this is none of my business, but I think we have to keep this incident between ourselves."

I recognised that haughty tone of voice. She was pissed, but Christ, I was falling apart here. Ellie wasn't just some random woman; she was important, and I didn't want to lose her.

"All this time I've been going out of my mind, thinking I was the worst person on the planet…fuck, Mack—I mean… what's your name again?"

"Tobias."

"Yes, Tobias. I'm so angry right now that I just want to scream. God," she shouted, threw off her covers and started picking her clothes up off the floor, not caring for the world that she was pretty much naked. Claire smirked and I stood there watching as she tried to dress quickly. My hormones were raging and I wanted to finish what we started. Hearing her say my real name lit something in my chest. I felt so alive with her.

"Ellie, I owe you an—"

"Shut up, just shut the fuck up. I want exclusive access to the whole story and to the case," she said, walking up to me, poking me in the chest with her small finger. Her eyes were on fire, her brow pulled down, her cheeks, ears and neck flushed. She was pissed. I'd seen her turned on and watched that fire burn, but I had never seen her like this. Her eyes changed to a whisky-amber from their usual hazel colour. She was seething anger from every pore and had every right to feel it. How could I object to her fury when it was deserved?

"Hold on—what story? What is she talking about, Tobias?" Claire asked, instantly alerted.

Ellie

Claire was staring at Mack, expecting answers. I didn't want her to know that I went to the strip club and got the job there in order to get a story. This whole mad episode sounded unbelievable, like some poorly written soap opera. It was completely crazy but somehow thrilling—I would get my exclusive after all. I nearly had a heart attack when I saw her at the door a few minutes ago. My head was spinning, and on top of that, Claire saw me being fucked by Tobias. This was the most mortifying moment in my life.

That bastard hadn't told Claire anything. He hadn't said that I found out Adrian's dirty secrets.

"Ellie, please, this isn't the right—"

"Oh no, you're not taking this away from me, not right now, not after all this." I cut him off, angry that he was actually daring to question me. Okay, so I had a clear conscience. I wasn't sleeping with a married man anymore, but I was fucking a police detective. A man that wasn't even called Mack but freaking Tobias. When he finally shut up, I started going through my own story. I told Claire about my work on the paper, about that night in the club when I followed Adrian—she didn't quite believe me when I mentioned that I was a decent pole dancer—finally getting to that part when I found out that Adrian was a drug smuggler.

"Shit, Tobias. This is huge; she probably knows more than we do," Claire said, looking dumbfounded. Mack was working his jaw, glaring at me with frustration. I ignored the desire flaring inside me and blamed it on the elation of the story. We met, he gave me a few orgasms; we had some fun and I thought we had something real—but now I couldn't quite believe that he wasn't officially tied down in a loveless marriage, that he was a free agent. I wanted to shut up my stupid brain. I didn't know anything about him. Maybe he was married to a real woman that was out there somewhere. Maybe he had a girlfriend or even kids. I knew Mack, I loved being with Mack, but I knew nothing of this Tobias.

"I think we all should take a deep breath and calm down. Ellie still can't get involved in our operation. This whole thing is too dangerous, even you know—"

"Fuck you," I shouted at him. He had crossed the line and I lost control. I was done with all his bullshit and his warnings. It was time to let him know where I stood. "We had sex, Ma—Tobias. That in no way entitles you to tell me what to do. Adrian fancies me and we can all use this to our advantage, to play him and find more solid evidence. I'm telling you, I won't be kept out of this, especially not after what I just heard in here."

"Darling, calm down," Claire said. "Tobias is stubborn and he's probably worried about you, but I guess you're right. This is a good idea. We need someone inside, someone that Adrian can trust." At least she was talking with some sense.

Mack was stuck up his own ass, but I was ready to put myself on the line for this, for my goal.

Phil could go to hell for all I cared. This was huge, even bigger than I expected.

"Claire, don't get her involved. This is against the—"

"Oh come on. Don't tell me that you care about rules. You've been sleeping with her since the beginning. The superintendent could demote your ass for this," Claire argued.

I folded my arms over my chest, watching as Tobias's face changed. He was so hot and on top of that he had a good name.

"I took a risk," Tobias mumbled, clenching his fists. "This is too dangerous. I'll report myself if I have to, but I'm not letting her do this."

"Well, you have nothing to say, loverboy, because I've just agreed to be part of it," I said, still not quite believing that he wanted to keep me out of it. This was a national story, something that could take my career to the next level. "Once you tell me what you need from me, I want full exclusivity assurances in writing. I can't believe that this has been happening under my nose all this time and I didn't figure it out. Unbelievable!"

"I think this could work," Claire said. "Lurkin likes her. He was flirting with her during the evening in our apartment. Think about Johnny Hodges! She was close to him too."

A cold shiver passed down my spine when I thought about my ex. Andrew was involved in this whole thing and he was making money by supplying and distributing drugs. There was a lot that I could share with them, but I wasn't ready to tell them stuff about my personal life. The tiny voice in my head told me that if I wanted this story I had to forget about my wounded pride and tell them everything they needed to know.

"Ellie, please, don't do this just because you're angry with me. I couldn't reveal the truth. You're important to me. After so many weeks you must realise that."

Hearing him say this, my heart raced. Claire sighed loudly and then said that she was going to give us a minute.

When she left us alone, the silence hung between us and for the first time I didn't know what to say. He didn't need to apologise. There was nothing he could say. We were done. I swallowed hard, feeling like my anger was fading away slowly. Yes, I had to admit it was a relief that he wasn't married. This meant that we could have had a shot, a real shot, but I told myself that I wasn't supposed to think about this stuff. Love existed only in fairy tales. Tobias wasn't for me.

"No, Tobias. I'm already part of this whether you like it or not. Let's forget about tonight. Call Claire and let's discuss the details. I want this story and I'll do anything to bury my ex, to ruin him."

Twenty-Two

Ellie

"I'm not letting you put your life in danger," he spat as he started putting the rest of his clothes on, looking furious. I was fully aware of that burning sensation in my stomach filled with need and desire. I was so relieved, knowing that he wasn't married, but deep down I knew that this was only going to complicate things more than I anticipated. One-night stands usually didn't go anywhere.

"I'm sorry, Tobias. I've made up my mind."

He shot me a furious look, picked his handcuffs up off the dresser and stormed out, passing Claire in the entrance. I didn't even know why he was so angry. I offered my help and he was behaving like I had no idea what I was talking about. He didn't consider the fact that it was me who had been worried sick over the past two months about sleeping with a married man. He had probably already forgotten about that.

"Don't worry about him. He's angry that he can't control you, frustrated that this whole thing is taking so long," Claire said walking back to the room. I was expecting her to tell me off, or to judge me, but she seemed sympathetic. Maybe I was thinking too much about what went on in here. I had a story, a real story, and if I played my cards right, I would gain a lot from it.

"I want to help, and I want my ex to pay for what he did to me," I said, ignoring her comment. All of a sudden I felt a little emotional when I thought about Tobias. I sat down on the chair, feeling lightheaded. It was probably the shock, but then, I hadn't eaten anything since I showed up outside Tobias's work. When I saw Claire at the door, I thought I was going to have a heart attack. I felt like history was repeating itself, a redux of when Theresa caught me in bed with Andrew. I was mortified, but then I realised that Andrew had never cared about me either.

"I'll talk to him about this, but you need to know that Lurkin is conniving, manipulative and lethal. You will be putting your life at risk. This whole operation is dangerous and we have to be very careful."

"Please don't tell me that you're trying to talk me out of it," I said.

"No, but I have known Tobias for years and I know he doesn't want you involved. He has never reacted like that. We both know that he is impulsive, particularly when things don't go his way." She sighed.

I thought that Tobias cared for me, but he was never interested in anything serious. Our relationship had always been casual. We had never discussed what was going on between us and where it was leading. I wanted to ask her questions about him, but after a few seconds I abandoned that idea. I didn't want her to think that there was something real between us.

Claire didn't want to talk further about what I knew. She told me that she had to find Tobias and we were going to talk about the whole agenda tomorrow. For a second I wondered if she had any feelings for Tobias, but I knew that I was just being silly. She seemed all right with the whole situation.

When I was driving back to work several hours later, I felt a little better. For weeks, I had been worrying about sleeping with yet another married man and the relief I felt knowing that I wasn't was palpable. Tobias didn't have to lie to me, but he chose to. Sure, telling me would have broken the rules in his police work, but he'd already done that by continuing to have sex with me. He should have sensed I wouldn't have revealed his cover. I was there for him, but obviously he didn't trust me. I should have known that there was something wrong during that night at the party. Now everything was crystal clear.

At the newspaper offices everyone was looking tense. It was probably something to do with the latest deadlines introduced by Phil. In the huddle everyone wanted to throw ideas about, and for the first time, Jordan had nothing new to bring to the table. I kept my mouth shut about what I knew. This was my story, and I couldn't see myself staying at this paper when my boss didn't respect me. After I drank a litre of bad coffee, I got on with my work knowing that at least now I didn't have to worry about Claire or Tobias.

As I was working through my admin just before lunch, my phone started vibrating. When I saw the private number, my heart sank to my toes. I completely forgot about that bastard who was attempting to blackmail me. I had no choice but to answer. I couldn't risk another story in the paper, especially now after what I knew about Claire and Tobias.

"Hello."

I wasn't ready for this conversation, but I knew that I wasn't invisible. New hair and glasses wouldn't change the fact that I had been recognised.

"Ellie Grant, it's good to finally hear your voice. I'm glad that you have decided to answer the phone this time," said the deep voice that sounded like it was digitally enhanced for the purpose of disguise. It was the same man or a woman from the other day, the person that wanted five thousand pounds.

"I don't have that kind of money. My father disowned me and I lost everything," I said, my voice vibrating.

"Too bad, because I'm ready to send this short email to all the gossip sites in Glasgow and I have a nice picture of you with your new hair."

I swallowed hard, knowing that I couldn't let him do that. Tobias and Claire worked hard to get close to Adrian. If this story came out, Adrian would disappear.

"Fine, fine. I'll get the cash. Just don't send anything anywhere," I pleaded, wondering if I had a chance to buy any more time.

"You have four days. I'll be in contact with you then," he snapped and hung up. I gripped my iPhone tighter, thinking about people that were close to me, about my friends, anyone who might be able to loan me the money. For a split second I thought about Tobias and Claire, but I knew that they had more important things to worry about. Besides, I didn't want to ask for their help.

This was my problem that I had to take care of myself. My money was tight as it was, and whatever savings I had, went towards the service charge for the apartment. I had a thousand pounds and my mortgage payment was going to be taken out of that this month.

There was no way that I could magically get five thousand pounds, unless I got my father involved, which was highly unlikely. He had cut me off, but this was also about him. I knew that somehow I would need to take care of this problem very soon. I lost touch with my friends when I moved away, not one of them had tried to stay in touch, which was greatly disappointing.

When the workday was over, I hurried to my car and drove back home, thinking about the story and my earlier encounter with Tobias and Claire. Maybe I was making a mistake; maybe I shouldn't have agreed to be involved. Tobias was against it, and now I had some kind of stalker that wanted to blackmail money out of me.

My good friend Rebecca would most probably rescue me, but we hadn't spoken for a while. I hadn't told her or any of my other friends where I was living now. After thinking about this long and hard, I decided to call her. I was in such a hurry to get back to the apartment that I walked straight into someone in the corridor.

"Hello, beautiful, where are you rushing to?"

My heart leaped in my throat when I realised that it was Adrian. Crap, I wasn't ready for this. My head was all over the place. He looked really good, with his dark suit, his usual arrogant smirk playing on his lips. Tingles of bad vibes passed through my body when I thought that I agreed to play his girlfriend and the fact that Tobias was putting his life at risk just to catch this arsehole.

"Err…nowhere, just finished work," I mumbled, smiling lightly. I didn't need to be nervous around him; he had no idea that Claire and Tobias were on to him.

His eyes flashed with mischief and he licked his bottom lip, revealing sparkling white teeth and looking down my cleavage. I didn't know what was with this guy and my boobs.

Apparently size didn't matter since I had nothing to show, anyways.

"I have been meaning to talk to you about that drink, you know. This time I wanted to take you out properly," he said, leaning over to whisper 'a date' into my ear. I swallowed hard, staring at his emotionless, dark eyes, trying to keep calm. This was the opportunity, you idiot! Say yes, this was what I wanted.

"A date, oh…gee, I don't know," I said, scratching my head, pretending that I was hesitating. I needed to play hard to get; otherwise, he could lose interest; men did love the chase. With a bit of encouragement he might tell me all his secrets. I needed time to figure him out.

"Oh come on, I have a free evening and I can show you a good time. Besides, Mack wants to organise a boys' night. You know he works for me now, right?"

"Yes, Claire mentioned it." I nodded, trying to keep the space between us. His cologne was strong and it reminded me of that guy who tried to rape me that night at Harry's party. "That's very noble of you to help him out and give him a job. I know they were having trouble, you know, from the conversation that we both overheard."

He puffed his chest out and smiled widely. Oh yes, I had to stroke his ego; that was what men like Adrian needed to hear.

"Is that a yes then?" he asked.

"All right, but I can't be out very late. I have to be in the office early. What time should we meet?"

"In an hour. I'm just popping over to the shop. I'll knock on your door when I'm ready," he said and stepped into the elevator. My head was spinning and the sudden dose of excitement rushed over my bones.

"All right," I agreed.

I didn't have much time. It looked like I would have to deal with my stalker later on. This date was important and I needed to tell Claire. I wasn't ready to see Tobias just yet. I had no idea how I was supposed to behave around him, but I figured that they had to know what was going on.

No one answered when I knocked, and for some reason I felt relief that I didn't have to face the man that I truly wanted. My palms were damp with sweat when I slid the message under their door, letting them know what was going on. Yesterday, everything happened so fast that I didn't even have a chance to take Claire's number.

That was it. Now I just had to pick my outfit for later, for my first official night out with a gangster. This wouldn't end badly, right? Well, at least I was telling myself that.

***

"Gorgeous, absolutely gorgeous. I don't think I'll be able to take my eyes off you all evening," Adrian said when we were walking to the car. I bet he liked hearing the sound of his own voice, and he was trying hard to compliment me.

It was cold outside, the winter well on the way. I had no idea where he was planning to take me, but I decided to wear a miniskirt with opaque, purple tights and a chiffon blouse so my cleavage was on view. On top of that I picked out high heels that accentuated my long legs. I felt nervous and on edge when I sank into a comfy seat in his car. Adrian kept talking about his business, telling me about the stock that he was bringing from Spain.

"I like this new car, Adrian. Am I wrong, but didn't you have a different one a couple of weeks ago?"

"Yes, I had an Audi, but I got bored of it," he explained, winking at me. "What can I say, I like arriving in style. Hungry?"

"I'm starving," I admitted smiling widely. "Are you going to tell me where we are headed?"

If I wanted to play this game right, I needed to be careful. Tobias was building a case and insisted that Adrian was dangerous. I'd been thinking that he was only trying to have fun. He didn't strike me as a psychopath. He talked a lot about his accomplishments and successes, joked jovially and bragged that he partly owned the nightclub. Adrian was either a very good actor or confident that he was never going to be caught in any wrongdoings.

"It's a surprise. Do you like seafood?"

"Yes. I wouldn't be Scottish if I didn't like it," I responded.

"Good, because you will love what I had prepared for us."

He was driving fast, showing off a bit, asking questions about my work at the paper. I couldn't help but compare him to Tobias; he was so different. The way he drove, for example. Tobias nearly killed us in the traffic when he picked me up from outside the depot the day he saved me from being mugged. So seemingly reckless yet completely in control, as fast as we drove I felt safe, knowing that my life would never be put in deliberate danger by him.

Listening to Adrian talk about what he thought generally of newspapers gave me chance to think, as he didn't always need a response from me. It was officially my night off at the club and I prayed that Nathan wouldn't call this evening. I really didn't want to spoil the night like that. I knew that the club was quiet this week and they had just hired another dancer. I was glad that I didn't have to deal with performing on the pole as well this 'date'.I felt my phone vibrating in my bag. I checked it, and seeing that it was an unknown number, I rejected the call. A few minutes later the text message came through.

Cancel this immediately. This isn't a joke, Ellie. I'm worried about you.

I had no idea how Tobias managed to get my number, but as usual he was overreacting. I understood that he was worried, and that we hadn't managed to discuss the details, but this was our first real chance to get something out of Adrian. Adrian asked me out, and if I had said no, maybe we would never get another opportunity.

I decided to switch off my phone and just go with the flow. But I didn't like not knowing where we were going and what he had planned when we got there. I suddenly had a bad feeling about this whole thing.

When Adrian finally parked his car and let me out, I realised that we were at the marina. It was getting dark, but I recognised the dock front and a few of the moored boats that bobbed in the heavy tide coming in from the rough seas.

"Adrian, what's going on? Where are we?" I asked, confused and more than a little scared. I really didn't want to get out on the sea in weather like this.

"We're going on a romantic trip. Don't worry. I have everything planned out. You will love it," he said, and took my hand.

Sudden fear hit my stomach as we started walking. It took me a moment to realise that Adrian was serious. We were going on a boat, and out there I was on my own. I thought about calling Tobias or Claire, but Adrian was with me and I needed to act like I was really into him. Besides, there was no way I could explain exactly what was going on while he stood next to me. He was holding my hand the whole time, explaining that I was going to love what he had planned for us. Whether I liked it or not, I was going to be on the open sea where I had nowhere to escape.

Twenty-Three

Ellie

Minutes later, we stepped onto the large, luxury boat that was moored on the other side of the marina. Adrian led me in, telling me everything I needed to know about his 'baby'. The yacht had four guest cabins, all were en suite, a sheltered exterior deck, a fully functional kitchen—"or galley as real sailors call it with all the latest gadgets," he bragged. There was also a small bar and a comfortable living room with deep-seated sofas. I was speechless, thinking that this was the reaction he was expecting from me.

When he told me to sit down, someone else must have switched on the engine, because we started moving. My stomach was flipping over with nerves. I knew that I wasn't supposed to be worried, but this whole setup was overwhelming. I knew he wouldn't get suspicious of my nerves. After all, this was our first official date. Still, I couldn't help thinking about the worst-case scenario. Maybe he was already planning to murder me on the open sea and throw my body overboard.

"Are you going to tell me where you're taking me?" I asked, once I found my voice again.

"In time. Hold on, I'll be right back."

He vanished somewhere, keeping that mysterious smirk on his face. He returned a few minutes later with a bottle of champagne.

"It's so miserable outside and I didn't just want to do dinner. I thought that this would be more romantic, a short trip out on the wild sea," he explained and started wrestling with the bottle. When the cork was popped, he handed me a glass and poured the fizzing champagne, smiling broadly. If he hadn't been a dangerous drug smuggler, I would have said that I was impressed.

"You're terrible. It would have been easier to have a meal in a restaurant. You still have to feed me, you know," I said, looking around, worried that he chose this setup because he was planning to sleep with me tonight.

"My cousin is a chef, a very good one, and has prepared something already."

"Your cousin?" I questioned him.

"He is steering the yacht. Once we're away from the port, he will serve up dinner. Drink, Ellie. Relax. I promise, you will be home before ten and by that time you will want to do it again." Adrian grinned at his innuendo and sat down by me on the sofa. His eyes were lidded and heavy, sparkling with lust. He wanted me, there was no doubt about that, but I doubted Adrian could manage subtle. I really needed to relax. This was a date and I was supposed to be here to have a good time.

I could deal with flirting, maybe some kissing, but I wasn't sure if I really could go through with sex.

"Is this what you do normally? You know, when you take a girl out on a date?" I asked, tossing my hair behind me.

"No, so far I have only done this for you. I can't deny it—I have worked hard and I earn good money and I want to enjoy myself. My family is wealthy," he said, moving closer to me. "Don't be angry with me. This boat isn't mine, but one of my associate's. I just wanted this evening to be special."

Yeah, you have earned money, all of it from those addicted to drugs, I thought, trying not to lose the smile that had been plastered on my face since the moment I agreed to this date.

He seemed so confident, so cocky, even when I was asking him about his previous relationships, his family. It seemed to me that he had an answer for everything. We talked about his fast food chain. I didn't want to press too hard, but from what he said, I gathered that he had been very well connected from the time that he opened his first takeaway. I wondered why he thought that it was all right for him to carry on like that, thinking that he was never going to get caught.

After I came back from the bathroom, Adrian topped off my champagne and then he brushed his hand over my cheek. Goose pimples shot down my arms. I didn't know why I was nervous. I was a freaking reporter and sometimes I needed to do things that I didn't want to, like now, making out with Adrian Lurkin. Adrian obviously wanted to sleep with me. That was what this whole seduction was about, but after Tobias, I didn't think I could go through with it.

Just when he was about to kiss me, another man walked into the cabin. He was Asian too, much darker than Adrian and taller.

Adrian introduced me. "Ellie, meet my cousin Mo. He's an excellent chef."

The man nodded, giving me a shy smile. I didn't know why, but I noticed that Mo was quite tense around us. I didn't think that they were related, especially after Adrian started throwing orders at him. Something seemed off with those two, but I didn't want to come across intrusive. I was here to play the coquettish date, that's all. And I wasn't about to obey Tobias's orders. He was out of the picture right now. He was committed to his job. I was his distraction, and he would probably laugh if I told him that I wanted a relationship.

Mo prepared our meal of grilled lobster and it was delicious. Adrian kept chatting away, keeping the conversation flowing but oddly not really saying much of any substance. As Mo disappeared back into the kitchen, clearing our plates, we were finally alone.

I kept drinking, probably because I was still nervous. I didn't even realise when I got tipsy. Adrian started telling me about his extensive family. He seemed much more relaxed now than during the evening in the club. It was probably because he owned it. Now he had me on his terms, and here no one could interrupt us.

"I have four brothers and three sisters. My father opened the first takeaway almost twenty years ago," he said, when we moved back to the sofa. "None of my siblings wanted to get into that business. I was the oldest, and when my father died, I had to take over the company. I think it's easier that my family isn't involved. I like going ahead and doing what I think is right, rather than trying to please people."

"I have the same feelings about my family. My father and I don't get on," I told him.

"I run everything, take care of the books and employees. At the end of the month, they get their money. This works well for everyone," he said, smiling and moving his arm around my shoulders. We were alone and he wasn't wasting any time, caressing the skin on my arms with his fingers.

"And you run the chain all by yourself? It's a lot of responsibility."

"Yes, it is, but I enjoy it. My work gives me a lot of satisfaction. I don't really talk about it, but I have a partner. He lives in Glasgow. We have a distribution network there too, so he takes care of that."

God, he was so close now, looking straight at my lips, and I didn't know what to do. I wanted to ask him more questions about Andrew, but then he kissed me. It was quick and wet. He cupped my face with his palms and pressed his mouth over mine. His kisses were rough and surprisingly sensual. I panicked a little when he intensified the movements of his tongue. I closed my eyes and imagined that I was kissing Tobias and we were back in that room in the hotel.

Desire pooled between my legs, igniting the fire in my belly. It took me a few seconds and several heartbeats to realise that I was embraced in a passionate kiss with Adrian Lurkin, not Tobias.

His hand began to wander towards my thighs, his fingers creeping closer to the edge of my skirt. This whole evening was getting out of control. I couldn't let him touch me. Tobias owed me now and I didn't want another man.

I managed to wiggle myself out of his embrace, breathing hard.

"Can I have some more champagne?" I asked, breathless. Adrian grinned and got up, giving me his smug smile. He was turned on. I could tell from the bulge in his pants that was suddenly there. When he was pouring more champagne into my glass, his cousin showed up again and said something to him.

Adrian frowned, shook his head and then sent the other guy away.

"We need to go back. Mo had a warning from the coastguard. A strong storm is coming from the north, and it looks like we have to return to the marina," Adrian said, looking displeased. "I'll be right back. I just need to check something with him."

I exhaled in relief when I was finally alone. My heart was racing and I kept asking myself what I was doing. I played tough, determined Ellie, but deep down I didn't want to fuck Adrian. Before Tobias, I'd never had a one-night stand with anyone, and as the realisation settled in, I was ready to run as far as I could, but the truth was—I couldn't.

Tobias

I was going crazy, pacing around the room, waiting and checking the clock every few minutes. Ellie had gone out on a date without consulting with us first. This took me completely by surprise. I thought she understood that she needed to be briefed before any engagement with the suspect could take place. I wasn't even planning to let her go out with him, but I knew that I couldn't tell her what to do.

"Anything?" I barked at Claire. She was in front of the laptop, checking what was going on with the surveillance team.

"No, they can't trace her. She must be out of the area," Claire replied, and then she rolled her eyes. "Seriously, calm down. He won't hurt her. He wants her, but he isn't stupid enough to do anything bad right now, not when he is just about to make a few million pounds."

Claire had no idea what he could do to Ellie. Lurkin didn't care about anyone apart from himself, and I was worried, knowing that Ellie wouldn't know if she was in danger.

I wasn't in a very good mood when I came back to the apartment earlier tonight. Then, when I read that note from Ellie, I thought I was going to lose my fucking mind. Claire looked too calm, pretending that she was all right with all this and not doing anything useful.

I paced again, wanting to tear my hair out of my head, when we both heard a knock. I hurried to the door and opened it abruptly, the knot in my stomach letting go when I saw that it was Ellie and she was safe and sound. She looked fucking amazing with her black hair falling down on her arms, and she was showing off her legs with that miniskirt. I cursed when I realised she went out looking like that.

"Come on in, quick," I barked at her, wondering if something happened between them.

When I locked the door, Ellie stepped inside the living room and Claire shut down her laptop.

"So I guess that the date went well?" she asked Ellie.

I breathed, well, at least I was attempting to, feeling like my blood began circulating through my veins again. This woman had that kind of effect on me. I hated myself for being so weak, for wanting her. She was still fucking angry with me, because she didn't even look at me. This was absurd. I had a reason to be angry; I was the one who'd been worried sick about her.

"We went out on his luxury yacht," she explained. "His cousin made dinner for us and we drank champagne."

"A yacht? A fucking yacht?" I blurted out. "You shouldn't have gone out with him in the first place, before discussing the details with us, let alone out to sea on his fucking luxury yacht."

I was probably an inch away from losing control. Since that night in the hotel, I hadn't been sleeping well. I'd been dreaming about Charlotte—and then Ellie. This whole thing was so fucked up.

"What are you talking about, Tobias?" she asked, placing her hands on her hips.

"Claire failed to mention that you should have been briefed first."

"I'm sorry, but I have no idea how this whole thing works. I came home from work early and Adrian asked me out. You weren't here and I couldn't say no," she explained, looking at Claire. It looked like she was still pissed off with me lying about the fact that I wasn't married. I got it, I screwed up, but as a reporter, she should know that I had no other choice. When you go undercover, you go undercover to everyone, not a select few.

"It's all right, Ellie. I think we both know that Tobias is a little overdramatic. Just walk us through the date? What did you guys do?" Claire sniped in, and I shot her a sharp glare.

Ellie started telling us about the date, about how Lurkin took her to the port and the fact that she couldn't say no without appearing to be suspicious. The bastard probably thought that he could fuck her there. The fire inside my chest spread fast and I didn't think I could carry on listening to how cosy and comfortable he made her feel.

"I found out that it was his father that started the takeaway business. After he passed away, no one else was willing to take over from him, so Adrian volunteered. I didn't find out anything else. He wasn't very forthcoming, but he did mention his partner in Glasgow."

"That's interesting that he admitted to that. We ran background checks on his family, but there was nothing there that raised any alarms," Claire said, looking disappointed. I wasn't sure what she was expecting from Ellie.

"So did you fuck him on that luxury yacht?" I asked, more aggressively than I should have. Claire and Ellie looked at me with their jaws hanging open. I had no idea what was wrong with me, but I was ready to explode, thinking that Lurkin had touched her.

"No," Ellie replied, pressing her lips in a hard line. "I haven't slept with him, Tobias. I might look easy, but I'm not."

"What the hell, Tobias?" Claire shot at me. "That is none of your business. She offered to help, and the only way she could do that was for her to get closer to Lurkin, and—"

"I'm standing my ground on this. This is dangerous and Ellie is a civilian," I barked back, remembering our moments together, watching them run like a film on fast-forward in my head. Fuck, I really needed to see another shrink, but the truth was that I couldn't and didn't want to get her out of my head.

"Tobias, come on, we've been through this," Ellie said. "I'm involved now and I want this story."Then she looked at Claire. "Can you give us a minute, Claire? I think I need to have a chat with Tobias."

I smirked, shaking my head, not believing that we were going to go through the same shit again. Claire nodded, but just as she was about to close the door, she turned around and said, "Before I go, can I ask you something, Ellie?"

My Angel nodded.

"Do you think you would be able to get in touch with your ex?"

I couldn't fucking believe it. We had discussed this before. Hodges was mine to deal with and Ellie was already knee-deep in this shit.

"I'd rather not see him. I know that I would be the perfect person for this, but he has hurt me too much and I don't want to dig up the past."

Same as me, Angel, same as me.

Twenty-Four

Ellie

"Fair enough. I just thought I would ask," Claire said, nodded to Mack, and left with her laptop, shutting the door behind her.

I knew that this whole conversation was going to be difficult, especially after such an intimate, intense night at the hotel. When I looked at Tobias my heart started beating with overwhelming emotion. I was struggling to feel indifferent about him. He lied to me, yes, I couldn't deny it, but we had something here, something deep and precious. Now he was Tobias Stanley, a man with a new name but an old identity.

"Tobias, I want to do this. I know that you're trying to protect me, but I have made my choice," I said, trying to be calm. I didn't want to anger him. Yes, we had our issues, but we had to work together to lock Adrian up.

Tobias's expression wasn't revealing anything, but I knew he was mad. I could tell just by looking at the way he stood, the set of his shoulders, and the twitch near his eye. The temperature in my body shot up when he walked up to me.

"Did he kiss you? Tell me, Ellie, or I swear to God, I'll lose my fucking mind."

I swallowed, remembering how much Adrian wanted me. I didn't know why Tobias was so against me working with them. We were sleeping together and, although I wanted it, we both knew that we didn't have any future beyond that.

"Yes, we made out on the sofa, Tobias," I said, looking into his eyes. Whatever the odds were, it was hard for both of us to carry on like this. As soon as I said it, he reacted with a sharp intake of breath, the muscles on his face tightening.

"This isn't a game, Ellie. If you carry on, you will have to sleep with that piece of shit," he growled.

"I know what I'm doing, and I really don't think that it will come to that. You shouldn't act like you care. I gave you my whole being and you lied to me. I understand why, I get that you were bound to keep this as a secret, but I want the story. I'm sorry, but I won't change my mind."

I'd had to sacrifice my love, my career and my life before. Now I'd have to do it all over again once this was finished, but he was making this very difficult for me. Tobias and I—we were from two different worlds. This operation was going to be over soon, and I was stuck here in this complex. Tobias would move on to the next one. That was the reality of the situation and I accepted it.

"Ellie, I lost someone special to me already—my wife—and I'm not ready to go through that again," he said, looking at me with those grey eyes. I had seen the sadness in them before, but I wasn't expecting this. Tobias had been married before? I shouldn't be surprised. After all, I didn't know who he really was. Whatever facts he had told me in the past were fabricated. "I do care for you. We have this crazy connection and I lose my fucking head when I'm with you. Do you think it's easy for me to stand here and pretend that I'm all right with you going out with him?"

A storm of emotions passed through me and I wanted to throw myself into his arms. Heat scorched me when I thought about what we shared, the passion and lust. When we were together it was like fireworks exploding through my body.

This whole situation was complicated enough and, although I wanted him badly, I couldn't allow myself to be pulled under his spell. He had too much power over me and he could destroy me.

"What happened to your wife?" I asked.

"That's not relevant. All I want for you to do is to stay away and let us work. We are so close. Adrian will lead me to Hodges; there is no doubt about that."

"I'm sorry, but you know me well enough by now to see that I'm not planning to give up."

"So you're going to date him? Despite what's been going on between you and me?" he asked.

Oh God, why did he have to say things like this? I had thought he was married, and I still slept with him. Now that obstacle had been removed and another appeared.

"We both know that this way I'll be able to help with the operation."

"The only way for you to help is to get in touch with your ex. I can't ask you this, because it's unfair," Tobias said and sat down on the sofa like he was done talking to me. I hated when he became so distant and cold, hated that he could switch to being closed off within moments.

I was torn between my newly formed feelings for him and the fact that I wanted to achieve something in my life. I was repulsed even thinking about touching Adrian again, but I knew Claire was counting on me.

"Tobias, please keep me in the loop. This isn't straightforward anymore and I want to be part of this," I said.

"Whatever, Angel, just go. Claire will be in touch. You've obviously made up your mind."

He was right. I knew what I had to do, but it was killing me that he was so indifferent suddenly.

I picked up my stuff and left, knowing that we weren't going back to being okay.

Tobias

When she was gone, I sat there wondering if we could have had a chance if I'd met her under normal circumstances. She did something to me and I felt I needed to stay close to her. Maybe I even loved her.

Claire came back to the room but didn't say a word to me. I was pissed off that she thought it was above board for us to use Ellie like this. Yeah, I was determined to get into Lurkin and Hodges's inner circle, but this whole thing was getting complicated and I felt guilty for putting Ellie in unnecessary danger. I knew that the sooner we built the case, the sooner I would be able to move on.

But was I ready to move on and just forget about her?

I didn't think I would ever be.

Hours later when Claire went to bed, I stayed up, switching through the channels on the TV. We hadn't spoken further about Ellie. She probably realised that it was a sensitive subject.

I went to bed at twelve, knowing that I wouldn't get much sleep anyway. The nights that I spent with Ellie were restful and gave me peace so that I woke up refreshed in the morning. Without her, I tossed and turned for several hours before I finally drifted off. Lying in bed thinking of Ellie and her soft vanilla smell, wishing I were lying next to her caused another problem. This time it was my dick that was a problem. I masturbated, but that didn't give me any relief. That deep connection I had with her, both of us being completely sated and exhausted, the scent of sex in the air just wasn't there when I was alone.

In the morning I woke up feeling like shit after very little sleep, but my mood brightened a little when I read the text messages from Lurkin.

He asked me to show up at some address once I was done with my shift, and that sounded like progress. I didn't dare to ask about Hodges, not yet. He needed more time to trust me. Lurkin was most probably hiding more skeletons in the closet and I needed to pull all of them out one by one.

That name 'Hodges'" boiled my blood. I couldn't wait to find him and make him pay for what he had done.

I was reluctant to talk to Ellie about Charlotte, and I didn't want her to know that the man that she had an affair with was involved in my wife's murder. She wouldn't take this well. She was already upset over the fact that I deceived her. Maybe I had to accept that we were both too damaged to even consider a future together.

Claire was already working when I showed up in the living room. I told her about the text and we agreed to inform the team to put surveillance in the area. We needed to get some results fast, so I hoped that tonight I would find out more.

When I left my apartment at seven in the morning, I collided with Ellie. She was just leaving her apartment, probably to get to work. She saw me, paled a bit and then quickly vanished behind the door that led to the stairs. She was running away from me. Well, that realisation hurt like a bitch, but I guess after our last conversation I deserved it.

I dragged my hand through my hair when I got into the car. My cock was at half-mast all the way to the depot. I had never experienced this kind of frustration before, this kind of longing for someone I'd just met. I wanted to punish her, fuck her hard until she ached, begging me to stop. I needed to end these kinds of thoughts. I couldn't expect her to continue to fuck me, and it was obvious that she didn't want me anymore.

Once I arrived at work, I chatted with the guys for some time, asking them about the stock, when Lurkin showed up and asked me to walk with him to his office. I didn't expect to see him today, especially after last night.

"I need you to take the other truck. I have an urgent order that needs to be delivered," he told me, grinning like it was fucking Christmas. I didn't like that smile on his face.

"What's in that truck that you're asking me to change my usual schedule?"

He winked and smiled again before he continued. "I need you to focus today, because you will be going to Newcastle. I realise that this is pretty short notice, but another driver bailed on me and you have proven to me that you can be trusted with more delicate assignments."

"I'm ready, whatever, just give me directions," I assured him, thinking about the moment when I could cuff him and throw him into the prison cell.

An hour later I was on the road heading to deliver what was probably a significant amount of drugs. Maybe it was a good thing that Claire was tracking my phone. At some point, I needed to check the truck, to make sure that it contained exactly what I was expecting. This was a step forward and I was getting closer.

The roads were busy, traffic was terrible, and by the time I managed to stop it was late, almost lunchtime, and I was very close to my destination. I opened the back and went inside. The truck was filled with Asian food products: spices, cans and packets of dry seeds. It didn't take me long to figure out that Lurkin was putting coke into the spices. He had wrapped small balls of coke covered in cling film typically known as an eight ball and dropped it into the bags of spice. I took some pictures, knowing that this was good, but not good enough. I needed to find out where he kept all the paperwork and the name of his contact in Spain. The team was looking into the Irish Brothers. I had learned that body parts in a box meant that there was a dead body out there somewhere. I knew that once we tracked the body we would be able to link it to the Irish Brothers. That was their M.O. To keep a body part as proof for loved ones.

Lurkin was a great actor. He hadn't been caught after all this time, but his time was running out. For years he thought he had been careful, making sure that his private life was separate from his business and the drugs. He wanted Ellie too, probably to add her to his collection of conquests. It drove me insane that she was so deeply involved.

This delivery was straightforward. There was someone waiting for me in the city. He picked up the delivery, signed the paperwork, chatted to me for a bit, and then I was on my way back to Edinburgh.

By the time I was done with work, I was fucking exhausted. Lurkin wanted me to show up at the club. I called Claire instantly and told her to keep Ellie out of there for tonight.

I headed to the club, knowing that there was probably going to be an initiation of some sort. When I got there, Ellie was on all the CCTV cameras; if Lurkin was the owner, he was going to see her sooner rather than later. I was fucking worried out of my mind about her. I had never come across anyone so stubborn.

It was Thursday night and the club was dead, except for a few intoxicated youngsters by the door. I headed straight to the private offices, when some guy showed up.

"Anything I can help you with?"

"Mr. Lurkin invited me over here," I told him. Didn't want to waste any more time.

"Oh yes, the party. Please follow me," he added, with that stupid smile. The party—what the hell did he mean?

I really wasn't up for drinking tonight. I had shitloads to do, checking out the files on other members of his crew. Claire had some gems, but still nothing on that Johnny fucking Hodges.

I followed him through the long corridor, passing the private rooms on the way, and remembered what had happened behind one of the doors. Ellie's mouth around my cock, sucking until I exploded. She was amazing.

Finally he led me through a wide brown door to a room filled with people. The music was loud, pumping its heavy bass line through hidden speakers.

I was surprised to see that Lurkin had organised a full-on party. Quite a lot of members of his team were there. On top of that, I spotted a few people there that weren't supposed to be in the country.

Topless girls walked around serving drinks. There were a few Asian men there too.

"Mack, you managed to make it. Everything went smoothly?" the prick asked, patting me on the back like we were best fucking buddies. He looked high; his pupils were massively dilated. This astonished me because I hadn't expected this from him. It seemed he liked control too much.

"Yes, Jonas seemed happy with the stock."

"Superb. Now let's get you a drink, and maybe a little something extra." He grinned. My pulse was speeding and I wanted to smash my fists into that perfect face.

He slapped a girl's arse as we were passing by and winked at me. Something was wrong here and I sensed that the party had only just started. I asked for a pint of beer when the topless hostess showed up and went back to the lounge where Adrian was sitting with some other guy.

"This is Stew. He works closely with one of my partners," he said, introducing me to the ginger fellow, who didn't look too pleased to be here. I shook his hand and sat down next to Lurkin. "By the way, we made a great profit last week and as a thank you I thought that I would throw this party for everyone."

He was almost bouncing out of his seat talking about people that he had invited to come. I tried to chat to Stew, but Lurkin kept interfering. After a while he took a bag of white powder out of his pocket and spread some of it on the table, chopping it into thin lines with his credit card. Of course, I should have noticed it sooner—he was as high as a fucking kite.

"I guess this is from the stock?" I asked, casually watching him as he carried on dividing it, laughing at his own stupid joke.

"Straight from sunny Spain. My supplier there knows that I only want the best shit," Adrian replied, and pushed the mat with coke towards me. "You need to relax a bit, Mack. It's been a hell of a day," he said, as he rolled up a twenty- pound note into a tight tube and handed it to me.

I didn't move for a second, staring at him and wondering why the hell he wanted to drug me. There were too many people out here that were watching me. The Irish brothers were sitting on the other side of the room and their eyes were following me from the moment I showed up here.

I fucking hated drugs. I wasn't a saint, but I had seen enough shit in my life to know that I wasn't into getting high every day. Right now I didn't have a choice. Lurkin was waiting, and I didn't want to screw anything up now, so I leaned down and picked up the rolled note and inhaled a complete line.

Twenty-Five

Ellie

I sat there on my living room sofa pleased with how productive I'd been. I had already finished a really good outline for my story, and my date with Adrian had gone reasonably well. He'd been texting me a lot, and I arranged to go out with him again at the weekend. It seemed he liked me enough to take this further. I worked on my article whenever I had time. I managed to produce a solid, few hundred words. Hope burned through me when I reread the words that my future rested on so much. I had a feeling that I was making the right decision, that this story was going to be good. Phil was giving me the usual crap. I stopped complaining, knowing that it was just a matter of time before I would have an offer from a more established paper.

Things between Tobias and me were still pretty complicated. Claire had told me that he wasn't himself. On top of that he had been putting a lot of hours in at the depot, doing a few more deliveries to Newcastle. I was worried, but I knew that it was none of my business. We'd had fun, and now our careers were to take precedence.

The other day, after I purposely ran away from him I felt like an idiot. He had seen me and looked so shocked that I'd run away. I just couldn't bring myself to talk to him that day.

Heat vibrated through my cells when I thought about the last time we were together in that hotel room—me handcuffed to the bed, panting with anticipation. I wanted more of him, but I knew I couldn't let myself believe that we could be together after this operation was over.

My phone buzzed, pulling me away from my daydreams. It was the private number again. My throat tightened with the sudden realisation that whoever was blackmailing me was very persistent. Since the last phone call I hadn't had time to think about this. I had too much on my plate as it was. Whoever was on the other side of the phone wasn't bluffing. I couldn't afford another scandal, plus, the future of Tobias and Claire's operation weighed on me. If my identity was leaked to the papers, it could ruin everything. Tobias was putting his life on the line and I couldn't jeopardise it, not after everything we'd been through.

"Hello." I answered the phone feeling like I had a massive lump in my throat.

"Check your email, bitch. Get the cash together. I will let you know when and where I want it; otherwise, these pictures will go to the press tonight," said the digitally-altered voice again.

My stomach dropped when I thought about the awful microscope I was put under when the paparazzi had been following me everywhere, hounding me for more juicy details, trying to smear my name further. The look on people's faces when I showed up at parties with friends. I hated hearing the snickers and whispers everywhere I went.

"No, wait please. I have the money."

"Good to hear it. Just follow my instructions and no one will know. You will get the final email from me soon. Stick to the plan. Otherwise your new life will end sooner than it began."

He hung up not letting me say anything else. I instantly logged back onto my laptop. My pulse started racing when I saw an email titled 'Your Lies'.In all the pictures I recognised myself. Now it didn't matter that I had died my hair, changed my style, and wore glasses. People who knew me would easily recognise me in these pictures.

All the tabloids claimed that I ran away and, if this story got out, all the hard work that Tobias and Claire had put in would be for nothing, as my presence would cause the media to investigate and put a spotlight on them as my new friends. Adrian would probably run. Too many people were tangled up in his business and he couldn't afford such exposure.

I'd made a fair chunk of money during my performances at the club, but it wasn't enough. I knew that I had to speak to Tobias and Claire about this. They needed to know what was going on. There was no way I could get this kind of money together on my own.

I tried to work on my story, but thoughts about this blackmail threat were in my head all the time. I thought about all the people that I could get the money from and realised that I should have been more independent earlier in my life. I had relied on my father for almost everything financially, and now I had nothing of my own.

A few hours later, after running out of options, I put some decent clothes on and headed to the apartment that was two doors away from mine. Nervous excitement fluttered in my stomach at the thought of seeing Tobias when I remembered that morning I took the stairs just to avoid speaking to him. I felt pathetic, knowing that now I was here to ask for his help. He most probably wouldn't be happy to see me.

Standing in front of their door, I took a deep breath and then knocked. I nearly cursed when Tobias answered the door. Lustful waves of heat riddled through me as his eyes met mine.

"Well, well, well…who do we have here today?" he said, folding his arms over his chest, pinning me in place with his striking eyes. Tobias looked tired. I noticed large, dark circles under his eyes. I just needed to tell him about the emails and get it over and done with.

"Please don't be an arse, Tobias. I really need to talk to you and Claire," I said, trying to be serious, but my heart threw itself against my ribcage. Things between us were still awkward. I missed him like crazy, but I wasn't planning to admit that to him.

"Come inside. We can't have this conversation out in the corridor," he said. I walked in, trying to breathe normally. Claire was in the living room, working on her laptop. She smiled when she saw me. I couldn't help being amazed that she hadn't held a grudge against me. This whole thing was so weird. A few days ago I was perfectly convinced that she was Tobias's wife.

"Ellie wants to talk," Tobias said, going back to the sofa and switching on the TV. I should have expected that. He was pissed off with me, about Adrian and probably about that other morning.

"Can I talk to you in private?" I asked him, not even knowing where this came from. It'd been a while since we had been alone, and I felt like it was time to start communicating again. Tobias was a very handsome man, and he had this aura of power around him. I needed to focus though and address the problem at hand. Claire didn't say anything. She pretended that she didn't hear me, or she probably sensed that things between us were tense and awkward.

“I need to have an early night tonight, so this better be quick,” Tobias said. He got up and walked towards one of the rooms, obviously expecting me to follow him. I glanced at Claire.

“He's had a rough couple of days. If he’s harsh, don’t worry, it’s probably not you.”

She was nice enough to warn me that Tobias was in one of those moods today. I walked into his bedroom and closed the door. The room was very masculine. The bed wasn’t made. His clothes were thrown haphazardly on a chair and the air was infused with his cologne. It was clear that Claire had never slept here.

“What can I do for you, Ellie?”

I hated that he was so formal all of a sudden. The usual warmth was gone and I knew that it was my fault. I cleared my throat and sat beside him. He shifted on the bed. I didn’t want to make a big deal out of this whole thing, and instead of explaining, I took my phone out and played the first voicemail that I'd saved in my inbox. Tobias listened, and when it ended, he exhaled loudly.

“I had another phone call today and an email with some photos of me. I’m here because I wasn’t sure what to do.”

“You made the right decision telling me about this. Do you have any idea who might have a grudge or have a reason to blackmail you?”

“No,” I admitted. “No one knows that I moved here to the complex. I dyed my hair, changed my style a bit, just to make sure that people wouldn’t recognise me as the society girl in the papers.”

He ran his hand over his jaw, looking away.

"I need to be careful who I'm going to talk to about this. I should be able to give my team access to your phone log and they can generate a number and account details from your incoming calls or at least triangulate the nearest connection mast to help isolate locations. They should be able to track whoever is toying with you," he said, sounding like he was thinking out loud. "Lurkin must not know who you really are, so it's a good thing you told me about this. We can't afford to lose him now that we're so close."

I wanted to caress his face, to comfort him and ease the stress in his eyes. The lies didn't matter. He was putting his life in danger for me.

"Tobias, are you okay?" I asked. "You look tried."

"Why? Don't pretend that you're concerned about my well-being all of a sudden."

"Of course I care about you! I felt used and I was angry. I said some things that I didn't mean because I was hurting from your lies," I explained, knowing that we needed to start working together. Tobias needed to acknowledge that I could be useful. "And I'm sorry that I ran away when I saw you a couple of days ago. That was childish, but I just couldn't face you."

Tobias's eyes softened and he lifted his palm and placed it on my thigh. The spark of electricity charged through me instantly, melting whatever anger I still had inside me.

"I'm fine, Angel. Don't worry about me. I had a long shift last night and I haven't slept yet. On top of that, two days ago I went to a party," he said with a heavy sigh. "Lurkin got high, then one thing led to another, and I was forced to taste some of his white powder."

God, Adrian forced him to take drugs so he could prove to him that he was loyal. This whole thing was getting way out of control. We were talking about serious stuff and Tobias was confessing his concerns to me, but I had trouble breathing and concentrating when his palm was on my thigh.

"What else happened there?" I asked.

"He convinced me that I was right about him all along," he explained.

Tobias

I was hard again, while we were discussing something so far removed from being sexy, but she had that effect on me. We weren't expecting anyone today and I was surprised to see Ellie at the door. I felt like shit, but she instantly brightened my mood. It'd been days since I'd seen her. I had been recovering. Lurkin's coke was good quality, not cut with baking powder to lower its purity, and the party itself had been a fucking nightmare.

I hated drugs. For me it was a sign of weakness. When I was in high school, I smoked some weed, just to impress my mates, peer pressure I suppose. Being at the party, though, when I took that high-grade coke that party quickly got out of hand. I lost touch with reality and started having vivid thoughts about Charlotte. I was hallucinating, thinking that she was still there, sitting next to me. I guess he dropped me some LSD somehow, maybe in my drink. Whatever it was, it was a bad trip.

Lurkin had introduced me to a few people that night, men that worked for him and some strippers that hung over his shoulder for most of the evening. I didn't want to tell Ellie any of that. She worked at the club and she probably knew some of the hostesses that were forced to walk around half-naked to entertain Lurkin's guests.

Sometime after taking the coke, I felt euphoric. All of a sudden, I was talking, about anything and everything. I was the centre of the party. People were listening, women were amused. It was the greatest feeling in the world. I didn't have any problems, the case no longer mattered, Ellie no longer mattered. I didn't care about Lurkin, Claire, or the superintendent.

The whole night seemed surreal when I tried to recall it, as if it happened to someone else. I didn't remember half of the things I said. In that moment Lurkin was one of my mates and we were drinking together.

"Are you going to tell me what happened at that party?" Ellie asked, pulling me back to the present day. I hated myself then, thinking that I was all right.

"Lurkin crossed the line."

The memories from that night were hazy, but I knew they were accurate. I remembered patting Lurkin on the back, telling him that he was my best mate. Someone bought me another pint, so I grabbed it and took a few generous mouthfuls. Lurkin was yapping, laughing at what seemed to be his own pathetic jokes. Every few minutes he was introducing me to new people.

I'd had no idea how much time had passed since I sat down. I felt good in my own skin, and I had nothing to worry about. Everything was going great. I spread out on the chair, closing my eyes, while Lurkin kept talking. I wanted to dance, thinking about Ellie, knowing that she would have enjoyed herself in here.

"Hey, hey… are you even listening to me? This guy, he's the best. He knows the trick," Lurkin kept saying, snarling his words, snapping his fingers in front of my face.

"What trick? What are you talking about, mate?" I asked, staring at some Asian dude who was at our table. I didn't remember when he sat down. God, something was definitely wrong with me. I needed to pull myself together.

"Mr. Lurkin, would you like—"

Adrian was distracted, and he didn't see the topless hostess approaching our table with a tray filled with drinks. He waved his arm and smacked into her. The whole thing spilled all over his suit. In a matter of seconds he was soaked, and the hostess was on the floor, pale and disorientated. I wanted to laugh, thinking about turning this whole thing into a joke.

"You stupid bitch, you fucking ruined my suit," he roared all of a sudden and stormed towards her. He reached down to pick her up from the floor, grabbing her by her throat. His eyes were wide, pupils fully dilated. My pulse started to race, my heart pumping too much blood through my veins.

"Fucking cunt, embarrassing me in front of my people. I'm going to fuck you up," he kept saying, blocking her airway. She was choking, trying to unhook his grip from her throat, but it seemed to me like Lurkin was in some kind of trance—he wanted to kill her. People started gathering around us. The music was still playing. I stood there, staring blankly as he was slowly killing her, feeling hopeless, not reacting.

"Cunt! This is my party and you're wasting my fucking money!"

"Adrian, let her go. You're going to suffocate her, buddy."

It was one of the Irish brothers that reacted first, trying to stop him. Lurkin fought with him, until he pulled away, breathing heavily.

"He went crazy when one of the hostesses spilled drinks all over him," I said to Ellie, shaking off that fucked up memory. "He nearly killed her. I should have never gone to that party. It was a tactical error, and I don't want to know what would've happened if he had killed her. I didn't remember much from the rest of the night. Lurkin started to buy me more drinks, then I was drinking and drinking until I passed out somewhere in the corner."

"That's why I want to help you. We can let him—"

"Ellie, don't you get it? He's dangerous, a lethal motherfucker. I hate going over this," I snarled, shaking my head that she still wanted to carry on with her stupid plan.

"Shh, don't be angry, please, Tobias," she said and leaned over to me, laying her head against my arm. My whole body tensed and I dragged some more air into my lungs. "I want to drive to Glasgow. I have to speak to my father about the voicemail and the email. Will you…I realise that you have a lot on your plate, but will you go with me?"

Twenty-Six

Tobias

I was ready to go anywhere with her as long as it ensured that it would keep her away from Lurkin. She didn't owe anything to her father, but for sure this whole thing couldn't leak out now, when I was so tight with Lurkin.

These nightshifts were slowly killing me, but I needed to go with her. I needed to protect her—even from her father. The voicemail and emails made me nervous. In any other circumstance I would have dealt with it differently, called some people and tracked whoever was trying to earn quick cash, but right then I needed it to go away quietly, so I was ready to pay.

"You don't need to ask, Angel. I would make a deal with Satan if that was necessary," I said, kissing her forehead. Sure, I wanted to tie her up to the bed again and fuck her, but we had more important things to worry about than sex. She asked for my help. After that day I thought that she wouldn't even want to talk to me, but now she lifted my shitty mood.

"I don't know what to do anymore. I tried calling my father, but he isn't taking any of my phone calls."

“You shouldn’t be concerned about your father. Lurkin has proven to us that he wants what’s mine,” I said, happy to admit that Ellie was important to me. I had no idea where this jealousy came from, but the past few days were a nightmare.

“Tobias, if I give him the money, he or she will ask for more,” she said.

“It’s a temporary solution. Don’t worry. I’ll deal with it, somehow,” I told her, just to keep her at ease. “We will go on Monday. Take a day off at work.”

She smiled and my cock strained against my trousers. I don't know what happened then. Maybe it was the combination of lust and anger, or maybe it was the fact that I hadn't touched her for days, but I lost the battle and kissed her. An overwhelming desire pulled me down into a world of pleasure. Her lips were soft and wet and I caressed them with my own, tasting her again. My balls were burning, as I felt her body crush against mine when I wrapped my arm around her tiny waist.

“Tobias, oh God, I missed you,” she moaned as I sucked and nibbled her bottom lip, needing to spread her legs wide and plunge my stiff cock deep inside her until she was writhing with pleasure. Her body needed to be possessed. Lurkin was a scum; he would never deserve her. I hated that she had been willing to surrender herself to him.

Her hands were in my hair and our mouths were all over each other, teasing and reacquainting ourselves. I pulled away knowing that I was being unfair. Claire was next door. I knew that I was inches away from taking Ellie back to her apartment and losing myself in her. This was too dangerous, and Claire and I needed to keep the whole undercover facade believable.

"I need to speak to Claire about this. We have a bit of time to get the money together, but she's—"

"Tobias, there is another reason that I'm going to see my father. I don't have five thousand pounds. When I bought this apartment, I put all my available money into the service charges," she explained, staring down at her nails. She didn't need to be embarrassed. We were in it together.

"Angel, look at me."

She did, and those eyes—fuck me, she captivated me. They were mesmerising, making me want do things to her, to claim her like an animal.

"Don't worry about the money. We are, as you said, in this together. There is a contingency budget for this kind of thing. I'm confident that we can get that money back. That piece of shit has no idea who he is messing with. Trust me on this."

"Thank you, Tobias. I appreciate it. I guess I better be going before we do something we won't be able to stop and will lead to regret later. I have a lot of respect for Claire, and I don't want to offend her."

"She hasn't seen me with another woman since my wife died," I told her, sharing something meaningful, something that I kept to myself most of the time. "Claire is married and wants to get promoted badly, so I guess she's ready to do anything to catch Lurkin and get back to her husband."

"It must be hard on her too," Ellie admitted.

"It is, but we have to finish what we started."

I couldn't even imagine leaving this whole thing behind unresolved. We both knew that her ex-boyfriend, Johnny Hodges, was also vital to the case. I had to make sure that he paid for everything he had done. It felt like fate had a hand in bringing me and Ellie together, and I have never regretted rescuing her at that party all these weeks ago. Without her, we wouldn't be as close as we were to getting this whole thing sewn up. I didn't have a plan yet, but I knew that if I got her fully involved I was risking more than just being her lover.

Ellie said her goodbyes and disappeared into her own apartment after we agreed to go to Glasgow on Monday.

Claire wasn't my type at all, but she was intelligent, bright, and she didn't give a fuck what other people thought about her. That was why we became friends in the first place.

"Tobias, how long are you going to pretend that this woman doesn't mean anything to you? I know this operation is important—it's important to both of us—but you have to cut yourself some slack once in a while."

She was going off on some kind of rant again and I wasn't ready to have this conversation, not right now. Love wasn't for me. I had given my heart to someone before and I lost her. I couldn't face that pain again.

"Things with Ellie are complicated. You know that yourself. She's scared and I'm fucked up, damaged. We both know that once this is over, I'll be moving on," I said. It fucking pained me to admit that, but I was planning to request a transfer abroad with Interpol. Ease up on this kind of case. Maybe visit my cousins in Belfast. At the same time, I didn't want to be away from my Angel.

That probably meant that I was in love with her. Charlotte had been the only one, and now… no, it couldn't be possible.

"This woman cares deeply for you, Tobias. You're blind not to see it," she muttered, shaking her head. "I know you don't want to talk about it, so I'll drop it. Say whatever you need to, because I need to go out soon."

Ellie

Adrian knocked on my door later the same night that I chatted with Tobias. I hated when he stood at my door, expecting me to invite him in. I didn't particularly want to deal with him tonight. I was just so tired. These last few months had left me feeling so emotional and completely drained.

"Ellie, I missed you, but I have bad news. I need to go away to London and I just came to say goodbye," he said, running his finger over my arm. Goose pimples shot over my skin and I swallowed hard. I couldn't do this right now.

"For business?" I asked casually.

"Yes, I have some things that I need to take care of. Will you miss me?"

"Of course. I was looking forward to our next date," I told him, and then yawned. It was late and I was hinting that I was planning to have an early night.

That didn't stop him throwing himself at me. When I looked deep into his eyes I saw his hunger and desire. It was hard to switch off, when I just had been kissed by Tobias. The man that my heart was beating loudly for.

"I'm looking forward to an evening with you. I'm already planning our next date. I hope you'll agree to let me take you away for a couple of days."

"Days?" I questioned. Fear shuddered through my bones and I wondered what the hell he had in mind. Then he kissed me and I wasn't ready. His tongue speared its way into my mouth, teasing, and I knew that I just had to get on with it. When he was done, he brushed the hair off my cheek and winked at me.

"I'll be thinking about you," he added and then vanished. I shut the door, feeling slightly sick and telling myself that he was going to be rotting in prison soon. It was just a matter of time.

***

The next couple of days passed quietly without incident. Phil wasn't too keen on the idea of me taking time off when our deadline was approaching, but eventually he agreed. It was clear that he didn't have anyone else but me to finish the usual crap for him.

I had yet another email from the coward who was blackmailing me. This time I was given the location details of where I was supposed to drop the money. Tobias told me not to worry, that he had already contacted his team and they were doing what they could to identify the blackmailer's location.

"Give me the keys, Ellie. I'll drive," he said to me on Monday morning after we left the building.

I didn't want to argue with him, and on top of that I was really nervous. I had no idea how my father was going to react upon seeing me. I thought about what I was going to tell him, playing the whole conversation in my head, thinking about Andrew and our relationship. Tobias did everything he could to try to distract me. He asked questions about my life in Glasgow, about my friends and my time at University.

The drive didn't take long, and as we got closer, my confidence shrank. When we arrived outside my father's building, I felt anxious and unwell. I had good memories associated with that place, and some very bad ones. Now, after almost two months, I was going to see my father again, and I knew that he wasn't planning to welcome me with open arms.

"I think it's better if you wait here," I said, knowing that Tobias couldn't afford to be exposed.

"Ellie, Claire did say that you can't tell him anything specific. Your father is an intelligent man and he will figure this out. Just tell him about the blackmail and the fact that you can handle it."

"Yes, I understand. I just need to know if anyone has contacted him about me, but to be honest, I don't even know if he will talk to me," I said, knowing my father and the way he reacted when I disappointed him. Tobias probably didn't understand why I wanted to be loyal to a man who cut me out of his life. Either way, I needed to close that chapter of my life and move forward.

"All right, I'll wait here," he assured me with a smile. "Call me if you have any problems."

I got out of the car and started walking towards the building. Every step took me closer to the man that hated me. I took the lift to the top floor and walked into the elegant lobby.

Anna was at the reception desk. She nearly dropped the phone when she saw me.

"Ellie! Oh my God," she said, springing out of her chair and rushing towards me. I knew that she had been sleeping with my father for the last eighteen months. I didn't care, and it wasn't my place to judge her. Besides, I liked her. She'd always been nice to me, even when everyone else treated me like something they had stepped in.

"Hi, Anna, is my father around? I need to speak to him," I said, trying to keep my voice from wavering. I told myself that I had nothing to worry about. I was strong, and soon my name would be respected. I could show my father that he didn't have to be embarrassed about me anymore.

"You know that I would be in huge trouble if I let you in," she warned me, looking uneasy. Anna was a bit older than me and she had dark hair. From the photographs I had seen, she reminded me a lot of my mother. Maybe that was why my father had an affair with her.

"Don't tell him. I'm just going to walk in there, without being announced. Just tell me—is he alone?" I asked. My heart was jackhammering between my ribs.

She nodded. Last time I called, I spoke to a new woman named Marcy. Dad was in court, and when she passed him the message, I heard him telling her that he wasn't willing to talk to me.

"Don't get me fired, Ellie. You know that he can be very unpleasant if he wants to be," she reminded me. I knew exactly what she was talking about. My father could be very aggressive and commanding. I never knew what kind of mood he might be in when he was working.

I took a few deep breaths and walked through tall, oak doors that led me to his office. He was at his desk when I stepped in, looking like his usual busy self. He lifted his head and stopped what he was doing in an instant, eyeing me sharply with disdain.

"Ellie, I think I have made myself clear. You aren't welcome here," he stated and then went back to whatever he was doing.

Yeah, I knew this was going to be difficult.

Twenty-Seven

Ellie

"Dad, someone is blackmailing me. I'm here because I know that you can't afford another scandal. I'm here to warn you," I explained, getting straight to the point, knowing that he wasn't looking for an apology. My father would view an apology as a sign of weakness and he detested any kind of weakness, especially from me. On top of that he was brutally honest.

He hadn't always been so focused. The past shaped him into the man that he was today—not affectionate, indifferent. I usually had trouble reading his emotions, and right then, standing in front of him, I had no idea what he was thinking. He inhaled, closed the book, and stood up. He was very tall, over six foot five, with broad shoulders and deep lines on his cheeks. People often told me that I was the spitting image of him, but he never acknowledged it.

"That wouldn't surprise me, Ellie. People don't forget about things like your indiscretion, but we both know that we can't afford another scandal. I thought the last catastrophe would have taught you a lesson, but I guess I was wrong." He sighed his disappointment. I just stood there, ready for anything. I wasn't stupid; I knew he wouldn't simply forget about what happened, but this time, the blackmail was directly connected to him and seemingly manageable.

"I have had to use a different surname in order to sustain myself financially, but I think that someone recognised me. I didn't come here for sympathy. I needed to warn you, so here I am," I said bitterly, hoping that he was at least ready to listen to me. He was working with Andrew, who couldn't be trusted.

"You don't need to warn me, Ellie. It's probably nothing. You're exag—"

"For God's sake, Dad, Hamilton can't be trusted. I found out things that could ruin your whole career forever. You need to understand that he used me to get to you. How can you be so blind not to see it?" I cut him off, shaking with rage. I had no idea what happened, but I just snapped. Before now, I wouldn't even dare to interrupt him, and now I was shouting at him in his office. He didn't realise that he had a new Ellie in front of him, someone who was ready to fight.

"First you barge in here, when I ordered you to stay away from this building, and now you're bringing up that whole affair again, telling me some unbelievable tale about Andrew?"

"They aren't tales, Dad. I'm a reporter now and my job is to investigate cases that might not have credibility without real evidence. I find that evidence, Dad. Andrew wants you to represent him in court, in case something goes wrong. He doesn't work in finance; don't be a fool. He has his hands in more pies than fraud," I continued, keeping my voice low and controlled. Last time I tried to talk to him I was crying and shouting, and that irritated my father. He hated when I threw tantrums, but now I was calm, speaking to him like an adult.

He kept looking at me intensely, looking slightly surprised, probably because he didn't recognise the new me.

"You know that I don't like empty words. False accusations like that can hurt a man's reputation, unless you have proof. Have you got any proof?"

"Yes, I do, but this is my case. Someone knows about me, about the fact that I'm using a new surname."

"What do you expect me to do? You made your bed, so now you have to lie in it. "

"I don't disagree. I am disappointed in myself that I fell for this man and allowed him to manipulate me, but I have learned my lesson. I'm asking you to keep him away from your main cases. Andrew Hamilton used the affair to his own advantage and he can't be trusted with too much freedom. Yes, I accept responsibility, but this time you have to believe me."

My father was quiet then, running his hand through his thick beard. This whole conversation wasn't going the way I had planned it. Last time, he lost his normally cool temper with me. He'd called me a whore and told me to get out of his sight forever. This time my words and demeanor made him think. He had this ability to see through people, but Andrew had managed to fool him.

"A reporter? So I'm guessing that you're not thinking about law at all?"

I had this urge to roll my eyes, but I forced myself not to. He was starting this again, trying to figure out if I was ever going to get back to law. I guessed it was time to end this conversation. I didn't know what I was expecting when I came here.

Maybe it was the fact that I missed him. Yes, we didn't get on, but we had this familial bond that worked well when it came to his cases. I did enjoy helping him, but only because we were very close with prejudging people.

“I'm a journalist, Father. This won't change. I'm sticking to what I said earlier. Andrew is deceiving you. He expects you to protect him because of attorney-client privilege and he could pull you into this shit with him, if you're not vigilant. I still care for you enough to let you know that you have to be cautious.”

“In that case we have nothing else that we should be discussing, Ellie. I have work to do, a lot of work,” he said, switching back to that indifferent tone of voice and returning to his work.

“This is about Kathy, isn't it? That's why you're treating me like this, because you can't get over the fact that she isn't here anymore.”

I didn't really know why I said that. We had never discussed it and I thought that at this point my father didn't even care about the scandal anymore. Yes, he had disowned me, but it was because I was weak in his eyes. He was impulsive, but I never thought he meant to keep me away.

“Don't even go there, Ellie,” he snapped at me.

“This wasn't my fault and you know it. I'm a human being and I made a mistake. I miss her too, you know, but you never understood that. I don't think you will ever understand it.”

I couldn't do this anymore. I didn't let him get on top of me, so I picked up my bag and stormed out of the office, swallowing my tears. I couldn't catch my breath. Anna was shouting after me, but I didn't want to talk to her. I achieved nothing by coming here. He obviously didn't believe me.

I ran to the stairs, thinking about my little sister, about how much I missed her. That terrible fire all those years ago destroyed our family. Deep down my father didn't care about the affair. He turned his back on me because I embarrassed him. His reputation was all that was important to him.

I never really understood him. Maybe he was just a sad, old man who blamed himself for what happened eighteen years ago. I ran down the staircase, my breaths coming in short, ragged pants. I felt claustrophobic, like I was trapped. My head was throbbing, because finally I understood what Andrew wanted all along—to push me away so Dad had no one left to support him. Dad's reputation was damaged and Andrew probably offered him support. Slimy bastard. I couldn't believe it.

What were the odds that I would move next door to Andrew's partner in crime, Adrian Lurkin? God, all of this was so messed up.

After taking control of my shaking body, I stepped outside, glad that Tobias came with me. Maybe I shouldn't have asked him to be there with me, but I felt a bit more secure knowing that he was close in the car.

"Ellie?"

I stopped in my tracks, hearing that voice, and slowly turned around. Andrew stood by the entrance, smoking a cigarette and looking straight at me. The dark clouds of my insecurity started gathering over my head, but I swallowed hard, telling myself that he was just a guy I slept with, and soon enough he would be rotting in prison.

Andrew looked even better than the last time I saw him, wearing a black fitted suit and his usual brilliant smile.

No wonder my father acted the way he did. Dad was probably expecting him.

"Hi, Andrew," I said, trying to act confident, like his presence didn't affect me. Part of me was slowly dying and the other part wanted to rip his face off. I had given him so much love and he just used me in the most manipulative and disgusting way.

"God, you look amazing. I have been trying to get in touch with you, but I think you must have changed your number," he said, approaching me and invading my personal space again. I glanced back at the road. I knew that Tobias could see me from there, and I was certain that he was aware that I was talking to my scum ex.

My heart threw itself against my ribcage, and all my remembered emotions of Andrew stormed right through me reminding me how miserable I was once I found out that I didn't mean anything to him. He lied to me, and now it turned out that he was a wanted drug smuggler, connected to my neighbour.

"You were obviously busy, Andrew. Besides, there is nothing that we need to talk about," I said, my rage keeping me immune to his usual charm. His eyes flickered with challenge, moving down my cleavage.

"We have plenty to talk about, darling. We had fun, but we both knew we couldn't carry on like that," he said, moving his finger over my face. "I was going through a lot at the time. You know, the divorce. Theresa has been a nightmare."

I just couldn't believe this guy. He was acting like nothing happened, like he had never promised to love and marry me, like he hadn't told everyone lies about me seducing him. Anger made me clench my fists so hard that my fingernails cut discs into my palms.

He was perfect—the clothes, body, and that tanned skin—but behind his facade he was simply a criminal who didn't care about anyone but himself.

"I don't have time for this, Andrew. Someone is waiting for me and I have to go. I came back because I needed to speak to my father about something," I said, indicating that this conversation was over and I was ready to leave. Then he came closer and I found myself between him and the wall. I felt nauseous all of a sudden, aware that he still wanted me.

When I glanced towards my car I saw Tobias; he was already getting out of the car. I had to be careful. Tobias couldn't afford any sort of confrontation at this stage of the investigation. The scent of Andrew's cologne reminded me of my tears that last time I slept in the bed we'd shared—and of how hard I cried after finding out everything he said was a lie. My throat was so tight I felt like I was choking on my own misery.

"Ellie, you're sexy as fuck and you don't know how much I missed you," he growled and leaned over, kissing my neck. Fear shut down my defence mechanism. I could have easily slapped Andrew, but I had to play my cards right, behave like the old Ellie—so clueless and naïve—that was ready to do anything for him.

"Yeah, you were missing me so much that you had to get engaged to a six-foot-two blond supermodel," I snarled, being very close to losing it.

His eyes darkened, but his pathetic, cocky smile didn't disappear.

"What are you doing here, Ellie? We both know that your father doesn't want to see you." He replaced his smooth tone with the one that he used when his wife caught us in their bedroom.

"He doesn't want to see me because of you!" I spat back, knowing that I needed to choose my next words very carefully, as he still had no idea that I had discovered his little secret. "I will accept it for now, but if I were you I would watch out. You never know what's around the corner."

He chuckled, looking at me like he didn't believe that I just said that.

"Is that a threat?"

"No, a warning," I added, turned around, and walked away. That piece of shit thought that he was above the law, that no one could touch him; well, he was going to have the biggest wake-up call in the history of mankind. I was looking forward to his tragic end. When I approached Tobias at the car, his jaw was tight and his eyes focused on the space behind me. He was staring at Andrew with pure hatred in his eyes.

"You were just talking to your ex, Johnny Hodges," he stated. I nodded, knowing that something wasn't right. Tobias exhaled loudly and handed me the car keys. "Drive. Let's get out of here before I explode."

He opened the door and slid inside the car, and I stood in the middle of the pavement, confused. My head was spinning, but I realised that something was not right with him, as he stared vacantly at the road ahead.

"Are you all right, Tobias?" I asked, once we were driving away, fading into the upcoming traffic.

When he began to bang his fists into the dashboard, I realised that I shouldn't have asked this question.

"Tobias, tell me what's wrong. Please. You're scaring me," I kept asking when he finally stopped and sat there breathing heavily next to me.

"I can't take it that a piece of shit like him walks free and that he keeps getting richer. She's gone, Ellie. She's gone because of him."

I didn't get what he was talking about. Maybe he was angry that we had a relationship. Seeing him so emotionally vulnerable shocked me, but I was surprised that I was so calm about this whole thing that I handled it the way I did.

"Tobias, I don't understand. What are you talking about?"

"Charlotte, my ex-wife. She was brutally murdered during a raid that went terribly wrong," he said. I couldn't take the way he said this, with so much anger and fury, like he was breaking into small pieces.

"Breathe, Tobias, breathe," I soothed, knowing that this was the best way to handle whatever he was going through right now.

"She was raped. That scumbag wanted to make an example of her, so he told the guy that she was investigating to do that, to hurt her."

My heart stopped.

"Oh my God, Tobias, I'm so—"

"It was Hodges. He made the call; he told that bastard to make sure that she was almost dead by the time the special unit arrived."

Twenty-Eight

Tobias

My head felt like it was about to explode. I couldn't fucking catch my breath and my heart was beating faster, then slower, then faster again. My vision was blurring, making me dizzy. Ellie's palm on my back was comforting, but I told myself that I couldn't lose control, not now, not here. I didn't want to show any weakness. That scumbag was certain that he was above the law, that no one could discover his secret.

After several deep breaths, I leaned my head against the headrest and shut my eyes, bringing more oxygen into my lungs. The car wasn't moving anymore. Ellie had stopped on some random backstreet.

Charlotte was dead, but the waves of misery continued washing over me, taking away my control slowly day by day and night by night, never ending. I should have told Ellie that Charlotte was raped and murdered. I felt so weak functioning without her. It was supposed to be me, not her. I failed in protecting her and now God was punishing me for it.

"What do you mean that he gave him an order?" Ellie whispered. I looked into her beautiful eyes, expecting to see pity, but instead there was a concern and warmth. I didn't expect to fall apart like that tonight.

"One of the guys I worked with in Lurkin's business told me stuff about his past. It turned out that he grew up on a council estate. He heard a story from his cousin about this female police officer who got trapped in one of the bungalows along with a few drug dealers," I said, failing to keep my voice from becoming sharp, but I had to continue. She needed to understand everything. "I instantly knew who he was talking about, and when he mentioned Hodges giving the order, I could barely keep myself from losing it before the end of the shift."

Ellie swallowed hard, paling as if she just saw a ghost. Was she finally understanding that her ex was far worse than Lurkin? Worse than any other criminal that existed in this screwed-up world for what he told them to do to Charlotte.

"Andrew...but...oh my God, Tobias." She broke down in tears.

I inhaled sharply, arching my head backwards. I found it hard talking about it and I didn't want to discuss the hell I went through when I found out.

"I have studied the files, listened to the transcripts from the original interrogation. It was only a few weeks ago that I finally understood what happened that day."

"I'm so sorry. My father ran some checks on him. That was his wa—"

"Don't, Ellie, please. None of this was your fault. He created this new identity for himself and continued to work with Lurkin. I wish I had known sooner."

"You said...you said that she was raped?" she asked hesitantly. I had never broken down in front of someone like that before. Even when I was talking to my shrink, I could still hide my true emotions. Fuck, I didn't want anyone to feel sorry for me. Charlotte was gone, and I had moved on. At least that was what I'd been telling myself.

That fucked up dream that I had a couple of weeks ago ruined me. I felt like I was in a fog most of the time. Claire witnessed it. She was a good detective, but we were both needed on this case. I couldn't afford for my attention to be pulled away. I needed to end Lurkin and Hodges.

"The guy that did it tore her apart, raped her and beat her and tortured her so much that she couldn't have survived."

Ellie reached out for my palm and squeezed it. Her touch made me feel better, calmer, but she wasn't the answer for everything.

"Tobias, I…I don't know what to say. Did they lock up the guy that—"

"He escaped, but then his body was found a few days after the boost. There had been riots in that area and someone shot him." I cut her off remembering that moment like it was yesterday. I wanted to get out, find him and tear him apart. When the doctors had confirmed that she was dead, the pain just kept spreading and spreading, burning through me.

"Tobias, I'm sorry…I had no idea. I can't imagine what you went through."

"I'll remember that awful day forever. Do you remember when I said that I had been shot?"

"Yes."

"I lied. I was shot, but it wasn't during a burglary. We were out in the field, trying to capture the dealers on one of the estates in Glasgow. Claire wasn't involved at the time. I blamed her for what happened to Charlotte, so we hadn't been speaking at all. I got hit and went down pretty fast," I continued, knowing that she needed to see that I was a wreck, that our relationship couldn't have any future, that I was cowardly enough that I wished to be dead.

"What happened after that?"

"I was glad that God had finally given me the chance to leave this fucked up world. My life was in shambles and I was ready to give up."

She didn't respond, and I was waiting for the moment when she called me pathetic and told me to go to hell. The silence stretched for several seconds.

Then she said, "I lost my little sister in a fire, Tobias. I know that it can't compare to what happened to your wife, but I get why you wanted to end it all."

God, death had harvested people that we both loved. I moved my arm and wrapped it around her, wondering why I hadn't seen that she was damaged too.

"What's happened? Do you want to talk about it?"

"I can talk about it now, only because I have learnt to live with it. We were only around ten when it happened. My father just popped out to borrow something from the neighbour. The cat knocked over a candle in the living room…that's how it started. Before I knew it the flames were everywhere. I couldn't find my sister. The smoke was suffocating me and I was panicking, calling for her, but she wouldn't come. I looked upstairs, but the smoke was so thick—"

Ellie broke off and covered her face with her hands. I didn't realise that she had experienced something so terrible.

"It's okay, Angel. You don't need to say anymore."

"I was rescued by a stranger, while Kathy was still trapped inside. I shouted to him that he needed to rescue her too, but by the time we got outside it was too late. My father came screaming, asking me where Kathy was, and I couldn't answer. I didn't remember much from that night, but I knew that I let her die in that fire. That's when Dad changed, became distant and cold. He blamed me, he always blamed me that I didn't find her."

I clenched my fists and brought her closer, thinking about my own tragedy. I should have asked questions about her life sooner. This wasn't fair.

"It wasn't your fault. Your father was grieving. He couldn't blame anyone else, so he chose to blame you."

"Maybe, but it was a terrible tragedy. My father loved my sister very much. After that, he was never the same."

"I can relate to his pain, to that dark period in my life. Charlotte meant everything to me and then in one moment she was taken away from me. We all say things that we don't mean in anger. After I got shot, my father knew that I wasn't right. He asked the doctors to transfer me to the psychiatric ward."

"He did the right thing. You needed all the support that you could get at the time," she said, wiping away her tears. "I get it. I understand all the lies now and I'm not angry with you."

She saw through me and through my pain. God, I didn't deserve her, but I couldn't deny these feelings any longer. I fucking loved her. In that moment, it finally hit me that I didn't want to be without her.

"Let's go home. I fucking hate this city. It brings too many terrible memories," I said, getting cold feet. I didn't want to dwell on the past. "And I'm sorry about your sister. I'm sorry that you had to go through it. I need you to remember, it wasn't your fault."

Ellie knew now and it was up to her to decide if she wanted to pursue whatever was going on between us. I kept telling myself that it couldn't be love, that it must be desire. I was planning to prove to myself that it was just sex, later on, when we got back to the complex.

"Your ex, that son of a bitch, has not only hurt you, but he also hurt me. I'll find his connection to Lurkin and then I'll kill him."

"Tobias, please don't say that. He has to be brought to justice the right way," she said, shaking her head. "I understand that you're hurting, but you have suffered enough. A prison cell won't bring you peace."

I nodded, without saying anymore. Hodges didn't deserve prison, he deserved much worse than that. Ellie didn't need to know what I was planning. She was my perfect distraction from this terrible pain and as long I could devour her pussy I could forget about my painful hatred. This wasn't normal, and maybe I was losing my mind. I couldn't love her. I was toxic and she needed to know that—before I hurt her too.

Ellie

Over the past twenty-four hours, I figured out who Tobias Stanley really was, but now I was sitting with a completely different man. He had gone through hell, first losing his wife, then getting shot and now being so close to arresting the man that had caused so much suffering in his life.

Heavy silence ascended between us as he drove home. I could never have imagined what I was getting into that first night when I kissed him in my kitchen. I had guessed he was over thirty, and I knew that he was damaged, but I had no idea to what extent. It was a lot to take in and I felt like we had taken a few steps backwards, not forward.

He was still suffering deep inside, and it explained why he wasn't ready to let me in. I had feelings for him; I couldn't deny it. It had been over two months since that night in my apartment, the night we had slept together for the first time.

I had been used by a man who was leading a double life, but he had been through so much more than I had realised. I was too scared to ask any questions about where this was going, about us. The sex was beyond amazing, mind- blowing, but I doubted that he wanted to take this further.

"Adrian is away until tomorrow," I finally said when we arrived outside our building. "Tomorrow is the last day for me to confirm that I'm bringing the cash to that scumbag who wants to sell me out to the papers."

Tobias sighed loudly. I hated that I had to get him involved. He had enough on his plate already.

"Don't worry. I'll be there. The guys from the team are waiting for the go ahead. We will get whoever is trying to mess with you."

"Thank you, for everything, for confiding in me about your wife."

Tobias looked at me then, lifted his hand and brushed his finger over my cheek, sending heat waves down through my core, stoking the fire that burned inside me only for him. I wanted and needed to feel him close to me.

"I couldn't keep lying. I hated that I couldn't tell you that Claire wasn't my wife," he admitted. "But now you know and I hope you realise that I never meant to hurt you."

"Tobias, Adrian wants to take me out on Wednesday night again," I said, knowing that I couldn't keep this away from him. I was part of this operation and we both knew there was no other choice. Tobias didn't say anything as we walked back to the complex, but I sensed that he wasn't happy about what I just said. He called up the lift, and we stepped inside it. I wondered if this whole thing was over between us.

"I don't like sharing, Angel," he whispered, leaning close to my ear. His warm breath caused a shiver to run through me and lust curled up my toes. I looked at him, trying to assess if he was angry or disappointed that I kept bringing Adrian back into the conversation.

"We have discussed this, Tobias. I can find the evidence, but that means that I have to get close to Adrian," I insisted, knowing that this could easily turn into another argument. We'd both had a tough day and I didn't want to play with his emotions.

Suddenly without warning the tension spiked between us, shifting the lingering anger, lifting the hair on the back of my neck. I didn't know if it was the elevator, or my way of saying to him that I still needed him, but the desire exploded between us, pushing the anguish and pain away.

Tobias moved fast, hitting the 'stop lift' button, and pinned me against the metal door.

"I'm going to show you in just a moment how dissatisfied I am with your behaviour, Angel," he said, tracing my ear with his lips. He clasped his hands around mine, pulling them behind my back. His harsh tone encouraged my need for him, making me wet in a heartbeat.

The change into being a sexual dominant again was instant and he wanted me to play the submissive. I didn't know how to deal with the desire that suddenly was fluttering through me like confetti. He was jealous, there was no doubt about that, but what was I supposed to do? I desperately needed that story and now I wanted to bring Andrew down, more than ever before.

"Do you want to fuck me here in the elevator?" I rasped, panting with a sudden dose of anticipation. My pussy was soaking wet, throbbing to be touched, my knees weak. There were so many things that I wanted to do to him, but as always, he was planning to take full control of my orgasm and I liked it.

Tobias spun me around, so I couldn't see what he was doing. He kicked my legs wide apart with his boot and ran his hand down my spine, lingering over my arse cheeks, and stopped between my thighs, cupping my sex.

"Angel, you can't even imagine what I'm planning to do to that sweet pussy of yours. Last time we were interrupted, but now we have all the time in the world," he added and pushed his hips against my backside grinding them into my heat. I whimpered, feeling his hard cock pressing against me.

He spun me around again and kissed me hard until I was out of breath, my lips swollen, demanding more and more.

"I'll show you right here that I'm the only man for you. It drives me crazy knowing that you will be touched by that arsehole, that he would dare to touch that sweet little pussy that belongs to me. That pussy is mine, Ellie. I make you come; I make you scream. Only I can lick it, stroke it, touch it, or fuck it," he said, gripping my arse and pulling me against him. The friction on my clit was delicious as he thrust against me with each word.

"Tobias, please, you know that—"

"Shut up. I'm the one talking now. Turn around, put your hands on the door above your head and spread your legs."

I swallowed hard and turned slowly, keeping eye contact until I had to break it to face forward doing exactly what he asked for. My mouth dried as I awaited his next command, my need increasing, and I was unable to squeeze my thighs for momentary relief. My heart was thumping loudly in my chest, my breathing laboured. There was something in his voice, that dominant tone that turned me on, making me so wet and needy.

We were in the lift, deliberately stopped. Surely someone in concierge must see that one of the lifts had stopped working. He couldn't fuck me here. We could get caught.

Tobias squeezed my arse, pressing himself against me. I needed him to ease the tension, the throbbing between my legs. Fuck, he was making this difficult for me. He knelt down and lifted my dress to my knees running his hands up my calves to do so, stopping at the top and licking the back of my knee. The unexpected tingle made me gasp and I felt my pussy squeeze, needing to be touched. Holding my dress above his face he lifted it slowly, tracing a path with his tongue, flicking my pebbled flesh until he reached the cusp of my arse. He stood and pulled the skirt of the dress to the front of my body and tucked it into the front opening making a knot, keeping my dress up and my lower body exposed. I felt him move away and I started to tremble in anticipation. I heard nothing behind me.

I wanted to turn so desperately, but I knew this game now. I counted to fifty-five before he spoke again

"So beautiful, baby. Your arse is stunning and I could stare at it all day long," he said. I heard the sound of his zipper and belt, and my temperature increased—he was going to fuck me in this lift.

Oh God, I ached for his beautiful cock to fill me, for his fingers to touch and tease me. A few moments passed and I heard his breath stutter and the unmistakable sound of him touching himself. I looked over my shoulder at him and saw his hand wrapped around his thickness, slowly stroking the shaft up and down spreading that glossy pre-cum over the length.

My breath caught in my throat and I moaned ever so slightly, "Tobias, please, let me do that."

He smirked at me before answering. "Angel, you can have this," he said indicating his dick, "if you don't let anyone have this." He thrust two fingers into my wetness. Christ, that felt good. He turned his wrist left and right to rotate his fingers without any thrusting motion. I rocked my hips back onto his thick fingers in complete ecstasy, fucking his hand. I could hear how wet I was, how much he affected me without even trying.

"You have to be quiet, Angel. You don't want to bring attention to us. Someone from concierge could bring this lift down at any moment," Tobias muttered.

I felt his sweet breath on my ear, and the sudden contact made me tremble. He removed his fingers and I whimpered loudly. When I looked over my shoulder again to see what was next, he offered me those fingers to taste. As his fingers touched my tongue, he kissed me around them so we both shared the taste. Removing his fingers from my mouth, he continued kissing me as he ripped the cups of my bra down, pushing my hardened nipples against the cold metal of the lift doors. He ripped his mouth away and pulled my hips back to him and kicked my feet further apart. He knelt between my thighs and bit the gusset of my knickers, pulling the soaked material away from me, and let go so the elastic of the lace snapped back and hit my clit eliciting a sharp gasp from me. He tucked his fingers under the material and pulled until it gave way completely.

I bit my lip when he positioned himself and blew a cold breath into my sex. God, he loved torturing me like this, but then again, I loved everything he did to me.

"You belong to me," he said, pinching my clit gently. "Say it, I want to hear you say it."

"Yes, Tobias, I'm yours, only yours," I kept saying.

"Good, because this time I'm not planning to hold back, not at all."

Twenty-Nine

Tobias

I slid my fingers over her magnificent heart-shaped arse. Her skin was soft and perfect. My heart hammered loudly, as the blood rushed through my veins pounding a beat in my eardrums. She belonged to me and I wasn't going to fucking share her, especially not with scum like Lurkin. I smelled her arousal and loved how wet she was for me, that she wanted me to touch her clit, to fill her up with my stiff cock.

"Oh, Tobias, please touch me," she purred. I didn't want to pleasure her, I wanted to punish her for thinking about that arsehole, but I didn't think that I could hold on any longer. I owned her pleasure, her sex, and tried to fight those unfamiliar emotions of love that rocked through me.

I bent down on my knees and breathed out over her clit. Her whole body shuddered and I smiled to myself. I stood up and pressed my body over to hers, kissing her neck, nibbling small bites on the back of her neck. I bet her cold nipples were aching against that hard metal door, eager to be teased by my mouth. Her skin smelled divine, like fresh rain in the summer mixed with her distinct vanilla perfume.

Fuck, what's gotten into me? I shouldn't be feeling like this, so euphoric and high on my desire. This was just sex and I couldn't let myself fall for her. She probably didn't even feel the same way, and I knew that I couldn't stay in Edinburgh.

"Keep your hands on the wall. I'm planning to fuck your wet pussy hard, but remember this is for me, not you." I moaned and then proceeded to drop my trousers.

My dick twitched in response. I was so hard that I had trouble keeping calm. This wasn't my first rodeo, but I had to keep taking steady breaths to calm myself. I needed to kill off the feelings that had been growing for her with each passionate moment between us. She was my healer, my calm in the storm, my safe haven, and even though it was the sex that brought us together, even when I wanted to lose control and fuck her, it was with love.

I grabbed my cock and started teasing her, rubbing it against her entrance, sliding up over her sensitive clit. I was ready to thrust myself inside her, but after a moment I went down on my knees, wanting to tease her for a bit longer. I had no idea when I would fuck her again, if ever, and I wanted to keep that memory for myself, to reflect on in the future.

I flicked my tongue over her wet pussy, and she cried out. This wasn't how this whole thing was supposed pan out. Her pleasure was mine and only mine.

"Angel, be quiet; otherwise, I will leave you here stranded."

"Tobias. I need to have you inside me."

"Your wish is my command," I growled, quickly tearing the condom and put it on, lifting myself up and thrusting my cock inside her. She felt unbelievable. I gripped her hips and started thrusting deep and hard, panting as I was just about to explode. I dug my nails into her hips, pounding into her hard, and she kept moaning.

"Oh, Tobias, this is—"

"Be quiet. Remember this when you think about fucking another man," I said, angry that she was still considering seducing Lurkin. She felt so good, and my cock responded in appreciation, fucking her faster. I leaned back and watched as my dick entered her, seeing us joined together as one. Her arse pushing back against me, that perfect untainted arse. I slapped it hard, hearing her beg me for more. I was riding her sweet pussy, making her feel things that other men would never give her. Sweat broke over the back of my neck, but I didn't stop until I was coming, arching my head backwards. She felt amazing hanging there, panting for me.

I wiped the sweat away and pulled out, after heat slammed through me, easing off the pressure that I had felt all day. I stood back and watched as she slumped forward, head down against the door.

"Good girl. Every time you think about someone other than me and get aroused, I will know, because I'm under your skin, baby," I told her, placing a kiss on her head and fixing her dress.

I restarted the elevator and we finally began to move. Ellie was leaning against the side of the lift, eyes closed and brows drawn; she was flushed, taking long pulls of air. This was a test and it looked like I didn't pass because I still wanted more from her than just fucking. I wanted to love her. I didn't have much time to think about that because, as soon as the door opened up, we were greeted by the porter from downstairs and Claire, who didn't look happy.

"Is everything all right, Mr. McCune?" he asked, looking from me to Ellie. Claire shook her head, hiding a smile. Yeah, yeah, she was intelligent enough to see that I was a needy bastard and I crashed the lift in order to fuck Ellie.

"Yes, I think it got stuck. I wouldn't bother calling an engineer. It was just a glitch, right, Miss Frasier?"

"Yes, it was a glitch."

She dropped her eyes, glanced at Claire and then headed out to her apartment, not looking back. I felt elated, but still angry that I couldn't control my feelings, that I couldn't control myself when it came to my Angel. The problem was—after all that, I still wanted her again.

Ellie

I sat in the car nervously waiting for the right moment to drop the bag of money into the bin on the corner of Church Street. This was the location that the blackmailer had asked for. He gave me very clear instructions: I had to drop the money at eight o'clock when the streets were abandoned and empty. I couldn't believe that I was prepared to give away five thousand pounds in order to silence someone.

Late last night I had another message with the details and I texted Tobias straight away. I was too embarrassed to knock on his door again, knowing that Claire was there. She had seen me all flustered right after Tobias and I had sex in the lift. She didn't need to say anything at the time. She knew what we were doing as soon as the door opened up.

I had no idea what Tobias wanted me to prove to him. He was so obsessive about Adrian. I had been squashing these feelings inside me, assuming that we were both using each other for sex because we were afraid to find out what would come next. I had committed to seeing Adrian again and dreaded how Tobias would react. Tobias's dead wife deserved to get justice. I was still coming to terms with what I now knew—Andrew was rotten to the core and I couldn't believe that I hadn't seen it.

I glanced at the clock realising that it was a minute after five.

My father hadn't called me back. I felt a little sad, because I honestly thought that I made some progress—that he finally was going to take me seriously. Growing up I had never paid attention to money, but since I started living alone I learnt to save. Bills were slowly getting on top of me and it was easy to keep spending what I didn't have.

The night was dark and cold, and the streets were empty. This was a rough part of the city. I wouldn't choose to come here on my own. Tobias assured me that this whole thing needed to be believable, and I had to follow the instructions. I took a deep breath, got out of the car and dropped the money into the trash. I didn't even look back when I was driving away. Tobias told me that I had to leave the money and get out of there as soon as I could.

Most people never cared about me; my friends weren't bothered when I moved away. It was obvious that money and status were more important than real friendship. I didn't make any new friends at work. Mimi was a bitch and Jordan, like the rest of the team, was stuck up in his own arse.

I drove back to the complex, thinking about the future. I swore to myself I'd never fall for anyone again and now I had been struck by Cupid harder than I realised. I didn't want to compare my feelings to the last time I was in love. The fact was I had to keep pretending that I was all right, making out with Adrian, but deep down all I could think of was Tobias and his endless sexual punishments, which I loved.

My phone started vibrating when I was pulling up outside the complex, and when I saw Adrian's face on the screen, my blood went cold. I needed to hurry this up, especially after finding out what happened with Tobias and his wife.

"Hey, beautiful, I've missed you. Please tell me that you're free tomorrow evening?" he asked, getting straight to the point. Claire had been trying to find out why he had to go to London the other day, but she wasn't getting anywhere, even with the bugs that had been installed in his car.

"I will be finishing at five as usual," I said.

I could hear people on the other side of the phone. He was probably at a party or in the depot.

"Sorry, hon, but I'm very busy. I just called to confirm everything for tomorrow. I'll pick you up at seven," he said and then hung up. My stomach made a funny jolt when I thought about telling Tobias about this. He was clear that he didn't want to share me with anyone, and especially not with Adrian.

I unlocked the door to my apartment and checked my house phone for messages. I didn't know why I kept doing this to myself. My father didn't care. Andrew must have told him that he saw me outside and he concluded that I was trying to discredit him because of what happened between us. I went there to give him a heads up in order to protect his business, his reputation, but he acted like he didn't believe me, that I was doing this because Andrew was now working with him.

That night, I went to bed early. I was up at five the following morning, wondering if Tobias was coming home at all. I needed to tell him that I was going to see Adrian, no matter what. He wanted me for himself, but I couldn't let him jeopardise this operation because of that. When I got to the office, I kept busy finishing all the articles from Phil and making slow progress on my own story. As soon as my day was over I drove home. Tobias liked working out in the afternoon and this was my chance to let Claire know that I was seeing Adrian tonight. It was a low blow, but I knew how he was going to react. I didn't need any drama right now.

"Hey, are you all right? Tobias has just popped out. He needed to speak to Adrian about something."

"Adrian is going to pick me up in an hour," I said, getting straight to the point.

"Okay, good, but before you go, I have to show you some photographs," she said.

"Photos, what photos?" I asked in confusion.

"A few potential associates. People that he is getting into business with. I have created a portfolio. You need to keep your eyes and ears open. If you recognise anyone from my list, then try to get their name."

I nodded and Claire quickly disappeared into the other room, leaving me a little stunned. It looked like she was fine with me going out with Adrian again. It was a good thing that Tobias wasn't here. I knew that he was going to seriously freak out once he found out where I had gone.

I started looking around their apartment, thinking about this evening, when I noticed a headed letter on the big cupboard by the door.

I took a step forward and picked it up. It was addressed to Tobias and it looked like something important.

Tobias,

I have received your resignation, and I don't want to believe that you're ready for this kind of transition. You have been a value member of my team and have served the police force for a number of years. No one wants to see you wasting yourself in Ireland, doing something that we both know you will hate.

Maybe you need some time to think about what's next. You should go on annual leave and reconsider your decision, then see me, so we can discuss it.

Moving away won't resolve your problems, and you won't be happy working at a desk rather than being out in the field. You have been a great officer. I value your work and commitment and I don't want to let you go.

Think about this. For now I have arranged the transfer to Belfast to begin next month, but I hope you will change your mind before that.

Walker

I re-read the letter a few times, trying to digest the message. Tobias resigned and requested a transfer, away from Scotland, away from me? But why? No, no, no, this was impossible. He couldn't do that to me after what we both had been through. I'd fallen in love with him, even knowing that there could never be anything between us. There I was again hoping for a fairy tale, but this was real life.

I put the letter away, just in time, because Claire came back to the room. She started showing me the photos, but I couldn't focus. All I could think of was Tobias, and the fact that he was leaving. He never said that we had a shot, but he did say that he cared for me. This letter clearly stated that once the operation was over our romance was too.

I kept looking at the men on the pictures, trying to memorise their features, but they were all very similar, all Asians. I told Claire, that I would have my eyes open and after an hour I went back to my own apartment. I should have known that this was going to happen. Tobias was never serious about me. We both agreed that we would fuck and then forget about it. That was my intention from the very beginning, but I didn't expect that I would fall in love.

I guessed that I was screwed more than ever before, because I'd fallen for my one-night stand guy.

Thirty

Tobias

I had been waiting for Lurkin for over an hour. He wasn't at the apartment, so I popped out hoping to speak to him now. We were supposed to discuss the next shipment, but I bet that the bastard forgot about it. Lurkin hadn't spoken to me since the party, and I was hoping that he would bring Hodges at some point. I was restless, waiting around for other people, waiting for him to make a mistake.

"Do you think that he'll be here soon?" I asked Raj, who was sitting in front of the computer, looking focused.

"He didn't call. As far as I knew I was expecting him tonight."

"I really can't be hanging around in here. Tell him that I'll be in tomorrow if he shows up, all right?"

"Yes, no problem. Mr. Lurkin might be occupied with another shipment that is coming from Spain tonight."

I clenched my fists and swore loudly in my head. Lurkin hadn't said anything about this, and I was worried that he wasn't planning to involve me this time around. I was frustrated with how things had progressed since I started working here. I needed him to lead me to Hodges, but it looked like he had other plans. I stood at the door contemplating what to do next.

"Does Lurkin work with someone other than you? Don't get me wrong, mate. I know that he trusts you, but he must be working with other people, someone who takes care of all the dirty work."

Raj was a simple guy, and he liked doing everything by the book. I didn't think that he knew about the drugs and other businesses that Lurkin was involved in. He was loyal and that was the problem, but sometimes even the most loyal fanatics had their weaknesses.

"Mr. Hodges, he's Mr. Lurkin's partner, but he doesn't come in here." Raj waffled, speaking quietly, like he didn't want to be overheard.

"Then how do you know about him?"

"I speak to him often over the phone. He calls to check if everything is all right," Raj added. I was considering starting early one day. I needed some time alone in Lurkin's office to see if I could find any paperwork with Hodges's name on it.

"Maybe you can put in a good word for me, you know," I said. I needed to sound desperate. This way I would not only get an ally, but also his respect. Unfortunately, this question didn't go down too well.

"Mack, I'm not supposed to talk about Mr. Hodges at all. Mr. Lurkin deals with him direct. Maybe it's better if you go now. I'm still waiting for Marvin."

"All right, no worries, boss. It's your call," I said, picked up my stuff and left, thinking that Raj was just a pussy. I bet he was related to Lurkin, and he was here to make sure that everyone was doing what they were supposed to do. Hodges was careful, and this whole slow progress was suddenly fucking me off. I couldn't ask Ellie to get in contact with her ex. I had a hell of a job trying to keep her away from Lurkin.

Last night Ellie left the money in the trash and then drove off. My team was already tracking the white male who picked up the black bag a few minutes later, then headed for the subway. In about a day or two the boys in the IT would get the lead. Ellie asked for my help; she made the right call telling me about the voicemails and emails.

I thought about her when I left the depot a few minutes later. I knew that tonight was a complete waste of time. I needed to ask Claire to run a check on Raj, to see what his deal was. He was married, had two kids and liked his job. Maybe he was getting a share from the shipment, to keep his mouth shut. On the way back to the complex I stopped at the newsagent to pick up some drinks for tonight. I knew that Claire was going to be on my case about the evidence and connection between Lurkin and Hodges, but I was stuck, and for now she just needed to be patient.

My transfer to Belfast had been authorised. I needed this. I couldn't stay here after this operation was over. I'd fly back for the trial, but after that I'd stay in Belfast. I fucking hated the fact that I'd fallen for Ellie. I was too screwed up to even consider a relationship. That's why I was leaving. I didn't want to ruin her life. She deserved someone better than me.

Ellie was at home, and when the lift took me to my floor, I was ready to knock at her door. The burning fire in my stomach was there, demanding attention.

I didn't knock. I stood and looked at her door for a few moments, but I didn't knock. Eventually I opened the door to my and Claire's apartment and went inside. Claire wasn't in the living room, and after a moment I heard the shower going. I sat down on the sofa and opened a beer, hoping to have a quiet evening. I noticed some files on the table with photos, but I didn't bother looking through them. Claire liked keeping her stuff to herself.

I started changing the channels on the TV, looking for something interesting, but my mind kept drifting back to Ellie. I was making this difficult for myself, fucking her in the lift, drowning in her sweet scent. I was falling apart most of time, my mind full of memories and regrets, but when I was with her she gave me relief. She made me forget the monster in my chest burning for revenge. I forgot about the stress of the day or whatever else had been bothering me. I even told her about Charlotte and the connection to Lurkin and why I wanted to finally get him behind bars—or if the opportunity arose, six feet underground—and she didn't freak out.

"I thought that you would be out late," Claire said. She had a white robe on and her hair was damp.

"I waited for Lurkin, but he didn't show up. He blew me off, so I left."

"He didn't blow you off. He has a date with Ellie tonight. She came here an hour ago," she said. "I showed her a few photos with people that are associating with him. I'm hoping she will have something tonight."

I nearly choked on my beer when she said that and started coughing. Claire couldn't be fucking serious.

"What? She has gone out with him? I thought that she was supposed to run everything by us first?" I asked, feeling like someone just threw a bucket of cold water all over me.

Claire placed her hands on her hips and looked at me like I couldn't be serious.

"She did run this by me. You weren't here. Lurkin called her when she was at work. They are going out to the cinema or something."

"Fuck, Claire. I don't want her anywhere near him. We both know that this is too dangerous. Call her mobile and tell her that she has to come back."

"What? You can't be serious right now. She's already too deep to call this whole thing off. I get that this might be difficult for you to digest that she's with him, but we need any help we can get. Ellie is smart and she will be fine."

"This isn't about me, Claire," I insisted, asking myself why the hell I needed to leave just then. I could have stopped her.

"They left an hour ago, Tobias," Claire said, when I started to pace around the room, thinking about calling her.

"If something happens to her, I swear to God, I'll not forgive you this time."

Ellie

Adrian was on time. He picked me up outside at exactly seven o'clock. I let him pick the movie, boosting his ego. He paid for the tickets and refreshments and headed into the screening room. It didn't surprise me when he picked a back row.

Halfway through the film his hand started wandering over my thigh, and he began whispering what he was planning to do to me once we got back. I was gradually regretting that I told Claire I was all right with this. My recent encounter with Tobias was hard to forget. He ravaged me, and now I was cosying up to another man that could never mean anything to me. On the way to the cinema, Adrian tried his best to woo me, regaling me with the plans he had for us, telling me that he wanted to take me to Paris and Venice. At first I thought it was some patter that he used on his conquests, but slowly I began to realise that he was serious, or at least he was making out that he was interested in pursuing a relationship, not just sex.

When the film ended, I suggested that we have a few drinks in the nearby bar.

"Have you got any plans for Christmas?" he asked, placing a mojito in front of me.

"No, I don't, not at the moment anyway, why?"

"I have a few friends in Spain. One of them owns this beautiful villa on the coast. I was thinking that if you don't have any plans, we could go there together and get out of this gloomy weather, catch some sun. I bet you look amazing in a bikini."

There was something in his tone of voice that told me he didn't want me to say no. I kept wondering what the hell was wrong with him tonight. First he was talking about Paris, and now about Spain.

"I love Spain," I blurted out, sounding pathetic, but judging from his smile, my answer satisfied him. He leaned over and started kissing my neck, moving his fingers down towards the edge of my thigh. Panic seized me, but I didn't move. I was supposed to be into him. Tobias wasn't here, but I remembered what he told me when we were together in the elevator.

Adrian ran his tongue over my lips and then he kissed me. It was obvious that he wanted to sleep with me tonight, but I didn't think that I could go through with it. This whole thing was moving too quickly, but I was afraid to do something that might raise suspicion.

"Good, because I'm planning to take you there soon," he whispered, then leaned back and took a sip of his drink.

"What does your friend do, you know, the one that owns the villa?" I asked, trying to switch the subject to a more serious one, but Adrian didn't take the hint.

"He's a businessman like me," he said, and brushed his lips over mine. "Ellie, I can't fucking take this anymore. I want you. I haven't been able to stop thinking about you since that evening on the boat."

Adrian was sober, he had barely touched his drink, and I was stunned that he could be so direct. Immediately my thoughts started to race and panic began to set in. I didn't know what to say.

"We barely know each other," I finally said, drinking some more of the cocktail. I misjudged him. He did just want to fuck me; that was what this whole thing was about, this grand seduction. This whole talk about Paris and Spain was to encourage me to give in to his charm.

"I respect you so much, Ellie. You're intelligent and funny. We have a real connection and I think we should fuck," Adrian said, smiling.

I wanted to ask him if that line had worked for all the other women that he had been out with, but I bit my tongue. I was hoping that he would take me back to the club, so I could meet some of his associates, but that was looking more and more unlikely. From the very beginning this whole thing was about sex.

"I'm not that easy, darling," I said.

"Of course, of course. I didn't say you were." He backed down. Then his phone started buzzing and I exhaled sharply, thinking that maybe this conversation was finally over. Adrian looked at the screen and instantly rejected the call.

"Maybe you should take it," I told him when the phone started going off again. His eyes darkened. He looked at the screen again and shook his head, switching the phone off.

"I hate being interrupted. This can wait. I'm sure it's nothing important." He chuckled and tucked a stray lock of my hair behind my ear. "Come on, drink up. I'll order one more round for us."

"If I didn't know you, I'd think that you were trying to get me drunk, Mr. Lurkin," I giggled, finishing my mojito.

"That's not my style," he muttered and asked me to choose another cocktail. I went for Long Island Ice Tea, knowing that I was already a little tipsy. We talked about my work in the paper, about the fact that my boss was a pig, and about Adrian's extended family. After an hour I went to the ladies' room, and when I was done with my business, Adrian was waiting for me outside the bathroom.

"We're leaving," he said, not saying anything else. He handed me my coat and started heading towards the exit. He didn't give me a chance to ask him why he was in such a hurry.

"Adrian, are you okay? I thought we were having fun," I said, when we reached the car. I didn't understand what was going on. One minute he was perfectly fine, and the next he was storming out of the pub.

"I'm fine, Ellie, just tired. Can't wait to get home and take you to my bed," he said in that seductive tone of voice. I felt so warm, goose pimples shot down my arms and my heartbeat was speeding erratically. I'd had way too much to drink and Adrian wasn't going to let me go home alone. He wanted to sleep with me, and I kept wondering if Tobias was at home. I couldn't do this to him, but Claire was counting on me. I was so screwed.

I didn't remember much from the drive home. Adrian was talking to me about his business. I had no idea what was in that cocktail, but I felt so drained and sleepy. I must have dozed off for a bit, because when I opened my eyes, he was kissing me.

"Oh, Ellie, you're so sexy," he purred, sliding his hand under my top. My head was buzzing in warning. He must have slipped something into my drink, because I had never felt so relaxed, my muscles so heavy.

"No Adrian, this is—"

"Shh, I want to touch you. Please let me," he kept saying, planting kisses on my breasts, rubbing his thumb over my clit. He was rough and I was ready to break. The world around me was spinning and I had no idea if this was happening for real or some horrible nightmare. When his fingers started caressing my sex, alarm bells started going off in my head. I couldn't let him fuck me in the car, but it looked like that was his intension.

"Adrian …wait. No, I don't want to do this."

"Of course you do. We're going to fuck, hard. This won't be quick, but trust me, you will enjoy it," he growled. I wanted to push him away, but my limbs felt so weak, like they weighed a ton. Then someone opened the door from the passenger side, and I launched backwards. Strong hands caught me, before I hit the ground. I nearly screamed when I saw Tobias staring at me with pure fury in his eyes.

Thirty-One

Tobias

I gave the bastard five seconds to stop touching my Angel and then I opened the passenger door, wrapped my arms around hers, and pulled her away from him. I spotted them in the car a minute ago, when I was walking towards the car park, hoping to drive around the city for a bit. For a moment I stood in front of their car, paralysed from head to toe. Anger began rolling through me in violent waves, my vision blurring with fury. I tried to stay away, watching them, but it was torture. I didn't want him to touch her, and he was doing more than that.

I had been trying to get through to Lurkin in the past hour, to let him know that his secret shipment had been boosted by the police. He didn't tell me that he had another truck coming from Spain, so I decided to turn this around in my favour. I called the base, filling them in with all the details. I needed an excuse to see if Lurkin was going to react, and if he was just about to lose his cool tonight. This whole thing was supposed to look like a random check-up, one that Lurkin didn't expect at all. I was fuming that Ellie went out with him, and I was pissed off with Claire that she let her go before running this by me.

"I'm sorry, Adrian, I didn't mean to intrude, but we have to talk. This is urgent," I said, more abruptly than I should have. He scrambled out of the car and stormed towards me. Ellie was giggling, still in the same position. Fuck, what was wrong with her? Was she drunk?

"I was in the middle of something. Are you out of your fucking mind?" he shouted. He looked livid; I could see the anger slipping through his normally cool facade. I remembered that expression from that day when he was strangling the topless hostess at the party. I needed to choose my next few words wisely, because I didn't want to fight with him, especially not in front of Ellie.

"I tried to call, several times, and when I saw your car I thought—"

He didn't even let me fucking finish; he was on me, slamming his chest into mine and grabbing me by the collar. At that point I already released Ellie so she didn't get hurt, but I wasn't fucking prepared for this sudden outburst of violence. He pushed me onto the back fender of the car, crushing my back against the solid metal body of the vehicle. I hissed with an unexpected sudden dose of pain.

"I don't answer to you, arsehole. You interrupted my fucking date," he roared, banging my head against the car. It took me several seconds to gather my strength and push him away, slamming my fists into his jaw. It looked like that was unavoidable, but it felt damn good.

"It's about the fucking shipment; someone highjacked your stock. Fuck your date, Lurkin!"

That finally got his full attention and he looked at me, staggered. Then he spit blood on the pavement, breathing like he was going through an asthma attack. Hell, my head was banging and Ellie was looking terrified with her jaw wide open. I was so glad that she was all right, that he didn't hurt her.

"What's going on? Why are you guys fighting?" she asked.

Adrian dragged his hand through his hair, looking at me like he was ready to throw another punch. He was either high or drunk, and he drove his car in this state while the fucker was with Ellie. I wanted to strangle him.

"It's all good, Ellie. Don't worry about it. We just need a minute alone, if you don't mind," I told her, ready to drag her back to her apartment, but I had to keep myself in line. He pushed me to the side, glancing at her.

"What the fuck are you talking about, Mack?"

"The truck from Spain. They were doing some spot checks on M5. They arrested one of the boys. I'm sorry about —"

"Fuck!" Lurkin shouted, searching through his pockets, probably looking for his phone. "This transport was important. Someone must have known about this."

"You didn't mention another shipment this week."

"I didn't think that I had to tell you about every single thing that is going on with my business, Mack," he growled, holding his bleeding nose. He needed a black eye in addition for his arrogance. "Ellie, I have to go. Something came up. I promise that I'll make it up to you next time."

I clenched my fists, as she was staring at both of us, looking uncertain. This was going to be the last time he touched her. I needed to make sure of that, because this operation was going to end tonight.

"Is everything all right?" she asked, picking her bag up and approaching both of us. I bet she was tipsy, letting him manipulate her into this. Fuck, I wanted to spank her arse until she couldn't sit down for a week.

"It's just something that I have to take care of at work," Lurkin said. "We will catch up next time. Now I really need to go."

Ellie looked at me like she wanted to say something more, but I shook my head, telling her to keep her nose out of this for now. She nodded, and Lurkin asked me to get into his car. Clearly he wasn't happy that I had found out about the shipment. We drove in silence for a good while until Lurkin cleared his throat.

"Listen, I was out of line back there," I said, remembering how good it felt smashing my fists into his jaw.

"Don't worry about it. I'm glad that you didn't wait around. There was two million pounds worth of coke in there."

"Who else knew about this?"

"Just a few people. I kept it low because I wanted to take care of it myself. This is going to hit me pretty hard, you know that, don't you?"

"I bet. I was waiting for you in the office. Raj mentioned the shipment and then Marvin showed up telling him about the truck being stopped by the police."

I was making this shit up as I went along. No one knew that the truck got pulled, but at this point I didn't care. Lurkin needed to know that he couldn't fuck with me. It had to come to this because he was claiming Ellie, and I couldn't just stand there and wait until he'd hurt her.

Lurkin asked me to put the phone on speaker and then asked me to find a contact listed as Johnny. He picked up after the second ring.

"Yes, Jason?" asked the voice on the other side of the phone.

"We have a problem. Police hijacked the truck with its contents. Someone must have talked. We lost everything," Adrian said. He was normally cool and collected, but I had never seen him so fucked off. I wondered if he had forgotten that I was sitting next to him.

"How much?"

"Two million."

"Christ, Jason, I counted on that money. The Russians will be furious," Hodges said. I heard the panic in his voice. This new development was starting to get interesting.

"I just got the message; I don't know how this happened. I'm heading over to my source to see if I can find out more," Lurkin said.

"Find whoever has been talking. If we've got a rat, get rid of the problem. We can't afford any prying into our business affairs. I also told you not to call me on this number."

"I had no fucking choice, mate. This was an emergency. We need to meet."

"Fine, whatever, I'll let you know. I can't believe that you messed this shit up," Hodges snarled and then hung up.

Lurkin cursed loudly, gripping the steering wheel tighter. I fucking knew that he would eventually have to get in touch with him. Now finally I had heard it myself, but this was just the beginning. Before this was over Lurkin was going to lead me to Johnny Hodges.

Ellie

"Tobias just dragged Adrian out of the car while we were making out in the car park," I said, storming into McCune's apartment several minutes later. I felt like shit. First I was woozy from the cocktails I had drunk earlier on. Then Tobias nearly gave me a heart attack when he punched Adrian outside, spiking my adrenaline. Now it was wearing off and my head was pounding.

"He did what?" Claire asked, dropping her jaw, putting her laptop aside. I started telling her about what happened outside on the car park. It was obvious that Tobias was jealous. He couldn't deal with the fact that I had gone out with Adrian after promising that I would reconsider seeing him again. This wasn't good, and he shouldn't have punched him. Claire did not look happy when I finished telling her what had happened. She was on her mobile, pacing around the room.

"Listen, Ellie, I need to leave, see if I can speak to the base about this. Tobias shouldn't have done that. He's crossed the line this time."

"What? I don't think you should do that. They were talking about some missing shipment. Adrian looked furious."

"Shipment? I thought that nothing was arriving this week?"

"I don't know, Claire. They were talking about it until they left. I don't know anything else."

Claire shook her head, looking on edge. I'd promised myself that nothing would be more important than this story, but now I began to think that I hadn't gotten my priorities in order. Tobias was risking his life because he was determined to catch my ex.

"Look, Tobias seemed to know what he was doing. Maybe we should wait for him here until he comes back?" I said.

"You're sweet, Ellie, but we both know that this investigation has turned into a damn circus. I want this whole thing to be over as much as he does. I'm married Ellie. I've a husband that I haven't seen for two months. He hates the fact that he has to wait for my phone call and that I have been unreachable for so long. We are close to resolving this case, but we're missing some very important pieces that connect Lurkin to Hodges."

"I saw the transfer letter earlier on. Once this whole thing is over, Tobias wants out. He seems convinced it's the right thing for him."

I didn't want to share with her that I read his private correspondence, but the whole stress of the situation was heightening my emotions, making me very sad. I thought I loved him and maybe that could be enough, but love was worthless, after all, and that childish dream was over. There was no point thinking about a future with Tobias, hell, any future with any man. He had ruined me.

"Ellie, I'm going to tell you something that I thought I would never say again. Tobias loves you. He loved Charlotte, his wife, but that was five years ago. Every time he's with you, he's changes, seems in high spirit. Trust me it's because of you."

I wanted to laugh. She couldn't be serious. Tobias asked to be transferred out to Belfast, and that was the end of the story.

Claire had no idea what she was talking about. He couldn't have any feelings for me.

"I don't believe it was love, Claire. It was just sex, very hot and kinky sex, that's all."

"Whatever. I thought you wouldn't want to believe me. You forget, I have known him for years. He's crazy about you and you're blind if you can't see it," she said, shrugging her shoulders. "I have to go. I'll see you later."

I told her that I would lock up the apartment for her. After I went back to my own place, I slumped on the sofa emotionally exhausted. I started wondering what was wrong with me. My life had been spinning out of control for so long I was dizzy with it all. I couldn't seem to see a straight path to my future anymore. I was in a mess. I'd made awful choices and had reaped the consequences because I got involved with the wrong guy. On top of that I had fallen in love with a man who didn't want me, which hurt more than I could say.

One thing was clear—Claire and Tobias needed to link Lurkin to my ex. I knew that I could get them what they wanted. A couple of months ago I was going through some papers in my father's office and discovered that Andrew owned a bachelor pad so he had somewhere to take his women. I couldn't believe that I didn't think about this before.

The apartment was in his father's name, but the deed was in his. Claire needed something for the court to prove that Johnny Hodges was the same person as Andrew Hamilton. This was it. This was what they were looking for. I finally got my 'eureka' moment.

I'd gotten to know Andrew quite well over the past year and I knew that he kept that apartment secret for a reason. There was probably something incriminating there that could help Tobias and Claire with their investigation. I knew that they had enough evidence to send Adrian straight to prison, but that would have been too easy. Tobias had a personal vendetta against Andrew and he didn't want to fail to arrest him because of lack of evidence after everything that happened to his wife.

I felt sick when I thought about it. Andrew had fooled not only me but also my father, and now he was fooling another woman. I needed to find something, anything that could bring him down and expose his crimes.

I made a quick coffee, hoping this would wake me up a little and allow me to think more clearly. It was the strongest espresso that I ever drank, but after an hour I felt more like myself. Drinking on an empty stomach wasn't such a good idea after all. I put on my old jeans and jumper. Half an hour later, I was walking towards the car park, thinking about my conflicted emotions and everything that had happened over the last two months.

Claire's words were burning in my head. I felt sad that Tobias was so shut down, that he was only interested in sex. Claire may have known him a long time, but she was wrong about Tobias this time. Tobias didn't love me; he was just doing his job. I was probably being incredibly foolish, but I wanted to do this for him. Once he had all the evidence he needed, he'd have his closure and he could leave. It was better to rip the plaster off in one go, the sooner he went, the sooner I could start to heal.

The drive to Glasgow didn't take long. There was barely any traffic on the road and it took me another twenty minutes to arrive at my destination. The building was old, Victorian with these huge windows. I got out of the car and looked around for a little bit. I needed a key; there was an intercom. I didn't want to risk buzzing some random apartment. I knew people in a posh place like this would be more vigilant.

After waiting in the car for another hour, I saw someone walking towards the entrance. I leapt out of the car and hurried to the door, pretending I was searching in my bag for a key. As I approached the door, the man was almost behind me, and I sighed and tutted my annoyance. The man chuckled and unlocked the door himself; I took that opportunity to sneak inside. The guy even held the door for me.

Pumped with excitement, I started searching for apartment twenty-eight. Andrew had fiercely guarded this place for years. His ex-wife had no idea that he owned it.

When I reached the bottom end of the corridor, where his apartment was, I noticed that the door wasn't quite shut properly. The latch hadn't been engaged. My heart skipped a beat. Someone was already inside and hadn't shut the door completely, or maybe Andrew's apartment was being burgled. I had two possibilities: I could either walk away or get in there and find out. Neither of these options was appealing. The only person that knew about this place was Andrew, and this was my chance. I had to get inside and confront him. I knew that he wouldn't hurt me. He was a coward and I was valuable to him. He needed my father's protection.

I took a few deep breaths feeling brave. I stood outside for a minute listening in, but whoever was inside was very quiet. My heart exploded when I thought about how stupid this whole thing was. I was intentionally putting myself in danger, but this way I could give Tobias and Claire the missing piece that they both needed to end this whole thing forever.

I made a split second decision and I sneaked inside. All the lights were on, but the apartment seemed empty. The whole place had been ransacked. It was a scene of utter destruction.

Cutlery was scattered, plates lay smashed on the floor; most of the furniture had been moved or turned upside down. It appeared to me that someone was looking for something specific in here.

"Ellie, is that you?"

I turned around abruptly, recognising the voice. I thought that I had scored some luck, but then the man came out of the shadows. I realised that it wasn't Andrew, but Adrian, and he knew about the apartment too.

Thirty-Two

Tobias

I was officially going crazy. It'd been twenty-four hours since I last saw Ellie. She vanished from her apartment last night, without a word. Her phone was off and my gut was telling me that something was very, very wrong.

Last night was a haze. I remembered driving around the city for some time, while Lurkin was on the phone to other people. After what seemed hours, he parked the car on a street unknown to me and got out to make another phone call, this time in private. The battery on my phone was dead, so I couldn't tell Claire what had gone on earlier.

"I need to drive somewhere, and I need to do this alone," he said when he came back. At first I thought that he was taking the piss, but when he threw me out of the car and drove off, it wasn't fucking funny.

Lurkin never behaved so irrationally and I knew that he was shitting himself about the shipment. He'd just lost two million pounds, and I had a feeling that most of this money didn't even belong to him.

It was just after eleven when I got back in the complex. Ellie's car wasn't parked in her usual spot, and that instantly concerned me.

"She must have gone to Glasgow to see her father," Claire said, looking like she wasn't bothered. For fuck's sake, she wasn't grasping the gravity of the situation. Ellie was missing. Lurkin hadn't come back to the Grange either, so something must have gone on between the two of them. Ellie wasn't impulsive, and she knew that I would worry. I didn't get why she hadn't left me a message or a note to say where she was. She was reckless, but not foolish.

"I don't know, Claire. I don't fucking like this. She took off in the middle of the night without a reason," I said, checking my phone again. I didn't sleep at all that night, listening and hoping that she'd gone out socially rather than being in danger.

"I don't know what to say, Tobias," Claire said, glancing at the clock. It was midday, early afternoon, and so far we had footage from CCTV that showed Ellie driving away half an hour after Claire left.

"Something must have happened to her," I insisted, slamming my fists on the table. I had to fucking find her. I was terrified at the prospect that she was with Lurkin.

"Tobias, we can't leave the case right now. Lurkin is with Hodges. We should pursue this to see if we can get them together. This is our chance. This case will finally be closed." Claire practically begged.

I lowered my head, trying to organise my thoughts about what the best course of action would be. Claire was right. I had no idea if Lurkin would crumble under pressure, once he realised that his most recent shipment really was boosted. Hodges had mentioned Russians, and that could mean only one thing—he and Lurkin must be absolutely shitting themselves. If the Russian Mafia had a presence in Edinburgh and they had gotten involved, then this whole operation just got international. No one liked messing with Mafia, especially in the UK.

I was going crazy stuck inside this flat, waiting, hoping that Ellie was all right. I couldn't imagine losing someone this special to me—not again. I fucking loved her, and I had to stop lying to myself, my foolish pride resisting my feelings for her.

Claire reported everything that had happened over the past twenty-four hours and now, because of her need to follow the rules, we were stuck in the apartment.

"This is absurd. I can't sit waiting around like this," I finally said, standing up.

Claire shifted on the sofa and closed the laptop. "What do you want to do?"

"We need to drive to Glasgow, speak to her father."

"Maybe we should call him first?"

"No, I need to see him face-to-face. Something must have happened. She hasn't worked at the club in weeks, and that guy Nathan said he didn't see her last night. I'm so fucking worried, Claire."

"Maybe she was angry with you over this incident in the car park and she decided that enough was enough, Tobias," Claire suggested, and I laughed. She didn't fucking get it. Ellie wouldn't just take off. She might have been pissed off, but she wasn't stupid.

"No, Claire, she must have found out something; otherwise, she would have waited for us," I said. "I'm going and it's up to you if you want to join me."

"We have clear orders, Tobias."

Fuck, she didn't need to remind me. A surveillance team was on it, looking for her, tracking her phone, but so far we had nothing.

"I don't give a fuck about my job. You can stay if you want to, but I'm going to look for her."

Claire was quiet. I knew that I was putting her in an uncomfortable position. She always followed the rules and I didn't expect her to understand my urgency. I grabbed my jacket and headed out. My head was banging and I was completely stressed, worrying about my Angel. Claire caught up with me in the car park when I was just about to drive off.

"We're in this together," she muttered, as she slid into the passenger seat next to me.

"This might cost you the promotion."

"I don't care. I'm worried about her too," she said, folding her arms over her chest. "For fuck's sake, Tobias, just admit that you're in love with her. I know that the first few years have been hard, but this is different. She means a lot to you."

I pulled a breath into my lungs, not looking at her. Silence stretched for a minute or so. Ellie was perfect for me and I didn't understand why I hadn't told her about my feelings earlier. I didn't want to believe that her life was in danger.

"Yes, I love her," I admitted. "Are you going to shut up now?"

I noticed that she was trying to hide a smile. Claire was a decent human being. It wasn't her fault that I was an asshole.

"We will find her. Get your head in the right space. You can't stress over it," she told me.

I hoped she was right, because my agitation grew as we got closer to Glasgow. Dark, terrifying thoughts were floating in my head. I was wondering if it was my fault that she was in danger. I should have protected her better. We were stuck in traffic as we got into the city, but half an hour later we arrived outside the building where her father worked. Claire wasn't too happy when I nearly hit the security guard downstairs. The fucker didn't want to let me in, so I shut him up with the badge.

"We shouldn't be exposing ourselves like that, Tobias," Claire reminded me.

"This was necessary," I said, as the lift took us up to the twelfth floor.

"What are we going to tell her father? We need to discuss this now," Claire continued. "He works with Hodges. You can't just barge into his office and lay in the whole truth, jeopardising months and months of work."

I cursed loudly, knowing that she was right. "What are you suggesting then?"

"Let me talk. I'll make the call on how much to reveal if this gets awkward."

"Either way, I know that he won't believe us. I was here with Ellie a week ago when she went to talk to him," I said. "I was downstairs in the car. Their conversation didn't go too well then."

Claire didn't say anything, but I knew that she was thinking about what I said. Jonathan Grant was a tough motherfucker and he was a barrister who would hide behind the law. He wouldn't take any bullshit from us. We had to give him something.

We both stepped out of the lift, heading towards reception. It was an old fashioned setup with a wide desk, wooden floors and chesterfield sofas.

"Can I help you?" asked the receptionist, smiling.

"We need to see Jonathan Grant," Claire said.

"Mr. Grant is having a meeting and I—"

She was interrupted by a door opening from the room to our right. Terror filled my stomach and blood rushed to my ears when I noticed the man that stood at the entrance.

Time stopped. I was staring at the piece of shit who was responsible for my wife's death. The man that I had been hunting since I arrived in Edinburgh.

Johnny fucking Hodges.

"Cath, is everything okay?" he asked the receptionist, looking directly at me. I was rooted to the spot, as fury rippled through me. I was ready to beat the shit out of him, in front of everyone. This was the moment I had been waiting for since I learned that he was responsible for my misery.

"Tobias, come on, let's go." Claire nudged me, and I looked at her like someone had just stabbed me. For a moment we both stared at each other, like there was no one around. It was like time fucking stopped. In that brief moment I was imagining that I had a knife in my hands, and I was cutting him to pieces, enjoying each time the knife sliced into his skin. Even that kind of death sounded too good. He needed to suffer like my wife had.

"Mr. Grant?" Claire said, stepping in front of me. It took me a second to realise that Ellie's father stood behind Hodges, eyeing me with interest.

"Yes," he replied, darting his eyes at Claire.

"We need to speak with you urgently. Tobias?" she said, kicking me in my calf.

"Yes, yes, we do, the sooner the better," I stuttered, forcing myself to stay calm. Jonathan Grant nodded to Claire and told us to come in. Hodges stepped away and then left. Never in my life had I been so torn between what I should do. I wanted to drag him back to the room and make him talk. When Claire shut the door and I finally snapped back to reality, my heart hammered in my chest. I was a wreck, but I told myself that this was about Ellie, not me.

"What can I do for you, Miss…"

"My name is Stanley," I introduced myself, stepping in front of Claire. "We are looking for your daughter, Mr. Grant. Have you see her today?"

I couldn't read anything from Grant's expression, but Claire sighed deeply. Yeah, yeah. We agreed that she would talk, but I couldn't fucking take this anymore. I needed to know where Ellie was.

Grant lifted his left eyebrow, but didn't reply straight away. Looking into his face, I could see features that reminded me of Ellie, although her eyes were much more striking.

"I'm sorry, but I think you need to explain who you are first. You barged in here without an appointment, asking me about my daughter?"

"She has been missing since yesterday," I growled, knowing that this was going to be difficult unless I told him everything. I hated that Claire was right, again.

"Missing? I don't think so, Mr. Stanley. As far as I know she stays in Edinburgh."

"All right, let's get this straight. I know that you don't give a flying fuck about her, but she disappeared from her apartment yesterday evening. We can't trace her phone. I need to know if she has been here at all."

"Tobias!" Claire said, raising her voice.

"You obviously know more than I, Mr. Stanley. I haven't seen my daughter since we spoke about a week ago and I don't believe that I'm particularly interested in what kind of trouble she got herself into this time," he said dismissively

I wanted to fuck him up, but I restrained myself. This guy was a piece of shit. He was protecting Hodges and didn't give a fuck about his own daughter.

"She's in danger, Mr. Grant."

"Please, calm down, Mr. Stanley, and please start from the beginning. I would be happy to tell you what I know, but you need to tell me first—what is this about?"

Claire laughed, took something from her jacket and slammed it on the table.

"Detective Claire Reynolds," Grant read. "I'm still confused, Ms. Reynolds. Why would law enforcement need to speak to my daughter?"

I had enough of this bullshit and this guy wasn't planning to play ball.

"For fuck's sake! We have been working undercover for the past three months, trying to build—"

I went on and on, telling him about our investigation. I told him about meeting Ellie at the party, about her work as a reporter, and Adrian Lurkin. I made sure that I never mentioned Hodges. He might have still been in the building and I didn't want to push my luck. Jonathan Grant appeared to finally become interested in what I had to say. At some point he stood up and started walking around his office. Then, I was done, and I was ready to explode. Claire didn't look happy and Grant was still silent.

"Mr. Grant, have you seen your daughter at all?"

"No, Mr. Stanley. I haven't seen her since the day she was here," Grant said softly. I exhaled sharply, feeling like rocks dropped down into my stomach. If Ellie wasn't with her father, then she was probably with Lurkin. His phone was off too and that wasn't good. He must have found out what she had been working on. "But I can help you find her."

"What do you mean?" Claire asked.

Grant smiled and sat back in his chair.

"My daughter and I had our differences, but I wouldn't let her leave without knowing if she was all right," he explained. "There is a tracker on her car. I believe that if we find the car, we should be able to find her too."

Ellie

I heard the squeaking noise somewhere near me, and my stomach dropped. I blinked rapidly, dragging sharp breaths into my lungs, trying to deal with the situation I found myself in. A sharp, stabbing pain shot through me, consuming me and making me lose my senses. My whole face throbbed in a regular beat with my pulse. I lifted my hand, tracing my fingers over the wounds on my cheeks, over the crusty dried blood. My eyes were bruised and swollen. My left one was closed completely. I couldn't imagine the horror show my refection would be in the mirror. As I began to shift, some of the barely closed wounds opened up. I had been locked up in here since Adrian found out that I wasn't interested in him romantically.

I thought back to the moment when I stood in Andrew's apartment, frozen, paralysed with fear and the realisation that I had made a mistake by going there.

"What the fuck are you doing here, Ellie?" he said, dropping the paperwork in his hands on the floor. I opened my mouth, but no sound came out. Adrian was still wearing the same clothes from when I left him in the car park. Gleaming sweat covered his forehead. I assumed that he was the one responsible for the mess in the apartment.

I wasn't planning to stay there and try to explain myself. No, that sounded like a very bad idea, so instead I turned around and ran for the door. I didn't get very far. Adrian caught me by the threshold, tackling me by my legs and throwing me straight down. I hit the floor hard, bruising my knee and smashing my forehead on the tiles. I had nowhere to run. I thought my life was over.

He dragged me back into the apartment and slammed the door behind him. There was an expression of utter madness on his face. His eyes were wild and unrecognisable.

"Fucking answer me! Have you followed me here?" he shouted.

"I used to date Andrew Hamilton," I mumbled.

"You used to fuck Andrew Hamilton?" he roared, grabbing me by my hair and yanking upwards, pulling my body taut so that I couldn't escape. My mind raced, trying to think of what I had to say in order to sound believable. "Tell me, what else do you know?"

"I don't know anything. I wanted to check out this place; I thought that he would be—"

I didn't finish my sentence, because he punched me right in my gut and I lost my breath for several seconds.

"Don't lie to me, bitch. It's the middle of the night. You came here for a reason."

The squawking and squealing sound near my head pulled me back to the present moment. Last night, I thought that I was going to die. Adrian wasn't satisfied with my answers. He kept punching me until I collapsed, leaving a fistful of my hair in his hand. Once I was curled up on the floor he began kicking me, slapping me, and then he tried repeatedly to suffocate me until I almost passed out, each time demanding answers, until I was forced to reveal to him that my surname wasn't Frasier, that it was Grant.

I didn't know why he didn't leave me to die in that apartment. Surely that would have been easier. He enjoyed inflicting pain, kicking me, slapping me, screaming names at me whilst smothering my face, trying to crush my spirit. I wanted to live, and I couldn't take another ounce of pain, so I told him everything. I revealed that he had been watched since he moved in, that he was going to rot in prison forever.

He went crazy then, and I thought it couldn't have gotten any worse. I thought that he would end my life. He didn't. He carried on slapping and kicking me, until I was vomiting blood. Sometime later I must have passed out, because when I stirred back to reality, we were on the move in his car. He was on the phone talking to someone.

It was a long drive, and I was bleeding. The pain was unbearable. I was certain that he'd broken a couple of my ribs, because every time I took a breath it was pure agony. My heartbeat pounded in my ears and I could no longer feel my legs. Then we stopped and I heard him getting out of the car. I tried to fight when he yanked me out and dragged me away, but he just laughed. The last thing I remembered was him locking the door to this container I lay in. Then the darkness took me, giving me some peace.

Now I was awake. I had no idea how much time had passed, but at least I was alive. I took in a deep breath and flinched with every move. Every breath was painful. I couldn't move freely, but I didn't want to stay here. I cried out when I attempted to lift myself up. Several attempts and many tears later, I was sitting up panting short, hard breaths.

Then I heard the clang of metal at the door. Someone was outside, coming for me. After a long moment, the light blinded me and I heard that voice.

"Wakey, wakey, sleeping beauty. It's time for me to play with your sweet pussy."

It was Adrian and he came to finish what he started.

Thirty-Three

Ellie

I wanted to pretend that I was dead, that he already crushed my spirit with his earlier tortures. The pain poured through my heart, burning deep in my soul, as every breath, every move brought on agony.

Maybe I deserved this, because I told Adrian what was really going on. Tobias was only trying to regain justice and find peace after his wife's horrific death, to close that painful chapter in his life. Now because of me, he was never going to move forward. Maybe this was just the way it was supposed to be. Andrew was getting away with his crimes and he was untouchable.

Adrian unlocked the container, stepped inside and pulled the door closed behind him. I closed my eyes dreading what was about to happen. I could hear his heavy steps and fear crept into my stomach. There was no point fighting anymore. I knew Adrian would want to end me in a way that got his rocks off. I'd thought that I was tough, but deep down I was petrified of what was coming.

"I know that you're awake, my little princess. Look at me or you will leave this container in a plastic bag," he said, leaning against the wall. A shiver of fear passed down my spine. I obeyed him. After all, I had no other choice. When Andrew hurt me, I didn't hate him. I was sad and disappointed. Now I finally knew how it felt to truly hate someone. Adrian Lurkin was a monster, the devil himself reincarnated.

When I lifted myself up from the floor, pain blinded me for a moment. The smell of blood made me nauseous. I needed to throw up, but I didn't think I could take the pain in my stomach. He looked at me, and in the shadow his expression was still, calm. He was a man who held power over me. To him I was an insect that he wanted to play with, pull its legs off one by one until he got bored, and then he could stamp on me, squash me until I was dead.

"Please, I can help you. Mack trusts me. You don't have to do this," I mumbled. My voice seemed so faint, almost inaudible.

Adrian smiled, but there was absolutely no warmth in that smile, just sick excitement. Absolute repulsion passed through me as I stood there, trying to keep my balance. There was no way that I could fight him in this condition. I tried last night after he stopped kicking me. I reached up and lashed out at him, giving him a deep scratch running down his cheek. For that he shoved me across the landing and I hit the wall, losing consciousness for several seconds.

"No, I have better plan. You made me wait for your pussy, teasing me, making me hard, then leaving me hanging. No one likes a prick tease. I always get what I want and now I'm going to take it." He brushed his finger over my cheek to my chin, then gripped it hard between his thumb and forefinger keeping my face turned to him. My body was trembling with fear and he smiled that awful icy grin as if my fear pleased him. I felt so naked standing before him, I shook painfully as if I were in freezing cold weather, unable to move. He was going to kill me, but he was planning to rape me first.

My legs trembled as he grabbed my arm and yanked me to his chest. There was blood in my mouth, and my lips quivered open as a silent scream left me from the pain that radiated all over my body. The thought of him touching me made me sick, so I started arching back, attempting to get away, but he only laughed. He ripped my top down the centre and tore it off my body, kissing my neck. I screamed, hitting him, but that didn't make any difference. Adrian didn't care that I found him repulsive.

He finally let go of me and I crashed on the floor, crying in agony. My vision was blurry, but then he was on top of me, his erection pressing against my core. I wanted to vomit on him, or rip his throat out with my teeth—do anything that would stop him. My salty tears burned my wounds as they fell down my cheeks. My strength was fading away and there was nothing else left for me to do, other than take my punishment.

He was fighting with the zipper of my jeans, grabbing my arse, panting. I kept telling myself that this whole thing would be over quickly, that the pain would go away soon. I was going to end up like Tobias's wife. I should have listened to him and stayed away from Adrian.

"I bet you always wanted to feel my cock inside you. Now you will have the opportunity, you cheap white slut. I'm going to rip—"

He stopped talking, freezing on top of me. I didn't dare to move, hoping that maybe he changed his mind. I was too scared to open my eyes, to see that revolting look of his desire. I wished that I could go back and change everything, warn Tobias that he should have stayed away from me.

"Come on, Pollack, finish your thought, because I really want to put a bullet into your head."

That voice. No, it was impossible; I must be hallucinating. Tobias wasn't really here.

I finally opened my eyes.

"Calm down, I wasn't planning to hurt her. I was only joking."

Tobias was standing behind Adrian. He had a gun pressed to his head. Tobias looked so calm. I opened my mouth, but no sound came out. He shook his head, letting me know that I didn't need to say anything.

"One more word and you're dead," Tobias growled. He sounded lethal, and I knew that he wanted to finish Lurkin off. His eyes still bored into mine intensely. I inhaled slowly waiting and expecting him to do it. Adrian had done things to me that were unspeakable.

Other people started to float inside the container, surrounding us. I held my breath waiting for the shot. Adrian's pupils were dilated, eyes begging me to influence Tobias. He could go to hell for all I cared.

"Stanley, don't be stupid," said another voice from my left. "This piece of garbage doesn't deserve the bullet. Handcuff him."

I had no sympathy for Adrian. Tobias glanced around, but he didn't lower his gun. My heart skipped a beat, and I sighed heavily, trying to dispel the tension building inside the container.

"You don't want to end up in prison, my friend, not for my sake. I admit I'd been stupid, thinking that I could trust you —"

"Shut up, shut your fucking mouth!"

"Tobias, please, don't do this. Let him rot in prison. Ellie needs medical attention. She's bleeding."

I couldn't believe that Claire was there too. Tears welled in my eyes, but I couldn't give up yet. I had to know if he was going to do it.

"The hell with this," Tobias snapped and pistol-whipped Adrian with the butt of his gun. Adrian slumped forward on the ground next to me. Then someone shouted, and blackness engulfed me.

I felt myself drifting in the darkness. My head hurt. So much pain. My body was on fire, and my lids were too heavy. I wanted to scream, but I had no voice. My entire existence was consumed by earth-shattering pain.

"Detective Stanley, let us do our job. She's bleeding." I heard a voice that I didn't recognise. I panicked, calling Tobias, but my throat was tight. I couldn't draw a breath.

"Ellie, I'm here. Don't talk… please. I'm here now and I will never leave you alone again, I promise," he was choking words out through short sobs. It was him. I smelled his cologne, the sea breeze, but I needed to sleep so much. I was so tired of all this pain.

"Tobias," I said, but I couldn't hear my own voice.

"Ellie, oh God, don't talk please. You will be okay and I love you. I just want you to know that. You're brave and perfect and I love you so much. I can't lose you."

This was in my head. He wasn't really saying all this to me. It must be a dream—what a great dream. But then I felt his hand, his big, calloused, warm hand touching mine, his fingers entwining mine. I believed him and I wanted to tell him that I loved him too, but I was lost to the fog, drifting into darkness again.

Tobias

"What's happening? She's not moving. Do something!" I shouted at the paramedic who was checking Ellie's pulse. I was dying inside. This couldn't be happening. That piece of shit had hurt her. I wished I had pulled the trigger.

"She lost consciousness, Detective Stanley; we need to get her to the hospital as soon as we can. She may have internal bleeding and might need surgery," the paramedic was saying, but I wasn't listening anymore.

We were in the ambulance and we'd be at the hospital any moment. I dropped my head and started praying, knowing that God couldn't punish me like this for the second time.

Minutes turned to hours. They didn't let me go with her when we arrived at the emergency room. The lead doctor was shouting to get me out of there as several nurses and doctors convened on Ellie. She was taken away and I sat down on the bench. I didn't know how much time had passed, but I couldn't sit still. I kept asking the nurse over and over if there was any news.

"How is she?"

It was Claire. I was surprised that she was here but relieved that I didn't have to go through this alone.

"She's in surgery. That bastard had beaten her so badly. Fuck! I wish I had shot that bullet into his head. God, why did I hesitate?" I shouted.

"Ssh, Tobias, calm down. She will be fine. She's a fighter. Pollack has been charged. There was nothing more that you could have done. We have the case."

"I don't care about the case. If I lose her, that's it. I will kill him myself," I growled, hiding my face in my palms.

Then the door opened up and the doctor came out.

"How is she? Goddamn it, tell me!"

"Stable but still in a high dependency state. Her injuries were numerous. She has a severe concussion, a broken arm, a few broken ribs, a twisted ankle and a cracked cheekbone. We were concerned about a potential hemorrhage on her brain but the bleeding was from a superficial cut. The most serious issue was internal damage. Her liver and kidneys are fine, just bruised, and her spleen is intact. She ruptured a smaller intestine, but we managed to take care of it."

"Thank God," I sighed and flopped back on the chair.

"She can't be disturbed just yet. You can see her in a few hours after she has left the recovery room. She will be on the HDU ward and she will stay there for a while," the doctor added.

My Ellie was alive. It was the most amazing news I'd heard. She was saved and I loved her.

"Tobias, listen to me. Hodges is still out there, but I managed to find out that he owes a few of million to the Russians. We can still get him, but I need you to help me."

I didn't want to listen to her. I couldn't leave Ellie. This whole thing had gone too far. I promised myself that Hodges would fucking pay for what he did, but there was no way I was going to chase anyone now.

"Not now, Claire. I'm done. I have to stay here. Hodges can go fuck himself for all I care."

Ellie

Eight weeks later

"Ellie, you don't have to do this. Tobias will rip me to shreds when he finds out that I put you in danger," Claire said.

"What he doesn't know won't hurt him, darling." I chuckled. Claire and I both knew how he would have reacted if we had presented this idea to him.

Andrew was still out there, living off drug money, enjoying the high life. Maybe Tobias could forget about it, but I certainly couldn't. There were rumours that he hadn't been seen since Adrian got sent down. He left my father's office that same afternoon, never to return again. I hadn't been sleeping very well in the past few days constantly thinking about him getting away with everything, and how not one of us got any closure.

"Ellie, please. I don't want to believe—"

"I asked you to do one thing for me, one thing, Claire, so you can't bail on me now. Everything is going to be fine. Just trust me," I said.

We were in the changing room in the club, when I was just about to dance for the final time. I went through a long and painful recovery. Tobias was beside me when I opened my eyes in the hospital eight weeks ago not remembering much at all. I couldn't move, staring straight at his face. He looked shattered, like he hadn't slept for days. He had large bags under his eyes, messy hair, and scruffy beard. His clothes were all greased up.

"Ellie, darling, please say something," he kept repeating, looking at me with utter disbelief. I was disorientated, but slowly everything came back to me. Adrian, the apartment, him on top of me in that dark container. All of a sudden I couldn't breathe, feeling suffocated by the memories.

Then it hit me what Tobias said to me just before I passed out. Those three words meant nothing. He was moving to Ireland, away from me.

"I thought that you would be gone. I thought that I would wake up and you wouldn't be here," I told him, feeling numb and sleepy.

"I wouldn't leave you. I promised. I will never leave you," he said, kissing my palms. I couldn't believe he was saying this, that he was beside me.

"I saw the transfer letter, Tobias. I know that you were supposed to leave when this whole shit show was over," I said.

He sighed heavily and moved closer. "Nosey Ellie…my place is here with you. I got scared, so I stupidly wrote my resignation. I love you, baby, and I died a thousand deaths in the past few days, thinking that I almost lost you."

I wanted to open my mouth, but my jaw was still sore. A comforting warmth spread through my body faster than a lightning strike, igniting the fire in my belly.

"I love you too, Tobias, probably since the moment I saw you."

"What are you smiling at? This is serious." Claire pulled me back to the real world, shaking me.

Since that day in the hospital I'd had problems getting on with normal life. The investigation had been completed, but the case hadn't been fully tried at court. True, they held Lurkin, whose real name was Pollack, on remand for attempted murder, but Andrew had gotten away. He vanished when he found out that Adrian was arrested. He left my father's office and hadn't been back since. He always was a coward, and I couldn't believe that Tobias didn't want to pursue this further.

It took me weeks to convince Tobias to look at the files again. He barely left my side. Claire visited me after my operation, apologising. I was an idiot turning up at that apartment, thinking that I could find something on my own.

"Nothing, I'm just concentrating," I assured her, knowing that this was our only chance. We had been working on this plan for days and I felt like a traitor thinking that I had to exclude Tobias, but these days he treated me like I was made of glass. "They are here, and Kim will lead them straight in."

"God, what am I doing?"Claire said. "Tobias will never forgive me if something happened to—"

"It will be fine and I won't be in any danger. Andrew's a coward. Come on, let's go."

Claire walked me to the door, going over our plan for the tenth time. I was a nervous wreck, my heart pounding, when I thought about seeing Andrew again, after all this time.

Tobias hadn't wanted to talk about it, but four weeks after that conversation in the hospital, I made a phone call to Nathan. He wasn't particularly interested in listening to what I had to say, considering that I cost him his job. My newspaper article insinuated that the club had been bought with drug money, and two weeks later the new owner had made the decision to shut it down.

I was looking forward seeing Andrew behind bars. Nathan hung up the phone once I gave him the overview of what I was planning. Then, a week later he called back. Apparently he was running a new strip club, but not affiliated with drugs and prostitution. He agreed to arrange something, as he still had contact with Andrew.

Nathan revealed that Adrian had promised cash bonuses to the staff but had never delivered on it. By the end of our chat I found out that one of the detectives implied that Nathan knew about everything that was going on in Coral but chose to keep quiet. He was going to go down, unless he was willing to help the department to lure Andrew out of hiding. Later on it turned out that Claire had been the detective that brought the charges against him. She probably knew that I wouldn't let it go, so she decided to offer Nathan a deal.

I suggested Nathan send a special invitation to Andrew. A private erotic dance from his favourite girl was supposed to encourage him to explore the new club. My ex was a party animal, and I knew that sooner or later he would come out of hiding, looking for an enticing performance with something extra.

Nathan was willing to help, in exchange for some more publicity in the future. He wanted to make a living and the club was turning a profit. I didn't say anything to Tobias, fearing that he might talk me out of it. He was staying in Edinburgh, and we were finally happy.

I put my mask on and waited a few minutes. My heart kicked me right in my chest, when I realised that Andrew had showed up. I was expecting him to be abroad, hiding in his large fancy mansion. It looked like he couldn't stay away from Coral, probably assuming that no one would look for him in Edinburgh. He flashed me a confident smile and complimented my sexy outfit. He was wearing my favourite suit.

The music started playing instantly and once he sat down I started moving my body, swaying my hips from left to right. Nathan had told me that Andrew asked for a lap dance. I just had to pretend that I was all right with it. Andrew brushed his fingers over his chin, shifting on the comfortable sofa, and unbuttoning his jacket.

"Gorgeous, you're amazing. I would love to see your face, babe," he said when I was in front of him, bending my knees, presenting my ass to him.

I took a few steps forward, bent all the way down and turned around ripping my mask off dramatically.

Andrew's face fell and he was on his feet within a second, looking astonished.

"Ellie? What the fuck are you doing here? What is this?"

"A lap dance. I thought that's what you wanted?" I asked, running my hand down my hip.

"Your father sent you, right?"

"No, no one sent me. I just wanted to let you know that I don't hold any grudge against you anymore, that we are okay."

"Please, don't be pathetic. I'm not going to apologise. We had a good time. I never promised you anything," he added, dropping on the sofa, shaking his head in disbelief.

"I'm not expecting an apology, but I have a surprise for you," I said. He raised his left eyebrow.

"Hmm, that sounds interesting." He chuckled. "The last dance?"

"Something like that, but first I need to get something. A surprise. Just stay here for a moment. I'll be right back," I said and slid through the door, my heart pounding in my chest. Outside, I came face-to-face with two large Russian men. They looked impatient, eyeing me with their hardened dark eyes.

"He's in there, alone," I muttered and began walking away as fast as I could, not looking back. Andrew was in deep shit with the Russian Mafia, and Claire managed to find out that they were looking for him. Apparently they invested heavily in the stock that Lurkin had arranged to be brought from Spain.

While Tobias had been busy nursing me, Claire carried on working. The Russians wanted their money back, and Claire found out that Andrew had lost everything when police seized Lurkin's truck. All his assets were assigned to his ex-wife and he was left with nothing except his flat, which the police seized as it was bought from the profits of drugs. Asset forfeiture they called it.

I figured out that I would get more satisfaction if I delivered Andrew straight to the Russians. Claire managed to leak that he was going to be in the club. One of the hostesses made a deal with us. She was supposed to bring the Russians to the performance room. I didn't even want to imagine Andrew's face when, instead of getting a lap dance, he had to explain himself to these very angry-looking men.

Claire was on her feet when I stepped back into the dressing room.

"All sorted. They are with him now. I guess he didn't see that coming. I think we should call Tobias now."

"You're right, but I'm not making that phone call. He will be furious."

I rolled my eyes and dialled Tobias's number. This was going to be a long conversation and I had to brace myself, because I knew that he was going to be pissed.

Epilogue

Ellie

"You know that I hate surprises," I told Tobias, pulling a face as we crossed the street in the centre of Edinburgh. He pretended that he didn't hear me, pressing his palm to my back.

He was probably still angry with me about the fact that I went faced Andrew without him. I had never seen him so mad in my life. He screamed and shouted for about ten minutes straight, his face the colour of an aubergine before he let me explain what happened that night. On a positive note, he promised to punish me and he indeed delivered on that. I was sore for almost a week.

That was three weeks ago and Tobias hadn't spoken to Claire since. I begged and pleaded, trying to tell him that it was my idea, but he was having none of it. Later on we found out that a few strippers had seen Andrew being dragged into a car by the Russian giants. I thought that I would feel sorry for him, but surprisingly I didn't feel anything. He deserved what was coming to him, and Claire was certain that it was nothing good. No one had seen him since then, and I had a feeling that it was the end of Andrew Hamilton.

Lurkin was sentenced to over twenty years in prison; the list of charges was long and very complicated. Tobias and Claire had to testify, and according to the prosecutor, they had collected a significant amount of evidence against him. On top of that, I resigned from my job and told Phil to go fuck himself, and that felt damn good.

I finished writing my groundbreaking exposé when I was in the hospital recovering from my injuries. The whole case was publicised nationally, and I was the first unemployed reporter to deliver a spectacular article with solid photos and great interviews. I had managed to secure a deal with one of the largest newspapers in Scotland that syndicated it to the whole of the UK. They hired me on the spot, and a few days later, my dream had come true. My story was published on the front page. This whole thing was still pretty surreal.

"Relax, Angel. You will like this," Tobias said. "I don't think you've been punished enough though. There is also a surprise waiting for you at home," he said with a twinkle in his eye.

I tried to stop thinking about the nights that we spent in my apartment. Officially Tobias moved into my place, unofficially he put an offer on the apartment that was two doors away from mine, after he received confirmation that he was able to be permanently placed in Edinburgh. We were together, and we were happy. Everything turned out great. He grabbed my hand as we walked into the restaurant.

"We have the table just at the back," Tobias whispered, leaning over while we waited for the waiter. I looked at him wondering what the hell he was planning now. "Oh, and I may have forgotten to tell you that my team caught the person that had been blackmailing you. It turned out that it was a woman from your old job named Mimi."

I looked at him struck dumb with shock.

"Mimi was the one that blackmailed me? How? Why?" I asked.

"She recognised you and was running behind with her credit card payments. She was desperate. Besides, she was an amateur. The team traced her pretty quickly."

I couldn't believe it, but it kind of made sense. Mimi never particularly liked me. I guessed she thought she had a chance to make some money off me and she took it.

After weeks in the hospital, I had forgotten about the whole blackmailing thing. Now I was kind of glad that Tobias managed to get to the bottom of it.

When the waiter took us to our table I thought that I was hallucinating. My father was sitting there facing us, reading a paper, but not just any paper—the edition from a week ago with my article on the front page. I hadn't spoken to him since the day I went to warn him about Andrew. He never tried to get in touch with me. I was so busy with recovering, starting my new job, and getting on with life that I assumed he didn't care. He rose from his seat when he saw us approaching.

"Ellie, forgive the intrusion, but I needed to congratulate you in person," he said, clearing his throat. God, what happened to him? He had never before congratulated me on anything that I had done. Looking up at his face, I could see that he was proud. I knew that my article created a storm. In the past few days the press wouldn't leave me alone, and a few television stations wanted to interview me. I achieved what I had wanted, and on top of that my man stood firmly behind me.

"Thank you," I said, blushing. It had been so weird to see my name on the front page, but I gained respect from the other staff reporters. No one seemed to want to write crap about me anymore.

We all sat down at the table. Tobias had this smug smile on his face, the smile that I knew so well. The waiter approached and Tobias was just about to order something when my father lifted his hand.

"Champagne, the best you have. We are celebrating," he stated. I leaned over to Tobias and asked him.

"You did this, right? You called him?"

"Actually, he called me. I have no idea how he got my number," he replied, looking at me with that familiar fire in his eyes. My father was busy looking at the paper. I had a feeling that it was his way of saying that he was proud of me, finally.

"Have you got any more surprises up your sleeve?"

Tobias ran his hand along his jaw and looked away. I hated when he did this, making me wait for his answer.

"Well, we are going to Shetland Islands. We'll be heading to the airport from here, Angel. Does that count as a surprise?"

I gasped at him and then kissed him, because I knew that things were going to be good from now on. Everything was finally perfect.

The End

Printed in Great Britain
by Amazon